A PENNY FOR YOUR THOUGHTS

Shannan,
Make a wish...

ROBERT FORD
MATT HAYWARD

POLTERGEIST PRESS

POLTERGEIST PRESS

Greatful acknowledgement is made to Gary Lee Conner, Greg Ginn and SST Records for permission to reprint an excert from "Girl Behind The Mask" by Screaming Trees. Copyright © 1987 by Cesstone Music. Used by permission. All rights reserved.

ISBN: 978-1-9993419-8-5

Artwork by Ben Baldwin

First Edition

www.poltergeistpress.com

This one is for you, the reader.
Our only wish is that you enjoy it.

Dear
Shannan,
Use the pennies
for emergency!

Barbara

Acknowledgements

Special thanks to Anna Hayward, Kelli Owen, Ben Baldwin, Melissa & Fionnuala Hayward, Nugget & Sauce, Patrick Lacey, Tim Meyer, Mary SanGiovanni, Brian Keene, Bryan Smith, John Boden, Paul Goblirsch, Tod Clark, D. Alexander Ward, Doug Murano, Rachel Autumn Deering, Jessica Deering, Josh Jabcuga, Mark McNally, Jeff Angell, Doug Metherell, John Stapleton, Tim Baker, and Mark Eaton.

A PENNY
FOR YOUR
THOUGHTS

CHAPTER ONE

WHENEVER I TAKE the Lowback Trail, I always find something different: unknown names carved into tree trunks, discarded briefs by overeager dippers, a smoldering pit left from weekend hikers—but today? Today I found a penny jar.

My parole officer warned me to stick to town, but a trailer park, one grocery store, and row of houses did not make for entertainment. Besides, the Lowback *was* town, at least to us locals, anyway. So, like every Saturday, I took a hike.

The clear air from last night's storm stung my lungs, and as a former *twenty-a-day* guy, that shit hurt. I shimmied through the ferns and passed the old fishing spot on the bridge—a trail the Lowback youth kept secret like a family heirloom. The dirt path wasn't much to begin with, but now, after the thunderstorm, nothing but thick mud slopped beneath my boots. Rainwater slipped from the high pines and slapped my face. I didn't mind. Being *inside* for eight years, I'd take a elderly drunkard spitting on my face for some relief...*Eight years*, man. Accomplice to robbery didn't make for the cleanest record, but I'd just happened to be parked by the street while my girl, Angie,

9

robbed a store at gunpoint, y'know? *Prove otherwise, Your Honor.* Angie, on the other hand, was still inside—and Lowback was a better place for it.

Rooks and insects chirped and chittered as I whistled and took the trail paralleling the rumbling tributary. High water smacked off the banks and rocks, dirty as a back-alley whore and just as fit to burst. Rumor had it those waters were home to a school of catfish so big they could eat a gaggle of kids and ask for seconds. I'd never been dumb enough to hop in and find out, but with the storm pushing water levels, I imagined those catfish might decide to emigrate to the woods come suppertime. I wanted to make it home before the rainclouds *really* popped, but then again, had I done that, I'd never have found my jar.

After kicking aside a pair of underwear large enough to fit a hippo with glandular problems, that's when I spotted the tree. The jagged trunk still smoked from lightning, and as the wind changed direction, sour air attacked my nostrils. I pressed my sleeve to my face as I jogged on over. The lone pine sat by the water's edge, shredded by the gods. A still-flaming branch sizzled on the riverbank. But strangest of all was the crater of blackened earth by the roots. If I didn't know any better, I'd say a tiny meteor had struck. Roots jutted from the scorched soil like tentacles, and I peeked below at the thing buried in the dirt. Rainwater rolled down the filthy glass. A jar.

My first thought turned to drugs. *Could someone have buried paraphernalia for a pickup? Would that attract lightning?*

Then (as stupid as it sounds) I thought: *silver. Did we have a millionaire Lowback hillbilly hiding treasures outside of town?* Parole officer be damned—my hands itched to find out.

A PENNY FOR YOUR THOUGHTS

I scanned the woods for hikers before hunkering down and pawing at the muck. The dirt came free in globs, gathering beneath my nails, but I soon shimmied my hands around the glass and pulled. The object *popped* free and I went *bassakwards* as the thing shot through the air, thumped the soggy ground and rolled as I scrambled to my feet and my treasure barreled toward the tributary.

"*Motherfuck!*"

I bolted and snatched the jar just as it started down the bank to the catfish. Then I caught my breath.

I took inventory of the woods once more. Only the sparrows and catfish knew my whereabouts, and the hissing rain cloaked my labored breathing. I hobbled to the shelter of a canopy, squatting back-against-bark as I rolled that cold jar about my open palms.

A seamed glass cookie jar—the very thing Pop used as a swear pot when I was growing up. Sometimes I think he cussed just to give me pocket money, the kinda man he was. "*Fuck, fuck, shit, cock, fuck, and there's your candy. Go on up to the store and grab me some tobacco while you're at it. Like magic.*"

"Like magic," I mumbled, and *popped* the lid before peering inside.

I expected a rank smell, maybe from a dead animal some psychotic child had shoved inside, but all I found was paper. *Lots* of paper. My brow creased. I wiped my hand on my jeans before slipping in two fingers and snatching a piece. Then I pulled a tiny, ripped scroll free and found myself surprised at the weight. Someone had shredded a notebook page before rolling the sections into tight little scrolls. The years only strengthened that fold, and once I unraveled a piece, I placed it on my knee and held it open. There lay a single penny taped next to handwriting.

"The fuck is goin' on here?"

I peeled the tape and held the coin up for inspection. A 1952 Lincoln wheat penny. *Pristine.*

I pocketed the coin before I studied the paper, cursing as raindrops marred the page. The scrawl reminded me of someone using their bad hand, or a drunkard's love letter. Then I realized what I was looking at: a *child's* handwriting.

'To whoever cares,' it read. 'I'm not asking for a RALEEEE! Just A BIKE-ANY BIKE! Stop Kasey making fun of me! Pleeeez! Is that too fuckn mush to ask?'

Well, goddamn—I couldn't help it, man. I laughed. I laughed *damn hard.*

I read it twice over before pocketing the thing and climbing to my feet. Shaking my head, I had one thought: what *else* had this kid wished for? The heavy jar promised lots of reading material, that's for sure, and I took off home as I recapped the lid. I didn't want a single page damaged.

What would I have wished for as a child? Probably a mountain of Fun Dip, Pop Rocks, and Everlasting Gobstoppers. Something stupid like that. But, *shit*, this kid had *balls*, man, and I needed to know more. I took off home with rockets in my boots.

Briarwood Estates Trailer Park emitted a soft glow as families wasted the afternoon binging TV. Pop's home sat at the far end by the welcome sign, no more than a trailer without wheels, and I beelined there as thunder cracked and pregnant clouds pissed ice-water. The wind had knocked June Randolf's SEEDS FOR SALE sign down, and I made a mental note to fix it come morning. Her and Pop always got along. Then Kenny Williams burst from his mobile home.

"Kenny, what's happenin'?"

A PENNY FOR YOUR THOUGHTS

He slogged across the lawn with that ball of beer-belly sloshing beneath his wife-beater. That man could run naked in the Arctic and still say '*it ain't that cold*'. He sniffled. "Hey, Joe. Uh...listen. I got a proposition to make."

"Now there's a word for a man like you. Shit, Kenny, you're gonna catch your death out here. Why not come over to Pop's place later? We'll talk."

Rain dripped from my nose and I made to leave when he said, "Well, see, I already been there."

Crap on a stick. If Pop caught wind of another infamous 'Kenny Williams get-rich-quick scheme', my parole officer would hop me faster than a dog in heat. Henderson wasn't a drill sergeant by any means, but the man had eyes for liars. I'd blagged my way onto his good side with each check-up, and you bet your pocket lint, I intended to stay there.

"Kenny, what did you go and do?"

"Nothin', man, nothin'. *Yeesh.* I got a guy out in the city movin' a bunch of repo'd shit. Junked cars, that kinda thing. I'm makin' a profit out here, just keeping food on the table, that kinda thing."

I thought of the time Kenny jacked pockets full of Parmesan from Walmart, planning to '*get a thrift-store suit and sell it to restaurants, all legit-like*', and stifled a laugh. I swear, he and Angie will be the death of me.

"Why were you at Pop's place?"

"Stuck something in the garage for you—for *free*, man. Free. Just provin' I'm movin' *serious* shit here."

"Oh, yeah? And what's the catch? Got the Denny brothers involved?"

He licked his lips, opened his arms wide. "Picture *big*, all right? Look, I got a junked '71 Chevelle that Bryan

13

put a new coat of paint on for me. Gonna pass it off—to *yeah*, the Denny brothers—for a grand. A grand, *easy*, Joe. I only paid four-hunnerd. You know how slow those knuckleheads are, they're a cash cow."

"And you want me to be your salesman."

"I'll give ya good money, cash in hand," he said in an exasperated manner, as if I were the slowest damn thing he ever did see. "You're good at this kinda shit, Joe. 'Member the time you sold the Denny brothers a green-painted bathtub because it looked—"

"—New-Age," I finished. "Yeah, I remember."

"So you *can* do it," he said, arms still out wide. "I'm pleadin'. It's real low-risk, Joe. Just a car."

"At first."

Rainwater slithered inside my jacket and I shivered as a harsh wind blew my hair. I *did* need the damn money. Pop's mill wage granted little comfort, the old house spoke to that. He lied he could handle the bills (*'ain't nothin', Joe'*) but I knew better. That man would give me the shirt off his back and ask if I needed more, even if I'd just broken his jaw with a wrench. I intended on pulling my weight, get settled by the time the weather cleared, and making Pop proud. No one would hire me because of my stint inside. No one *smart*, at least.

"All right, listen," I said. "I'll come around tonight. But stay away from Pop's. He doesn't need this shit."

Kenny flashed those nicotine-stained stubs. "Got it. Oh, uh, hey, can I get a cookie?"

I'd almost forgotten about my jar. I shook my head. "Get out of the rain, Kenny. I'll see you tonight."

"Right."

I kept my head low against the sheeting water as I rushed home. And that's when Kenny called out.

"Joe, it's a bike!"

I turned. "What?"

"It's a bike. What I left ya. A serious present for a *serious* deal. Thought you could take it up the Lowback sometime, y'know? Now that you're out and gettin' clean."

"A bike?" Something cold and hard twisted in my gut. "What kind?" I asked.

"A Raleigh," he said, and smiled. "Come on, who doesn't want a Raleigh?"

Pop sat at the kitchen table holding the morning newspaper. A cup of black coffee rested beside him (probably untouched), and room temperature at best. My father was nothing if not a creature of habit. He wore his weekend clothes—a flannel shirt, faded jeans, and scuffed moccasin slippers. Every other day of the week for the past twenty-two years, he donned his dark blue work clothes for the Lowback Feed Mill. Took every bit of overtime they offered if he could, and never took a day off. Hard-working man through and through, my dad. He glanced at me as I shut the door and stepped into the living room.

"Evenin', kid."

"Hey, Pop. How's the world this morning?"

"Going to hell in a handcart, that's how. Nothing gets my piss hot like reading about the government these days. Stupid sons o' bitches."

"Then why do you keep reading about it?" I crossed to the kitchen counter and poured a cup of coffee—black. I used to hate it that way, but when you're on the inside, sugar and creamer become valuable trading commodities. Now I look forward to the bitter taste.

Pop let the top of the newspaper fold and peered at me. "Because knowing and getting pissed off is better than walking around stupid."

I laughed and sipped the hot brew.

"Speakin' of stupid, Kenny stopped by after you left this morning." His gaze remained on me. "Acted all shifty and nervous like he does. You two up to something?"

"*Naaah*, Pop. You know how Kenny is. Nothing to worry about."

"Man's dumber than a box of shit and always has been. Don't get mixed up in any schemes he has cooking."

I nodded and swallowed another mouthful of coffee. "I won't. I know better."

Pop grunted and turned his focus back on the paper, flicking out the pages.

I headed toward my room and made it halfway down the hall before I realized I'd been hiding the penny jar at my side so Pop couldn't see. For the life of me, I had no idea why.

Pop called out as I made it to my room. "Kenny said he left you something in the garage, by the way."

"Thanks, Pop."

My father hadn't touched my bedroom at all during my time inside, and now that I was out, I didn't feel the need to change it. There was something comforting, something *safe*, about the posters on my wall. *Misfits* and *Dead Milkmen*. *Screaming Trees* and *Alice in Chains*. I was home again, yeah, but more importantly, it *felt* like home.

I sandwiched the jar between my bed and dresser and pushed a trashcan against it, then I appraised my work. *Nope. That wouldn't do.* I knelt and pulled out the bottom dresser drawer. Lots of band t-shirts and some hoodies I probably couldn't fit into anymore. I lifted them out and froze. A wave of nausea flowed through me and I felt like getting sick right there on my bedroom floor.

I pulled out a length of rubber tubing and held it in front of me. How many times had I used it to tie off and shoot up? I dropped it to the carpet and put the penny jar beneath the old clothes and pushed the drawer shut.

The tubing lay on the floor like a dead snake. I looked over at my bed and everything flooded back: throwing up over and over again until nothing but stomach bile burned my throat. The sweating, the *chills*. Muscle cramps through my entire body, twisting and knotting in places I didn't think could even *do* that sort of thing. Shitting and pissing myself. Snot running in rivers like it was abandoning ship. The leather belts buckled at my wrists and ankles holding me to my bedposts. *For my own good.*

And Pop. Through the whole thing, Pop. The expression on his face. The painful disappointment I had let something else control my life.

See, while Angie was busy shoving a .38 revolver at a teenaged cashier and demanding the cash from the register, I was sitting in a parked car, shaking in pain from being dopesick.

That's why I wasn't inside with her. *That's* why my sentence was reduced to an accomplice.

Because I was sicker than a dog, dealing with withdrawal.

After the arrest, Pop posted bail and brought me home while the courts lined up all the pre-trial and sentencing bullshit. But that night, the first night Pop took me home, he told me he loved me. Understand, he's a kind man, my father, but actually saying he loved me out in the open? More terrifying than getting arrested for robbery.

He told me he loved me and punched me with a right hook the hardest I've ever been hit. When I woke up, I was shirtless and wearing sweatpants and my wrists and ankles were buckled to the bedposts with leather belts.

And hell started. Hard and fast and so deep I thought it would never end.

But Pop got me clean. I'll give him that.

I begged and pleaded with him. I screamed so loud I lost my voice. I told him I *hated* him and cursed his name. Called him everything in the book. But he ignored it all and brought me water so I could throw it up again. Cleaned my piss and shit and puke so often I lost count.

When it was over, and I opened my eyes for the first time to find my body wasn't wracked with cramps, I loved him even more. I'd made it through to the other side. He'd gotten me clean before I went to prison.

With the tubing in my hand, I headed back to the kitchen. "Hey, uh...Pop?"

He grunted in acknowledgement but didn't look up.

"Pop, I don't know if you, y'know, go through my bedroom or not. I wouldn't blame you if you do, but I didn't want you to find this and think I..."

He peered up, his gaze zeroing in on the dangling tube. That expression I'd seen so long ago washed over his face. Disappointment, yeah, but more—it's like something sad and heavy he wanted to say but couldn't quite muster the words.

"I found it in my dresser with some old clothes and wanted to tell you. I didn't want you to find it and...I'm clean, Pop. I'm staying clean. I just—"

"All right, then." He nodded and flicked out the paper. "Cut it up. Toss it in the bin."

I waited a moment, dumbfounded. Then I did as he asked, slicing up the tube and throwing it on top of the used coffee filter in the trashcan. Done.

A PENNY FOR YOUR THOUGHTS

I swallowed the last of the coffee in my mug and headed to the garage. The door whined as I lifted it and—*sonuvabitch*—Kenny's words were true. I stood, staring.

There's a unique feeling when you step out of the gates of prison. It's freedom, of course, but it's more than that. It's an *uneasy* freedom, as if you'll be snatched back before you take one more step, the guards saying, "There's been a mistake." You don't trust it.

That's how I felt walking toward the Raleigh bike. It was *exquisite*. I didn't know where Kenny had gotten the thing but there wasn't even any wear on the grips. Besides some dirt on the tires from when Kenny had brought it over, the bike looked untouched. Brand new. The metal flake paint gleamed in the low light of the garage, and I couldn't help but grin.

It had been about ten years since I'd ridden a bike, but when I straddled that Raleigh, it fit me perfectly. I flipped up the kickstand with my foot and pedaled out into the drizzle, my heart picking up speed alongside the tires.

With the rain and wind on my face, I pedaled down Fishing Creek Road, smiling like a kid on the first day of summer vacation. It was the first time since I'd gotten out of prison I truly felt free.

CHAPTER TWO

I SHIVERED AS the warm house embraced me. Water dripped from my nose and I eased the door shut as I sniffled, our wooden *Welcome Home* sign greeting me from down the hall. Pop snored from his La-Z-Boy near the television while some over-excited goon asked for another vowel onscreen. A string of drool glistened from Pop's open mouth, and the electric heater by his feet cast his features in an orange glow. That damn thing *devoured* electricity, was a fire hazard, and I'd warned him to switch it off before falling asleep a thousand times before. I tiptoed across the room and clicked off the device before draping a blanket across him. That man could sleep through an avalanche.

"Sleep tight, Pop," I whispered, and snapped off his pride and joy—a homemade lamp we'd built together while he'd gotten me clean. Sturdy mahogany, *solid*, and he'd once said, "there's a metaphor there, but I ain't highfalutin enough to find it."

After a shower, I returned to my room and changed into fresh jeans and a shirt, still amazed at how great fabric softener smelled. Prison clothes never stunk of anything but hard water and sweat. I threw on a clean pair of socks for good measure. Let me tell you, the one thing people should never take for granted is a clean pair of socks.

With a couple of hours before my meeting with the Denny brothers, I decided I'd spend the downtime letting my muscles relax after the bike ride. I hadn't felt that good in forever. I bunched up my pillow, eased onto my back, and closed my eyes...And that damned jar called me like an alarm. I felt like a kid who'd snuck home some alcohol. My eyes twitched beneath their lids. I waited for another snore from Pop before hoisting myself upright and pulling the jar from the drawer. I rolled it over in my hands. Did I believe in fate? *No*, and I wasn't one for the paranormal, either. I left the ghost-hunting and spirit-guiding to the elderly and the phony intellectual neckbeards. But my Raleigh bike, man...I couldn't deny *that*.

"Coincidence," I muttered, and popped the lid once again. In the confines of the house, a hint of soil ghosted to my nose, pleasant and earthy. My stomach fizzed with excitement about the words I'd find, and I couldn't help but think of an alcoholic cracking a cold one in private. I imagined—if left unchecked—my little jar could become quite the addiction. And knowing my personality, this thing could soon become my best friend. My *only* friend.

"Coincidence," I repeated, and slipped my fingers inside. Paper grazed my index, and I pulled a sheet free. I clasped the jar between my thighs as I unfolded the cold parchment. As before, a spotless and 'like new' penny was taped to the left of some childish scrawl.

Fine. No Raleigh, it read. But then she doesn't get to have one neither. How about that? If I can't have one she can't! Bitch!

"Well, goddamn," I said with a laugh. "Someone's gotta potty mouth." I flipped over the paper to make sure

22

A PENNY FOR YOUR THOUGHTS

I hadn't missed any zingers, ready for another belly-laugh—when something *crashed* in the garage. I froze.

A stray, pregnant tabby had been prowling Briarwood since my release, exploring the garbage cans in hopes of some pot roast or a chicken bone. Residents didn't mind (they'd even named her Momma Fluff) but whatever crashed in the garage was no cat. I placed the jar down and got to my feet before swiping my Louisville Slugger, a seventeenth birthday present from Pop that only saw use in times of trouble.

Like that time Kenny came calling for Angie's head when she'd broken into his house on a high...

My fists tightened around the slick wood as I stalked the hall and peered in on Pop—still out cold. I entered the kitchen and pressed myself against the garage door. Something shuffled (*no fear of being heard*) as I counted to three...I took a deep breath and barged inside.

"On the fucking ground!"

I swung like a motherfucker. The bat cut the air with a *whoomp! whoomp!* as, across the garage, a young woman raised an eyebrow and folded her arms.

"What the...?" A swing threw me off-balance and I collided with Pop's car. She cocked her head.

A vintage *Throttle* tank-top clung to her scrawny frame and her wet hair was tied back in a tail. She chewed gum as she asked, "The fuck you doing with my bike, asshole?"

My heart thumped as I raced for the door to eased it shut, wincing as well as praying Pop hadn't heard a word. He was a patient man, understanding, but hearing I had someone come knocking for their stolen property would test his nerves. I cursed Kenny—*the moron!*—as I lay the bat across Pop's workbench. I showed my empty palms.

"Listen, I didn't take shit, okay?"

"No? Y'just borrowed my bike and stored it in your garage? Cause that's *taking my shit*. The nerve to go cycling out past my trailer on Leeds Mill with a stolen bike. My bike. You're lucky I didn't bring a goddamn knife."

"Fuck."

I rubbed my forehead, kept my voice low. "Look, my buddy Kenny, he's...he's a dumb sumbitch, okay? That's what he is. He took it to give me a present. But if I'd known he'd *stole* it from someone, I'd have turned him down and brought it back—honest. Woulda slapped his swollen head, too."

My excuse did not impress her. She hocked a wad of spit as wind billowed in from the yard, the garage door swinging like a drunkard on its broken hinges.

"Ah, shit. You really have to do that?"

"You really have to take my bike? Fair is fair."

"Suppose. Look, go on, take your damn bike. I didn't ask for any of this."

"Oh, I have permission to take my own damn property? How fuckin' kind of you, sir. And cut the 'woe-is-me' act, none of us asked for *any* of this."

"Kiss your fuckin' momma with that mouth?"

"Kissed yours down south and blew a raspberry."

She grabbed her bike and *yanked* it out the door before stalking down the yard, rain beating off her bare shoulders. Why folks around here refused to dress weather-appropriately, I'd never fucking know.

"You'll be hearing from the police," she shouted as she slipped onto the saddle, her trainer finding a pedal.

An invisible hand squeezed my guts.

Well, fuck me sideways.

"Whoa-whoa-whoa." I ran after her and placed a hand on her shoulder. Her eyes burned fire as she smacked my arm. "The *fuck* off me. Whatdya you think you're doin'?"

A PENNY FOR YOUR THOUGHTS

Rain soaked through my clean clothes but I held up my palms in surrender. "Sorry, I'm sorry, but...no cops. Please."

Her eyes relaxed as realization dawned. Then narrowed. I was dealing with no dummy. "Parole? Bein' a good boy?"

"I am. I really am."

She leaned across the handlebars, the gears in her head going *clank-clank-clank*. "What's in it for me?" she asked.

Jesus fuck...

"Look, please don't do this."

"Hey, I'm not the one who took somebody's bike and swung a baseball bat like a damn *maniac*, now am I? This is *your* problem, mister."

"What do you want?"

"Got money?"

"No."

"Got candy?"

"What? No."

"I'll have to think about it." She worked her sneaker on the pedal. "You'll be seein' me around."

She took off through the downpour as a rumble of thunder crackled in the clouds. My shoulders fell lax and my mouth dried as I watched her go. *Fucking Kenny. The hell had he gotten me into?* The girl peddled hard and fast out onto the street, and—

Tires *screeched*.

Just for a moment, the girl's head whipped sideways in a *'whazzat?'* before headlights lit her shocked face and then came a hard *thump*.

She crashed to the tarmac. Her bike skidded as she rolled to a stop in front of the grill of a beat-up Chevelle. Rain hissed and tapped the car's roof as the wipers slapped back and forth, back and forth—*eeeer, thump, eeeer, thump.*

"Goddammit..." I jogged across the lawn as someone stepped from the car. A man. I closed in and realized who. Not a man, *no*—a goddamn *moron.*

"The fuck have you done, Kenny?"

His mouth opened and closed like a salmon without oxygen and I slapped his chest. "Speak, man, speak!"

"I—I was comin' to see if you needed a lift before we meet the Denny brothers and she came outta nowhere and I—"

But his blubbering faded to white noise as I spied the bike. It lay crumpled before the now-dented car grill, the frame buckled and beaten as droplets fell to the road. Spokes jutted from the spinning back tire like crooked teeth, and the loose chain lay curled beside it. In my head flashed the note:

But then she doesn't get to have one neither. How about that? If I can't have one, she can't! Bitch!

"You *hearin'* me?" Kenny asked. "Dude, *answer* me."

"Huh?"

"I said she's awake! Ah, shit, I knew I shouldn'ta taken the stupid bike..."

I left Kenny rambling and rubbing his balding head as I approached the girl and got to one knee. She groaned and pushed herself upright.

"Hey," I said. "You all right?"

A couple of pebbles clung to the side of her face, embedded in her reddened skin, but I saw no blood. She winced. "Fuckin' leg. It's killin' me."

And your bike's totaled, too, I didn't add. *You don't get to have one neither. How about that?*

"Think it's broken."

A PENNY FOR YOUR THOUGHTS

"Aw, shit," Kenny cried, biting his lip as he approached. "Lady, I'm sorry, yeah? It's the damned rain, you just came outta nowhere and—"

"*You.*" I tell ya, if looks could kill..."You're the asshole who stole my damn bike, aren't you? Not good enough or somethin'? Had to wreck it, *too*?"

"Hey, I said I'm sorry, the...the heavy rain and the—"

Kenny was cut off as she screamed and her hands shot to her leg. I whipped my head toward Pop's, making sure he hadn't heard a thing. The thundering storm cloaked us well; besides, I'd watched that man sleep through wars before, he was dreaming of steaks and whiskey.

"You gotta take her to a hospital," I said. "Could be broken."

"What? *Me*? Dude, we gotta meet the Denny—"

"Can you shut your damn mouth, idiot?"

The girl watched us like we were the *Looney Tunes*. "A hospital," she said dryly. "A hospital now. And you're paying all of my bills, and you ain't arguin', and you ain't sayin' shit. And you're replacing my damn bike."

Kenny blew a breath. "I ain't paying nothin', lady. Nope."

"Then I hope you like having your license taken away and my boot in your balls."

"Yeah? Joke's on you, I don't even got a license."

Kenny...

She looked to me as if to say, *'seriously?'* and added, "Well, prison sounds great this time of year. Good food, good people. You'll like that."

I took a breath. "Kenny. I know you're thick as a Lowback pine, but take the girl to the damn hospital, okay?"

"Oh, and pay with what money?"

The Chevelle caught my eye, its grill dented but not beyond repair. Kenny scoffed and blew a '*ppfffff*'. "No damn way. Uh-uh. That's a grand between *us*. I need that."

"You need to stay out of prison and a brain that actually works, that's what *you* need."

"Thought you ain't got no money?" the girl said.

"Quiet."

Kenny scanned the road as if the answer lay in a bush somewhere. "Fine. Fine, okay. You're meeting the Denny brothers alone, then. I'll take her. That'll cover her bills and I'll get something else together for us when I get back. Shit."

The girl looked between us and that calculating look returned. I figured I'd grow to hate that stare. "What do you two have cooking?"

"Nothing."

"Bull. Shit."

Help me, Jesus, please.

"I want fifty percent of whatever it is."

"*She wants...*" Kenny wheezed a laugh. "Boy, howdy."

"Shoulda thought of that before you broke my damn leg and stole m'bike."

"She's got a point," I said.

"And a broken leg," she added.

"Look. Fine. Kenny comes up with any more brilliant ideas, you get fifty percent. Now go on. Kenny, take her to a hospital."

"I gotta go get my car. Can't take the Chevelle, you need it."

"Then *go*."

As he waddled off, I took a deep breath and ran a hand across my face. The girl stopped rubbing her leg.

"You okay?"

A PENNY FOR YOUR THOUGHTS

"Oh, I'm good," she said. "It's not damaged. But your dumb buddy is paying out big time."

"You *lied*? It's not broke?"

"Nah. And you, good sir, aren't saying a word to him, are ya? Because if you want the cops to stay out of this, then you're following *my* rules."

"And what does that mean?"

"Oh, I'll think of somethin'."

"Your parents never tell you that blackmail is wrong?"

"My parents? My mom's off fuckin' anything she can get a hold of and my daddy was just one of 'em. Gramma's in prison, and I've been living in the family trailer since I turned eighteen—*three years long*. If I see an olive branch, I'm grabbin' hold with both hands, Mister. And with you two boneheads, I see something that I want."

Great, I thought. *Just fucking great.*

Headlights cut through the rain as Kenny beeped the horn. I helped the young woman into the backseat and then sent them on their way. Kenny gunned the engine and I watched the angry brake lights flare before he hooked a left toward the highway. I crossed to the Chevelle, hopped inside, and slammed the door. The stink of air-freshener invaded my nose and made me gag. Kenny had all the sales subtly of a drunk pusher.

I had an hour to get to the Denny brothers and collect cash for a young woman I didn't even know. *A young woman who now has Kenny and I snared like a fox; all because that* idiot *stole her bike.* But that thought was soon drowned out by something much more frightening; something that made the walls of prison seem like a good idea. *That child's notes kept their word.*

CHAPTER THREE

THE DENNY BROTHERS liked shiny things.

I had known this before my little vacation on the inside and had used it to my advantage more than a few times when I used to buy their laced and dodgy bundles of smack. They bought with their eyes, and if it looked good, they wanted it—a new toy to play with for a while until they got good and bored and wanted something different. For an addict, they were a useful resource.

For as long as anyone could remember, the Denny family lived at the edge of Lowback on an overgrown fifty-acre plot littered with rusted cars, stacks of tires, and a smattering of busted toilets and old bathtubs (a *New-Age* green one among them). There were garbage piles scattered on the land, and often a column of smoke could be seen reaching for the sky as they burned things—their own things, and things other people wanted to 'disappear'. Word had it their house sat on tons of waste from *two* chemical companies...Explained why they looked like mutants.

When I was nine years old, Curtis Denny ran out into the road to fetch a rogue soccer ball. He was hit by a Lowback Quarry work truck and dragged a solid thirty feet along the cracked asphalt of Leeds Mill Road. Pops told me there was nothing left of that kid by the time the brakes of the dump truck kicked in.

Jerry and Raymond were the remaining brothers and I still remember standing on the front lawn of elementary school as the principal gave a speech in front of a freshly-planted cherry tree in memorial of Curtis.

Both brothers stood with their hands behind their back, listening but not listening, to the principal's words. At one point, Jerry snickered. For whatever reason, that always stuck in my craw, y'know? *How the hell could you be a snickering asshole at your brother's memorial?*

But, as I said, the Denny brothers were a useful resource for an addict. They knew how to get things. No, let me correct that, they knew how to get *anything*. That's where I got Angie's pistol from, but I could just as easily have asked them to get me a bazooka or a Sherman tank. Somehow, they always had a source. Angie had originally bought a pistol from her pusher but the damned idiot never even filed the barrel. For all their stupidity, the Dennys had a McDonald's-level system at work. Guns, drugs, cars, dogs, whatever you wanted.

They'd been dealing coke and smack for a long time and I had brought them watches, jewelry, stereos, cameras—whatever I could steal and trade to get a fix. As long as I made sure I polished it up ahead of time and made it *look* amazing, it was a done deal. As I said, they liked shiny things and they bought with their eyes.

I started the Chevelle, greeted by a throaty growl, and thought over my sales pitch to the Denny brothers as I took off.

Part of me felt greasy for going to meet them, like taking a hot shower and putting on gritty work clothes again. I *knew* I shouldn't be around them. It was too close to old habits. Made me feel queasy, like finding my old tie-off cord.

Pop had told me not to get mixed up with any of Kenny's schemes and here I was—right fucking in the middle of one. *And the girl.* Christ, I didn't even know her damned *name.* I had to give credit where credit was due, though. She saw an opportunity and was working us like a seasoned pro. All because of a stolen bike. "*Fuckin' Kenny.*"

I gripped the steering wheel tighter. Cairn Road was a stretch of curves and hillside and I punched the gas pedal to see what the Chevelle could do. It didn't disappoint. Once I crested the second hilltop, I let the car coast down the other side as I got closer to the Denny's driveway at the bottom.

The farmhouse sat back from the road a few football fields worth of length. In truth, I wish my Pops and I could have a place like it. No neighbors. No bullshit. Away from prying eyes.

But here, it felt different. It made my arms itch with yearning just pulling into the dirt drive. Back in the same old habits.

No, fuck that. I was here to sell the car, that was it. That was all.

I parked and killed the engine, dust swirling in my headlights. The farmhouse looked the same as it did before I went into prison. Whitewashed clapboard siding, flaking and untouched. Metal roof with snow-breakers spaced out on top. Brick chimney looking like it could use some attention before it fell down on itself.

I wanted to turn the Chevelle around and tear the fuck out of there, spinning a rooster tail of mud and gravel as I left the place in my rearview mirror. *I shouldn't be here. I shouldn't be here at all.*

The screen door swung open and Jerry sauntered onto the porch. He wore a loose tank top and tan cargo shorts. Dirtied white high-top sneakers and a flat-bill hat cocked to the side completed his wannabe Kid Rock ensemble.

I always did think he was a fucking idiot.

Raymond stepped out beside him and they both gawked at me from the porch. Raymond was dressed almost exactly like his brother, exception being he wore a black Anthrax t-shirt. He pulled a pack of cigarettes from his shorts and lit one up.

Fuck.

I gritted my teeth and ignored the itching in my arms, took a breath and got out of the car.

"Mornin', fellas. Been a long time."

"Mmmhmm." Jerry stepped from the porch and withdrew his own pack of smokes. He made a dramatic display of whipping open a Zippo (shiny, a new addition) to set fire to his cigarette before snapping the lighter shut and stuffing it in his shorts again. "How was your time?"

My mind flashed to Angie, still inside, but I shrugged. "It was time."

"Mmmhmm." Raymond stepped down to join his brother. "Kenny sent you, I guess."

"He got tied up this morning."

The two of them walked closer to the Chevelle, taking slow puffs off their cigarettes as they eyeballed the vehicle.

"I thought that cocknocker said it was a hotrod. *Kickass car*, Kenny said. I don't know. Bit of a disappointment in person."

And so it began. I knew the fucking drill. I'd been there before, *so* many times. I glanced back at the car. The morning rain still speckled the paint job like diamonds. The chrome rims gleamed. As it stood, the car could have been on a calendar photo. Kenny *was* a moron, but either the car had come this way, or he had done a damned good job of cleaning it up.

"Disappointment? You're fuckin' kidding me, right? You two already buzzed up today? This...this is *American muscle*. United States of America motor car."

They circled the vehicle like hyenas over a dead zebra. Their expressions phased from disgust to—at best—modest approval.

Jerry stopped at the driver's side door, knocked the chrome with his knuckle. "Give you a grand for it. Best I can do."

I glanced at Raymond, turned back and nodded to Jerry. I dangled the keys out in front of me so he could see and hear 'em jingle. "A *grand*? I could take it to the fuckin' high school and sell it for fifteen hundred to one of the football jocks. This car is American history, tried and true, for fuck's sake!"

I stalked to the driver's side and made a point of pausing in front of Jerry. "Excuse me," I said, "Got places to be."

He stepped back and I opened the door and got in, making sure they could hear the solid *thunk* as I closed the door again. I slid the key home and gunned the engine, giving the gas a couple solid gooses. The goddamn thing roared and I threw it into first gear.

Jerry stepped around front and put up a hand, silhouetted in the headlamps as smoke curled from his face.

That's it, you fucker. Nibble on the hook and take the bait.

I revved the engine one more time and he didn't move, so I twisted the keys and shut it off again. The hood ticked.

"Yeah?"

Jerry came around the side and leaned in through the driver's window. "I want to test drive it first, but...I'll give you two thousand for it. That's it."

I let out a long sigh, a real *'howcudya'*, and leaned my head back against the seat rest. "Two grand for this... *machine*? Goddammit, Jerry, two grand? This car is tighter than freshman homecomin' pussy. Do you have *any* idea what kind of jean-short splitbottoms are going to line up with you two driving around town in this? Any thought to how many mix-tapes Raymond could sell with it bumpin' out of this stereo? You both will be *swimming* in pussy."

I shook my head in disgust. "If it wasn't for our history... look, man, I'll *give* this car to you for two grand but you're gonna have to kick something else in."

Four bundles. Say it, Joe. Four bundles of smack. Just do it. You want it. You need it. Oh God, it would feel sooooo good.

I gritted my teeth as my smackhead mentality kicked in. When you're a junkie, your creativity is only matched by your selfishness. You find ways to leverage. To overcome. You don't really *want* to fuck people over, but you think quickly for your own outcome.

I suddenly realized if I sold the damned Chevelle, I had no way back home. Kenny and the girl were supposed to be headed to the hospital. And Pops? *Hell no.* No way I could call him to pick me up. He'd flay me alive for just being on the same property as the Dennys.

I lifted my head and took a quick survey of the farm. A yellow dirt bike lay against the side of the house.

"Throw in the dirt bike and...okay. I guess."

I hauled ass up the hillside away from the Denny brothers. I wore no helmet, goggles, or sunglasses as I squinted against the wind. The occasional BB-gun sting of bugs smacked my face but I didn't care. I had two grand in my pocket, one of which Kenny was going to find out about, and a new mode of transportation.

It wasn't until I breached the second hill and gunned the Suzuki into an outright scream that I realized I'd left my jar out on my bed and Pop was alone in the house.

CHAPTER FOUR

I PARKED THE Suzuki at Kenny's and made my way back to Pop's on foot. Stuffing my hands into my pockets, I cowered against the rain, praying the old man was still sleeping by the heater. I hopped the sidewalk and started across the lawn—when I found him in the open garage with my baseball bat at his side.

"About time you came home."

"Pop." I hurried out of the downpour and shivered. "I'm so sorry. I was just checking up on Kenny. He caught a cold, being out in that weather all day."

"Caught a cold, huh?" Pop tapped the bat against the concrete and clicked his tongue. "Why's this out on my workbench?"

"I..."

The old man was smarter than this. I couldn't insult his intelligence, not after all I'd put him through—but I still tried. "Heard a noise," I said. "That damn alley cat was back. Chased it off before I went to see Kenny."

He looked outside as if confirming the direction I'd come. I hated myself for lying, but I doubted he believed a word either way. He gave a curt nod, and the disappointment he emanated was almost too much. I couldn't meet his eye.

"Right," he said, stretching out the word. "Well, I'm just going to take this into my room from now on, okay? Y'know, I bought you this hoping you'd crack a few balls with Alan and Davey out in the old field. You remember that place? Those guys? They're both married now, Joe. Davey's got a kid."

Here we go, I thought. *The passive aggressive slap. Just use the bat and be done with it, Pop.*

"Right," I said, and swallowed the lump in my throat.

Pop shouldered the bat. "Right is right. Get inside. You got some explaining to do."

Ouch.

I cocked my head and followed him, hoping against all hell that damn girl wasn't waiting inside with a smug smile plastered across her face. She could ruin everything at the drop of a hat and—

"What's this?" Pop pointed with the bat to the jar on my bed. Dirt peppered the sheets. In my excitement, I'd never even cleaned the thing.

"That's...a jar, Pop."

"Don't be a fuckin' wiseass. What's the deal with it?"

I crossed the room and plucked it from the mattress, rolled it over in my hands. A penny clanged against the inside. "Found it out by the creek this morning, thought it looked kinda—what? Don't look at me like that, I'm not lyin'."

His brow creased together. "And what's inside?"

"I dunno, all these *wishes*. Little hopes from a little kid, far as I can tell."

He pulled something from his back pocket, and smiled. "Testing you. Needed to know you wouldn't lie. I know what's in there."

"How?"

A PENNY FOR YOUR THOUGHTS

A piece of rolled up paper sat in his open palm. "Grabbed one to see what you had there."

My mouth suddenly dried and I licked my lips. I thought of the Raleigh bike. I thought of the girl's crash.

But then she doesn't get to have one neither!

"A-and?" I said. "What does it say?"

"Says," he opened the paper and chuckled, "Says 'just a bite of luck.' Misspelled. Queer thing, huh? And y' just found it out by the creek?"

As Pop talked, his voice trailed off, replaced by a high-pitched ringing. He'd *read* one. A *bite* of luck. The hell could that even mean?

"Earth to Joey, y' listening to me, son?"

"Sorry, Pop, just...long day is all."

"Right. Well, I asked if you're planning on heading out again tonight."

"Just if Kenny needs something. Said I'd drop some painkillers. If he needs 'em."

"I see. Well, I gotta be at the mill tomorrow at seven, so I best get some sleep. And you've got a curfew. Eleven on the nose. Two hours, y' hear me? And I want the keys on the counter when you're back. I'll be checking, and don't think I won't."

I bit my tongue at being scorned like a child and reminded myself: *you did this to yourself.* So instead I said, "Yeah, Pop."

"Right." He let a beat pass before adding, "I love you, Joey."

"I love you, too, Pop."

He nodded and left as I eased myself onto the creaky mattress, feeling like the world's biggest pile of shit. That man deserved better, and each lie I'd told felt as if I'd actually smacked him. But I didn't have too much time to marinade. My phone buzzed.

The phone light ached my eyes as I pressed 'answer' and kept my voice low. "Kenny, you home?"

"Yeah," he said, "*We're* home."

"Shit. She not leaving?"

"Joe, she said she's setting up camp on my doorstep if I kick her out. Wants fifty on the Chevelle."

In the background, I heard her yell, "Damn right I do."

"Believe this shit?" Kenny lowered the phone. "That honey ain't for you, bitch, git your hands off my shit!" The line crinkled as he raised the device back to his ear. "Joey, tell me you got that hunka shit moved?"

"I got it, Kenny. A grand. Job done."

And another thousand for my troubles.

"Thank Hendrix. And what's this bike doing at my place?"

"That's mine. Compensation for going it alone. Don't touch it."

He sighed. "Look, I ain't babysitting this kid any longer, get over here and give her a cut to shut her trap. Leg wasn't even broken. Believe that? I paid two-hundred for a four-eyed Indian to tell me that while she snickered behind me. Meanin' I've *shit* left to my name once I give her fifty percent and—*will you stop going through my goddamn things?* Jesus Christ, Joey, help me out here."

"I'll be right over."

I hung up and stared at the too-bright screen for a long time...Kenny's situation took second rung on my priority ladder. My guts clenched as I pictured that note in Pop's hand. The damn vision refused to dislodge from my brain's cinema. I couldn't deny the two scribbles I'd read had come true, but part of me still considered that coincidence. I needed test subjects. A baseline. I wouldn't let any harm come to Pop. Not on my life.

A PENNY FOR YOUR THOUGHTS

The time on my sticker-covered digital read 20:54, and when I stashed my extra grand, grabbed the jar and left, it was 21:00. My thoughts remained on one thing, and it swelled with urgency: a bite of luck. I locked up and stepped out, keeping a close eye for anything with teeth.

"Happy now?"

Kenny planted his hands on his hips, watching the girl count her cash—making a point to *flick* each note. A pretzel hung in her mouth as she nodded, then, apparently satisfied, she pocketed the bulging wad and pulled the food from her lips. "Happy as a run-over girl can be."

"Stop that."

I sat at Kenny's kitchen table sipping a Coke. A low-wattage bulb hung overhead, caked in cobwebs, and taped posters of pin-ups decorated the walls. A bachelor pad, Kenny called it—a dump, I say. Grimy dishes filled the rusted sink and clothes were draped across every possible surface. Before me on the table sat the jar. I told the two we'd get around to that in time, but first, we needed to talk business. A grand could tide me over, sure, but with my parole officer coming, I needed proof of income, a payslip, something—*anything*—to get him off my back. Until we made our next move.

"Look," the girl said, and hopped onto the only clear space of the kitchen counter. She kicked her legs like a child on a swing set. "I need an income. You both need an income. Joe, you need payslips, and Kenny...well, you just need professional help."

"And you need a name," I said.

"Ava."

"Ava, right. Well, what is it you're thinking, Ava?"

Kenny balked and shook his head. "You gonna take whatever this chick says, Joey? She's a cheat."

"We're all cheats," I reminded him, and watched the girl chew her pretzel, her brow knitted together.

"I'm in a bind. And here you two come like a wrapped present on my doorstep. I'm takin' an opportunity when I see one. My grandma was put away three years ago. She got done for a crime back in the late sixties that she swears she didn't commit and—"

"Hold on," Kenny said with a chuckle. "Just hold on. They put away an old woman for something she did in the late sixties? And it was outta the papers? You're local and I never heard shit. Ain't buying it."

The girl's voice hardened, as did her features. "Yeah, well, why embarrass the woman at that stage in life, Kenny? She was already going away. They let her go without a scene. Granted her that much."

"What did she do?" I asked. I didn't know if I believed her, but thanks to Pop, I could read a good poker face.

"They *said* she killed her boyfriend. Both woulda been about sixteen at the time. Found his body out in the Lowback trail way back and—"

"I remember that!" Kenny spat.

The girl sighed. "Can ya let me fuckin' finish? They ran some new tech they got, much better than they had in those days. A 'cold case' or somethin' they called it. Skull had been bashed to shit and they managed to fingerprint the markings on the tarp he was wrapped in. Belonged to Grandma. Damn fingerprints were all over the place...A body wrapped in plastic and, all these years later, they can pull her prints from it, can you imagine? The poor bitch..."

"She do it?" I asked.

A PENNY FOR YOUR THOUGHTS

"What did I say? Like *hell* she did. One time I asked her, asked her straight up. She never answered but I saw it clear as day on her face, she didn't do shit. I know that woman better than myself. Tried approachin' it buncha other times, all sideways-like so she wouldn't see it coming, y'know? But she just stared at the table as if ghosts lived in the wood...But she raised me. She's my Gramma. Wouldn't flick a fly. So, she just let them take her off without a fight and that was that. She's still inside." She trailed off, seeing something neither myself nor Kenny could. Then she shook that vision free. "Look, that ain't the point. The point is, she was opening *Hole in the Dough* to try make enough to get me and her outta Briarwood once and for all."

"The scummy, old donut place?"

She threw Kenny a look that could stop a rodent's heart. "Yeah, the *scummy, old* donut place."

"But it's closed, how's that gonna help us?"

Ava rubbed her forehead as if Kenny's words ached her think-jelly. I didn't blame her. "Look. The place is closed, you both know it's dusted and locked. *But it's in my name.* Now, I don't know about you, but if Joey needs to claim a couple of hundred in wages to a parole officer with no paperwork, then he can be my guest. But I've got a better idea."

I couldn't help but smile. "We wash the money through your donut shop."

"All it takes is me switching that sign to *open*, ringing up receipts, and giving you an honest-to-God wage. Order supplies and materials with the dirty cash and mark up the sent payments a little. Just a little here and there, nothin' to raise any eyebrows. Your parole monkey just needs to know you're working, he won't pester you too much. They've got enough scum to check up on, believe me, I know."

"How's that?"

"Bad ex. Look, it'll keep them off your back, Joey. Clean as a whistle." Her eyes locked on me then. "I *need* this. Please."

"So we're selling donuts now?" Kenny asked.

Ava slapped her cheek. "Jesus, *Lord*, give me strength. No, you *idiot*, we *say* we're selling donuts so that our money is... Joey, help me out here?"

"I'll draw up a picture book to get it in his head, Ava, don't worry."

"All right, then. Look, all this, it'll prove useful when... *other* cashflows come our way."

She studied the countertop and chomped another bite of her pretzel. I watched as a dumb smile spread on Kenny's face.

"Kenny, what's she talking about? You two know something I don't?"

"I got an idea."

"When *don't* you have a fuckin' idea?" I said. "Spill."

Kenny pulled a stool closer to the table and plopped down all three-hundred pounds, his face containing the same excitement as a kid in a toy store. "So, the repo guy I got the Chevelle from? He tells me about these storage lots they got out in an industrial estate Downtown. He's all proud, see, 'cause he just picked up a second job replacing all the locks thanks to an ex-staff guy who cut all the keys. They don't tell the clients, don't get it in the papers, 'cause they don't want people pullin' their shit. Just change the locks, act like nothin' happened. He's got some of the keys on him. We're drinking, and he crashes on the couch the night he delivered the Chevelle. Well, I take one of the keys over to Leroy's place, and—"

"You got the keys cut," I finished.

"Right, but I ain't stupid, Joey, even if you say so. I only got *one* key cut. Only took the one. Unit used to belong to this pawnshop in South Philly by some guy named Samson. This dude is tellin' me all about it 'cause he had to open each lot to make sure the new keys worked. All unwanted piles of shit in there, he said. *Valuable* shit."

"You want to rob old pawnshop junk from a storage unit."

"And hawk it off to the Denny brothers and their friends."

"And wash it through Hole in the Dough," Ava added.

"Well, fuck me," I said. "This could actually work."

"I've got two ski masks and black spray paint for the cameras already," Kenny said. "If it even comes to that. Dude's just yappin' and telling me they ain't got shit for security. Half the cameras *don't even work!* So, look, I got the key to the place, and I just need a yes from you, Joe."

I shook my head. "It's like you were almost expecting me when I got out, huh, Kenny?"

"Oh, don't give me that shit. Don't act like I'm some kinda bad influence. You're just as bad as me, get off your high horse. Least I'm nowhere near as bad as *Angie*." His face twisted as if the word tasted of shit.

"The hell happened between you two anyway?" I asked.

"I don't want to talk about it."

"Fine." My head throbbed. The day had been too long. "Look, I've gotta get back soon, but let me think this 'idea' over."

"Little boy gotta go to bed?" Ava sang.

"Curfew."

She chuckled. "Curfew? How old are you?"

"I've got a parole officer and an angry Pop, lady, so *yeah*, I got a goddamn curfew. Shut it."

"And you got a jar," she said with a nod. "What's that all about?" She popped the last of the pretzel into her mouth and arched an eyebrow.

"Yeah, Joey, what's up with the jar?"

In all the excitement, I'd forgotten about my little acquisition. Now that I was here, my plan to use these two as human guinea pigs faltered. Then I recalled Pop's note and quickly dashed my doubts. I'd spent a lot of time since leaving the house watching for something I could interpret as a '*bite* of luck', just like those crazy conspiracists who interpreted old writings in abstract ways. But if these two read a note and something *did* come true—then I could not doubt my jar any longer. I *needed* the proof.

"It's like fortune cookies," I said. "Found it out in the woods today. Thought it would be a little fun for us, bond us together with our new business plan. Like those synergy exercises companies make you do."

"Bonding." Kenny squinted his eyes. "Don't sound like something you'd offer, man. What's your angle?"

"Angle?" I opened my arms and a nervous laugh escaped my lips. "Jesus, Kenny, it was just a bit of fun, that's all. Look, I'll take it home, it was just an idea I thought would be interesting."

I stood and grabbed the jar.

Just like with the Dennys, I thought: *that's it. Bite, little fishy.*

"Nah, nah, nah." Kenny grabbed my arm. "Sit down, come on now. I'm interested."

I sat.

"Okay, so what's in there?" Kenny cocked his head and eyed the dirty glass.

"Pieces of paper. Just something I found out by the river that I found amusing. Pop your fingers in and pick one out, tell me what it says." Distrust crossed Kenny's face, so I added, "That's all there is to it."

I wasn't lying, either. But as with Pop, it was only a half-truth.

"Well, go on."

Kenny looked to Ava who simply shrugged.

"You first," Kenny said, and folded his arms.

"Fine, you big baby." Ava stood and slid two fingers inside the jar. Her tongue poked from her mouth as she shuffled about the pages. "Got one. Here."

She withdrew a scroll and fell back on her seat, unfolding it as she crossed her legs. "There's a penny," she said. "Looks old." She scanned the page, eyes moving back and forth, back and forth. "Okay. It says...'Now she's got a puppy. How can she have a puppy and not me? I want one, I want one, I want one! Give me a puppy!'"

Ava lowered the page and jutted her lip. "That it? What's this gotta do with anything?"

"Just a bit of fun," I repeated. "That's all. I don't know who wrote these, but I was interested in what they said."

"Then why don't you just pull them all out?" Ava reached for the jar and I whipped it from the table, my heart slamming. "Cause that would ruin the surprise, wouldn't it? It's not every day you find a jar in the woods full of wishes...I wanna savor it."

She appeared to accept the answer and shrugged. "All right. I just think it's stupid."

"Well I don't care what you think," I said, and held out the jar to Kenny. "Go on, man. Your turn."

"Kid's gotta have wished for, like, a million dollars, right? What kid wouldn't wish for a million dollars?"

"Well, reach your hand in and see if you find it. You find the *million dollar* wish, and I'll even let you keep it if it comes true."

Kenny waggled his brow. "You're on, Joey."

He popped two meaty fingers down the glass throat before yanking out a page. Then he laughed as he sat back and the chair creaked. He unfurled the page and flicked the penny taped there. "Come on, my million. Let's be having you."

He began to read, his lips in motion as he mumbled the words.

"Kenny, you gotta read it out to us, those are the rules."

"Ah, fuck that noise." He slapped the page on the table before folding his arms in a huff. "That ain't funny, Joey. Just...some stupid little girl wishing for stupid little girl things. No million dollars in there."

"What's it say?" I reached for the page but Kenny slapped my hand.

"Dude." I tried again. Another smack.

"It's stupid, that's all. Just a stupid wish."

Ava's hand flashed across the table fast as a bullet. She yanked the note to her face and read as she dodged Kenny's paws. Then she burst out laughing. Kenny reddened.

"*What?*" I asked. "Jesus, will someone just tell me what it says!"

"It says..." Kenny sighed and scratched the back of his neck. "It says, 'I wish I had big boobies.' You happy?"

CHAPTER FIVE

EVER GET A big idea? A big ol' *Eureka!* thought, itching to make your head burst like a too-tight helium balloon? While you're sitting there, patting yourself on the back, blown away at your own genius, you either decide to jump right then and there and get down to it, or you take your time to consider the fine details and finesse of it all.

When Angie and I thought to rob a store, it was *not* a big idea. It was a junkhead dumbass plan of something along the lines of: *Mongo, point gun at man. Take money! Run, Mongo, run!*

On the 'inside', I heard a lot of dumbass plans from cons—it was how most of them ended up there in the first place. The *good* plans I heard, however (far and few between) all had one thing in common—they were uncomplicated, and the little things weren't overlooked.

Kenny's plan, *surprisingly*, was a good one. And *just* as surprisingly, Kenny wasn't pestering me every other hour asking when we were going to do the job. For someone with the enthusiasm of a new puppy, it was highly unusual.

Ava's idea of using Hole in the Dough as a front was pretty damned good as well, but it was a detail I couldn't afford to overlook. If my parole officer came sniffin' around the shop, it wouldn't do much good to have him peer through the glass and see the place covered in cobwebs and dust like an old woman's abandoned cooch.

When I got there, the shop door was already cracked open and I found Ava inside. I'd called Kenny and left a voicemail and texted him twice with no response.

"Where's Captain Smiley at?" Ava had lined up cleaning supplies on a dusty countertop near an ancient cash register.

"Probably sleeping off a hangover." It was an excuse but I knew better. His car wasn't there this morning when I walked by and took the dirt bike. Hard to say what the hell he was up to this time of morning but Kenny was never an early riser. He'd once said 'goodnight' to me at eight a.m.

"Well he'd better get his sad ass in here and help if he wants his cut, I don't care if he's the one who has the key to the kingdom or not." She pulled a backpack to the counter and unzipped the top, withdrawing two rolls of paper towels.

"He'll be here." I scanned the place and shook my head. It looked like it hadn't seen a bottle of Windex in a couple of decades. I took a deep breath and sighed. "Well, let's get to it."

We started from the top down, front of shop to back. The dust on the windowsills was as thick as rabbit fur, and more than a few times, Ava and I had to step outside in the middle of a sneezing fit to suck a breath of fresh air. I jammed a rubber wedge beneath the door to prop it open and keep the air flowing.

After a few hours, the place was starting to look *almost* presentable. A few dead flies still dotted the sills and the dust bunnies beneath the counter could eat a rodent whole, but we were getting there. The subtle scent of lemon cleaner lifted the room.

Ava withdrew a couple cans of beer from her backpack. She nodded at me and tossed one over. "Swiped these earlier. Figured they might come in handy today."

"Shouldn't you have a juice box or something instead?"

"Shouldn't *you*?"

"Huh?"

"Parole officer, dummy. They don't take too kindly to alcohol."

"Shit."

She cocked her head and cracked the tab on her can. "Go ahead. My ex had a decent one, he never minded a beer or two as long as you were keeping straight and narrow. If you trust the guy, then it's up to you. But I'm havin' a damn beer." She took a swig, burped lightly. "More importantly, we'll see how funny your parole officer thinks it is when you have a wad of cash and no reason why you should have it."

"Christ, don't get your panties in a bunch." I sipped my beer, relishing the taste as it fizzed down my throat. "Didn't know you were so testy about your age."

"I'm old enough to turn you both into my bitches a couple days ago." She set her can down on the counter, and then hopped off and dipped out of sight. I heard sweeping, gritty noises of a dust broom against the linoleum floor.

I leaned back against the wall and shook my head. I checked my phone and there was still no word from Kenny. *What was that fucker up to?*

As I called the moron again, soft clicking noises drew my attention to the front of the store. Where a small terrier-type dog sat on the sidewalk. It was mostly white, with brown and black patches on his face and upper back.

It had the floppy ears and loose-fitting pajama skin of a pup. The animal moved toward the threshold of the shop and then stopped, seeming to take inventory of the place. It took a few more steps, sniffed the rubber prop, and walked inside.

It glanced at me, then away, still turning its head to admire the place, as if hunting something specific.

The hell is this?

Ava rose from behind the counter, hair matted to her forehead with sweat as she set the dust broom down and—I swear—that goddamn puppy *smiled*. It ran the ten-foot distance to her with its tail wagging to beat all hell.

"Well hi there, puppers!" Ava bent to pick the dog up and it excitedly nuzzled its head against her, licking her neck. I shook my head again and watched her laugh as she hugged the dog close.

"Didn't take you for the type to have a dog. Figured you'd have some pissy Siamese cat or something."

She glanced up at me, smiling. "Neither."

I gulped another mouthful of lukewarm beer. "What do you mean?"

The dog was trying to roll over in her arms, so damned *overjoyed* to be near her. She laughed out loud and I had to admit, the girl had a great laugh. A *sincere* laugh. She looked at me, eyes wrinkled and arms full of the little mutt. She scratched beneath its chin. "Handsome little guy, isn't he, though?"

"Bullshit."

"What's bullshit?"

"That's not your dog?"

"I've never seen it in my life before just now. Honest." Ava set the canine down on the dirty floor before reaching inside her backpack. She withdrew a bag of chips, tore open the foil, and pulled free a single chip. The dog instantly lowered on its haunches, staring up at her. "You're *such* a good boy!" Ava stretched out her hand with the treat and the dog gingerly took it from her fingers, crunching it up. A line of spittle fell from its working jaws.

"You're screwin' with me."

I got to my feet and stepped outside to look around. No one was patrolling the area calling out for a beloved pet. Just another dismal gray day in Lowback. I glanced inside at Ava, now sitting on the floor beside the dog, petting him. There wasn't even a collar around its neck.

I want one, I want one, I want one! Give me a puppy!

The hair on the back of my neck stiffened as I remembered the wording on Ava's wish. I crossed back to the counter, stared at the cute furball beside her on the floor, and set down the half-empty can of beer. This wasn't a coincidence.

I checked my phone. Still nothing at all from Kenny. *Something was wrong.*

A bite of luck. "I gotta go, Ava."

The puppy crawled into her lap and Ava looked at me as her good-cheer vanished. Her expression wasn't one of frustration but of disappointment. Somewhere deep inside that black-hearted chest of hers, I think she was almost prideful we were cleaning up her grandmother's shop. "But... we're not done yet."

"I know, okay? I'll be back tomorrow. I just...I gotta go."

I slid the Suzuki to a stop beside Kenny's trailer. His car still wasn't here. I walked the bike to the side of the property, parked it, and then stepped onto his front porch and knocked on the door.

Nothing. Place was as quiet as a mouse fart.

Kenny, where the hell are you?

I stalked on back home with my thoughts reeling, and when I stepped inside, the smell of grilling steak greeted me. I hung my jacket up as movement flashed in the back yard through the sliding glass door. A bottle of McClelland scotch rested on our old picnic table, absent a few inches of liquor.

Snippets of lyrics came muted through the house, the melody an old Creedence Clearwater Revival song, though I couldn't remember the title.

Pop was...*singing*.

Now that may be a familiar thing for some—their parents singing—but not for me. I think the last time Pop sang was in 1989 when the Berlin wall came crashing down, and I honestly don't remember why in the hell he was singing then because we don't have a drop of German blood in our line.

The gas grill gave a metallic *clank* as Pop closed the lid. He wiped his hands with a towel before pulling the sliding door open and stepping into the kitchen, followed by the smoky aroma of charred food. A grin lifted his cheeks. "Good timing, boy. Sit down." He hummed as he opened the cupboard and pulled two plates—*the 'red ones', Mom's Christmas plates*—and laid the dinner table. He then got a glass from the cabinet before retrieving the food from the grill. "A man's dinner tonight. Steak and whiskey." He chuckled as he poured into the fresh glass and recapped the bottle.

"What's the, uh..." I lifted the glass and smelled. Truth be told, I was never a big fan of scotch, but right then and there, I took a swallow of the liquid lava. My nerves felt shot to hell. "Celebrating something today, Pop?"

A PENNY FOR YOUR THOUGHTS

He worked his steak knife over the grilled meat on his plate, slicing it into morsels. Stabbing a piece, he raised it toward his mouth, then paused. "Damndest thing happened today." He popped the meat past his lips, and released a satisfied sigh.

That feeling I had at Hole in the Dough washed over me again. Little whispers at the back of my neck, like freshly hatched spiders marching along my skin. "Oh yeah?" My voice came out weak but I don't think Pop heard the shakiness. I took another sip of the scotch.

Pop chewed his bite of meat and nodded. "That's damned good." He continued using his steak knife and glanced up at me. "You know the Connellys, right?"

"The mansion out at Woodmount Crossing? Yeah, Pop. *Everyone* in Lowback does."

He wasn't wearing his glasses, yet leaned forward with his brow wrinkling as if he was peering over them. "No need to be a smartass, but I get your point." Another bite of steak, another sigh. "Eat up, boy. It's better when it's hot."

I got to work on my own steak, the fibers tearing as easily as butter, and I had to admit—it smelled damned appetizing, even with my stomach doing flips.

"I was strolling down Woodmount when this walking *bedroom-slipper* of a dog came haulin' ass at me from the end of the Connelly's driveway. Snarlin' and growlin' so bad you'd have thought I was trying to rob the place. Latched onto my damned ankle like you wouldn't goddamned believe." Pop reached for his whiskey and closed his eyes as he savored a swallow to wash down the meat. "Mmmmm, *damn*. This stuff'll take you back home, all right."

"What did *you* do?"

"Well, I reached down and grabbed the little bastard off of my pants leg and he turned around and bit the hell right out of me." He laughed as he unbuttoned his sleeve and rolled it past his elbow. A bright white bandage covered a good nine inches, thick enough to cover his wrist and forearm.

"Jesus, Pop! How bad *is* it?"

"I've been hurt worse by watching dirty movies. But Maria Connelly didn't know that." He grinned as his eyes got a little sparkly and full of mischief as the whiskey made itself at home. "She came running down her lane at me almost as fast as that mutt of hers had done. Wearing nothing but an untied bathrobe and some sort of nightgown beneath, and waving a dog leash as she screamed, '*Pookie! Pookieeeee! Leave that man alone!*' like some kind of crazy woman. By the time she reached me, I was holding that snarling puffball out like a dead rat and had blood gushing down my arm. Mrs. Connelly ran out of the gates onto the sidewalk and yanked the dog right out of my hands."

"Pissed at you?"

"At the dog!" Pop leaned into the table, laughing. "I've never seen a woman slap a dog in the face, but you'd have thought she was scolding a toddler stealing candy at Carrington's General Goods."

"What happened then?" I pushed a bite of steak around on my plate but reached for the whiskey instead. My mind was trip-firing as Pop talked.

"Connelly clipped the leash onto the dog's collar, reached into a pocket of her robe and pulled out—*I shit you not*—her checkbook."

"From her *robe?*"

A PENNY FOR YOUR THOUGHTS

Pop nodded his head. "Rich people...I tell ya, kid." He speared a piece of meat, mopped it around his plate in the juices. "She starts yammerin' away at me, apologizing all over herself, eyes wide as saucers as she's lookin' at the blood running down my arm. Starts writing out a check for *fifteen hundred dollars* and hands it over to me, mumbling about medical bills and lawyers or something."

He reached for the whiskey then, poured another finger's worth into his glass before wiping his hands on the towel. "She hands me the check and I'm staring at it, and her, because her mouth is runnin' a mile a minute and she takes one look at my expression and takes the check back and tears it up. She's shaking her head and scolding herself as she's writing out another check and hands that one to me, this time for *twenty-five hundred*."

"Two and a half grand?"

"Yes, indeed, boy. Handed that check to me and took her dog back toward her house, yelling at that animal the entire time. All for a bite from Cujo's puppy." He held his bandaged arm out and looked it over like a war wound. "Shit, if I'd have known it was *this* easy to get money from rich folks, I'd have been walking past mansions with dogs years ago." He leaned back in his chair, patted his stomach and smirked. "Hell, I might go back again tomorrow."

"A bite of luck." I said the words out loud to myself.

"Wha—*Oh!*" Pop nodded and laughed. "Yeah, the penny thing. You damned right it is." He stood from the table and took his glass with him, swirling the contents. "Don't let that steak go to waste now. Finish eating and clean up for me, yeah?"

I nodded. "I will, Pop."

He left the room and settled into his lounge chair, the TV blurting to life with some gameshow or other. At the table, I sipped my whiskey. It wasn't long before Pop's breathing slipped into soft snoring as a burned-out actress on the tube tried to sell some miracle cream.

I stared at my dinner plate for a long time with my mind on Ava and Kenny. The steak was a good cut of meat but I'd lost my appetite for the day.

CHAPTER SIX

"I'M GONNA NEED you to do it in front of me."

I cocked my head at Officer Henderson, waiting for him to continue.

"Piss," he said. "In here."

I took the offered container with a slow reach, and then motioned to the house. "Out here, or do you wanna, y'know, come into my bedroom? Might be more comfortable."

He sighed. "Don't be a smartass. Sooner we get this over with, the sooner I can leave you to whatever it is you do."

A passing car slowed, the morning driver taking no effort to hide their curiosity. I gave them a wave as I jostled and unzipped. As I did, a thought slapped me hard as a calloused palm. "Shit, Officer Henderson, I had a beer a couple of nights ago and my dad gave me a whiskey with dinner when—"

He waved a hand in dismissal. "It's a NIDA 5, Joey. Amphetamines, cocaine, that kinda thing. You were a junkhead. The court doesn't much care if you washed your dinner down with a beer these days. More interested in your employment situation." He gave me a nod. "You impressed them, you know? Myself included. Can't deny your old man is solid, too, still want him to take me up on my fishin' offer one of these days."

"Pop's a creature of habit." I stuck my little fella in the container and squeezed out a few drops. Being watched while *draining the snake* came naturally from my time in prison, and for a while, I even wondered if I could go *without* someone breathing down my neck. "Here," I passed the man my piss before zipping up. Look, I liked Henderson—I did—but authority figures gave me as much pleasure as a rotting tooth.

He accepted the container with a grimace and slipped it inside a baggie before removing his rubber gloves. "Look, you're a good kid, Joey. I'm used to peacocking assholes with too much pride and overflowing entitlement on my route. Don't let me down now, okay? I'll be gone before you know it."

His encouraging words were lost on me, however, as, over his shoulder, Kenny popped from behind the corner of Pop's garage. He waved frantically, his wide eyes bursting with alarm. Officer Henderson caught my expression, spun, but Kenny ducked around the corner. He turned to me again with some suspicion. "Everything all right, Joey?"

I swallowed. "All...all good, man. All good. Hey, how about I take you over to Hole in the Dough and you can be on your way? I'll even talk to Pop about your fishing plans again. He needs a jolt sometimes."

He smiled at that. "Good plan, Joey. You just lead the way."

And lead the way I did, sticking to his right side so he'd face the street rather than the house. The day was nice, warm, and I took full advantage. I yammered on about something mundane as we strolled past the garage, and I forced my face to relax as I spotted Kenny hunkering behind my father's Daphnes. He was topless.

Now, this was nothing new for Kenny Williams. I'd watched that man wear a wife-beater in a deluge; saw him bare-chested in the sun, but never—and I mean *never*—had I seen him in a bra large enough to take two mice sailing downstream. Until now.

I couldn't help it. I gawped.

"Joey? Joey, what?"

Henderson turned and spotted the idiot pretending to trim the Daphnes...without a tool in-hand. Kenny whistled.

"My neighbor," I spat. "He's...look, Officer Henderson, he's a little touched, you know? Pop lets him think he's our gardener and throws him a couple of dollars once a week in good faith. Took a bad knock as a kid and never fully recovered. Now he's decided he likes to...likes to wear women's clothing, I guess."

Henderson shook his head. "Poor sonofabitch."

"Right," I agreed, matching his concern. "Poor, *dumb* sonofabitch."

Henderson cupped his mouth. "You're doing a great job. Keep it up, son."

I shouted, too. "Keep it up, Kenny. You're a machine. A big, well-oiled machine."

The moron stood and gave me a look hot enough to boil rice. I just shook my head. "Doesn't like me. I took his scissors away, see, last week when he started chasing the strays. Found him with two bare kittens and mounds of fur at his side. Miss Randolph down the street had to knit 'em sweaters after that."

"I see," Henderson said. "Well, let's leave the little man be. He's a good worker."

"Yeah. Let's leave him be."

I mouthed "sorry" to Kenny as we made for Hole in the Dough. I'd deal with that bra-donning ape in due time, but first I prayed Ava had the store in presentable condition. I needed all tracks covered.

"Nelly's at the Women's Correctional," Henderson said.

"Huh?"

"Nelson Novotny? You guys were chummy, right?"

I smiled at the name. *Ol' Nelly.* The only Corrections Officer who cut me slack. I missed the sumbitch. "Yeah, how's he doing these days?"

"Got a mustache fatter than a dead squirrel to go with the new job, but he seems to like the place. Did a good job convincing the board to get you out early. He's a good man, Nelly. Gets attached to the inmates, though, but you know he's a softy. So that Women's Correctional will either be a blessing or a curse, depending on where you're sitting."

I laughed at that—Ol' Nelly surrounded by hard-lined women looking for an out...And Angie, too, of course. I prayed they didn't cross paths.

"I remember correctly," Henderson said, "He vouched and said you'd have work faster than anyone after you got to the outside again. You fulfilling his promise?"

"Uh, the place just opened again recently," I explained as we crossed the street. "Taken over by the original owner's granddaughter. Nice kid, and I really believe in her business."

"Donuts?" he said with a laugh. "Joey, you don't have to lay it on *that* thick. A job is a job, right? That's all I care about."

"Right," I said, and pulled open the door as every muscle in my body tensed. Lemon cleaner and light music hit me.

Ava greeted us with a smile as she rounded the counter, hair tied back and an apron hugging her figure. She looked great—professional—and I breathed a sigh of relief. She shook hands with Officer Henderson and gave me a wink. "Joey, is this the man you told me about?"

"Officer Henderson, ma'am," he said. I noted the stammer in his voice.

"Henderson." She rolled the word about her tongue. "Cute name for a handsome man, I gotta tell you."

Henderson blushed. The bastard actually *blushed.*

"Well, we're not open just yet so I don't got a whole lot to show you, but Joey's been helping me get the place ready better than a team of coffee-fuelled strongmen, I gotta say. Even trucked out these stools from my source, went the extra mile."

Henderson laughed. "And, Miss..."

"Greenfield, but please, call me Ava."

"Ava, have you been *employing* Joey for the work? He has a paycheck, right?"

"Right as Lowback air, sir. First one due today, in fact." She rummaged about in her apron; like she hadn't planted it there for this very reason. "Here we are."

Henderson took the paper and scanned it over twice. Satisfied, he handed it my way. "Well, congratulations, Joey. I'm impressed. And I'll be sure to let the court know. Nelly, too. You're a working man now. I want to see you keep this up, okay? Next time I come back, I expect a double-glazed and change, understand?"

"Oh, I understand," I said, and accepted his firm handshake.

He nodded to Ava, cheeks still red. "Ma'am."

"Officer," she breathed with a wink, and then he was gone. I gave a sigh of relief, raking my fingers through my hair. I only noticed then that I'd been shaking. Four tables sat at equal spaces across from the counter, each one with a red-checkered cloth and surrounded by smart chairs. The countertop itself was shining and the register gleamed. Overhead, Ava had cleaned the glass bar that would soon contain pricing information for customers to peruse as they ordered. I admired her work.

The door squeaked open and Ava breathed an irritated breath before slapping down her arms. "Ain't open yet, dickwad, go find a cookie or somethin'."

The man disappeared fast as he'd come as Ava untied her apron in angry jerks. "Been suckin' in my gut for an hour. Fuck this noise. I've been up since five this morning, Joe, *five*. I ain't never woke before the sun and I don't intend to again. You fuckin' owe me. And—"

"Ava." I cleared my throat. Took a moment. "Ava, Kenny has tits."

"And the *bra*, Kenny?" Ava curled on Kenny's kitchen floor, clutching her stomach as tears streamed her cheeks. "Where the—where in the *fuck* did you find the *bra*?"

If looks could kill, Kenny would've toasted us there and then. He slumped over the table with a bottle of whiskey in one meaty fist. His stomach looked as if it were eating the table wood, his upper lip twitching. Some of his coarse back hair sat pinned beneath the bra straps. His tits were great, though, I gotta say.

A PENNY FOR YOUR THOUGHTS

"I hawked it from Missus Elmore's line at five in the mornin'."

"*Elmore?* The librarian?" If Ava heard anymore, I thought she'd explode.

"Yeah," he shouted. He smacked the table. "What about it?"

"Just didn't expect such a *handful* from her, that's all."

"Jesus, guys!" Kenny snatched the bottle, knuckles white. "I've got tits big enough to give a blind man a hard-on and you two just wanna giggle and shit? Joey, this is *your* fucking fault, fix this!"

I held my palms out. "Man, I swear, I would if I could, honestly. I don't know how."

"This was your jar's doin'. How is that even *possible*? It's bad mojo, man. You've got a *curse* on me or somethin'."

"Or somethin'," I agreed. I wanted to give that more thought but all I could think was *honk, honk!*

He shook his head in disbelief. "Let me get this straight. You found that thing in the woods. That much true?"

"Right. I swear."

"And then you *obviously* pulled one out and it came true, so you wanted to use us as, like, *test subjects* and make sure it wasn't a coincidence?"

"You got me."

Ava sat upright. "Damn, why couldn't I have gotten the boob wish?" She collapsed into giggles again as Kenny slapped a palm to his forehead.

"So what did *yours* say?"

"Mine? Mine was for a Raleigh bike."

"But...But I gave you the Raleigh bike?"

"I think that's how it works, man. It makes things... happen. I can't explain it. I just had to make sure it was real, you know? Ken—I swear—if I'd known whoever wrote them would've wished for big tits, I never would've—" *Fuck.* I couldn't finish the sentence. "I'm sorry."

Ava and I caught eyes and that's all it took, we bellied-over, unable to breathe. Tears streamed our cheeks and then Ava farted and we laughed some more. It took five full minutes for our engine to run dry. Kenny sat there, red-faced and seething, as he sipped from his bottle.

With her shoulders still *shaking*, Ava said, "Insane as this shit is, one thing's for sure: that wisher was a teenage girl."

"At one point, yeah." I wiped the tears from my face. "Other wishes were from *way* younger, though. Her handwriting changed. She's been wishing for stuff and sticking them in that jar for years. Possibly her whole childhood."

"And sticking pennies to the wishes," Ava added. "Why that?"

The mood shifted, darkened somehow.

"Payment?" I said. "I know as much as you guys. I swear I just found the thing."

Kenny's brow creased as he leaned forward, giving me a full view of his new meat-cushions. "Well, she's gotta have wished for a million dollars, right?" He looked between us both. "I know I said it already, but come on... what kid *wouldn't* wish for a million dollars?"

Before that train could take off, I interjected. "We're *not* taking any more wishes out." I thought of Pop's encounter with the angry mutt—*a bite of luck*—and waves of fear washed up my spine. Just *one* misspelling was all it took. One heat-of-the-moment outburst from a teenager, and we'd be in deep...All the while, my eyes refused to go anywhere but Kenny's chest. It was like a car crash, man, I couldn't look away.

A PENNY FOR YOUR THOUGHTS

"You're right, Kenny," I said. "It's bad mojo. We don't fuck with it anymore. You want to be 'pretty as a unicorn' so your tits look less out of place? It's a little girl's wishes. You don't fuck with that."

"So, what?" Kenny leaned back, his attempt to appear 'macho' counterbalanced by his bazookas. "I'm just stuck with these things? Feels like I'm carrying two watermelons on my gut. This is my life now?"

"Welcome to my world," Ava said.

"Hey, man, I told you—I know as much as you."

"Kenny." Ava got to her feet and planted a hand on his back. Her eyes were already glistening with mischief before she continued. "I know it sucks, and running is going to be hell from now on, but I'll help you pick out something nice, okay? Something to help with the back pain. Nice sports bra, yeah? And at the end of the day, when you're sweaty and hard-worked, *oh, boy*, there is *no greater feeling* than taking off that boulder-holder, trust me."

"See?" I said. "You've got friends here. We got you, buddy."

"Listen, you two fuck-nuggets. And, Joey, my eyes are up here, Padre. Before you forget, we got a storage unit to get to tonight and I'm the only one with wheels."

"Kenny," I said, "you go breaking into a storage unit with Double D's, trust me, the folks watching *America's Most Wanted* will remember."

"Then I'll *tape* the fuckers down," he growled. "Ava ain't takin' my wheels, and neither are you. I'm the one with keys to the place—so *I'm* going. Not havin' no one take the wheels in my house. Not anymore."

"What's that supposed to mean?"

"*That bitch of an ex of yours...*" he mumbled.

"What? What the hell happened between you and Angie, dude?"

He gave me a fiery 'god-help-me-if-you-talk-back' look before breathing deeply. Finding his 'Zen' place. With his face now red, he spoke slowly. "If either of you want in...I suggest we get planning."

Whatever had happened between him and Angie, I wasn't going to probe.

"Well, I'm out." Ava clapped her hands and stood. "I want a cut of the deals, that's *all* I said, remember? I clean the money—that's all. But you boys run into trouble, Kenny, don't forget to get the big guns out for security. A crop-top will help. You know how men are." She snickered and I watched her bite her lip to keep from erupting all over again.

I folded my arms. "I guess it's just you and me then, Jugs."

We didn't speak the whole ride over.

Kenny gripped the wheel, his teeth clenched as Waylon Jennings howled from the dashboard. While he had not 'taped the fuckers down', he had, in fact, gotten Ava to snag him a large sports bra from the mall. I said nothing about the fact, opting instead to eye the tarmac slipping beneath our tires. In the backseat, we had ski masks, three duffel bags, and a backpack.

We also had a key and a simple plan: at seven o'clock, security checked out. Unit owners were free to come and go as they pleased. We'd park out of sight of any roadside cameras and walk the rest of the way. Once at the storage units, we'd don our masks (*smile for the camera, boys*) grab the loot, and leave. Simple. We had a key, after all, and the industrial area lacked the foot-traffic of 'real' Downtown, especially in the late hours, so no one would be around to freak out on account our ski masks. I still had to be home for curfew by eleven, though. I told Pop that Ava needed help at Hole in the Dough and he seemed pleased—hell, he seemed pleased at *anything* now that he had two and a half grand burning a hole in his long-johns—but I still hated lying to his face.

We had one hour.

"You all right?"

Kenny pulled up behind a U-Haul at the sidewalk. He killed the engine and pocketed the key. An overhead streetlamp cast his features in heavy shadow.

"Yeah. We're good here, I think." He craned his neck for a look-see. Outside sat a dodgy-looking complex, its windows a checkerboard of on and off lights. The industrial estate sat two blocks up. Not a soul walked the streets. "Let's get moving."

I popped my door and climbed out into the night, the air still thick with moisture from the rain. Kenny slammed his door and ran a palm across his face before waddling to the back door and grabbing our things. He muttered something as he threw me a ski mask.

"You sure you're all right?" I asked again. We'd done jobs like this before, mainly the tourist cottages out by the lake that only housed occupants through the summer. With Angie on lookout, we'd typically grab watches or TVs—easily pawnable stuff—but the act was much the same as tonight.

"I'm good, Joe. Seriously. Let's just get a move on."

I allowed him to take the lead and studied his gait

as we moved up the street. Something felt *off*, and while Kenny might be stupid, the sonofabitch had his ways. I'd once watched him talk his way out of a parking ticket by offering the meter maid a bite of his sandwich. And, *yes*, that actually worked. Poor thing looked like she'd been on her feet all day and Kenny spotted what she needed, called it a 'trick up his sleeve,' and I imagined he had many more.

A block from the units, we paused at an intersection and scanned the road. In the distance to the right, a lustful red light winked as a beacon to late-night drinkers. If I strained my ears, I could hear country music and chatter from the bar, but down here, we were in the dark. Some bored teens had even busted most of the streetlights. This would be easy like Sunday morning.

I pointed to the industrial gate entrance. "Camera at the gate. Ski mask on here, we'll waltz in and out. They check the cameras, we've got nothing distinguishable besides your...ample bosom."

Kenny snarled before yanking on his ski mask (crooked) and I did the same. We crossed the street, picking up speed with each step. As we passed the security booth, I peeked inside out of instinct. Empty. Just an empty yogurt container by the CCTV monitors and a folded newspaper. Before us stood rows of locked units, their metal grates still glistening with rain. A white-painted number marked the right of each door, and I counted as we moved.

"Number 15," Kenny said, and took off without saying more. The less we spoke, the better, and when we reached the door, Kenny fished the key from his pocket and slipped it home.

"Almost seems too easy," I whispered, but Kenny ignored me as he yanked up the door. The metal banged as it rolled above our heads and we stepped inside, greeted by the musty odor of antiques and concrete. I rummaged for my phone and switched on the light.

Dust particles danced in my beam across three columns of cardboard boxes in the center. Random knick-knacks flanked the larger pieces. I was actually impressed with the load, and when I spotted a pristine Gibson SG in the corner, I jutted my lip and gave a nod of approval. Not bad. That guitar would net us nearly a thousand depending on the interior condition. Still, the boxes pulled my attention and I grabbed one. I sneezed as dust tickled my nose through the mask.

After ripping off the tape, I peered inside. "Two guitar pedals," I said, "Eighty apiece, easy."

I lifted out the units and placed them in my duffel. "A cigar box and an old game console." They also went into the bag. "Handful of DVDs...some porn, and..." I hoisted out a bag of clinking jewelry. "Jackpot."

I stuffed it all inside my duffel and moved onto the next box, working fast. Kenny did the same, and within a few minutes, our loot bags were fit to burst. My chest pounded and I glanced out at the lamp-lit lot more than once. After testing the weight, I shouldered the duffel, feeling as if a midget was trying to choke me out. I grabbed the Gibson with my free hand and waited for Kenny to lock up. In my head, I attempted a calculation of the score's value but gave up. If the jewelry was genuine, we could be looking at over ten thousand total. Not bad, at all.

"Let's move it," Kenny said, and once he slammed down the metal roller and locked up, we bucked it, keeping a close watch on the streets. Again, we passed no one on our way, with just our labored breathing and a subtle *buzz* from the lights for company. At the car, we slipped our stash into the trunk and the backseat. We were in the clear. I yanked off my ski mask as soon as I eased into the passenger seat and breathed crisp air, only realizing then I'd been sweating. I laughed as Kenny kicked the engine to life.

"Shit, Ken, we've got about ten Gs each here, holy shit." The smile stretched my cheeks but Kenny didn't reciprocate. His face was sour and shining as he pulled out and U-turned for the highway.

I slapped his shoulder. "What's up with you, man? You've been acting weird all night. You love it when a plan goes well." A memory sparked and I said, "Remember the night Angie got wind of that New York yuppie's place out at the lake? We lifted seven iPods and you were so fucking delighted you suggested we stop for, what was it, 'burglar burgers' at the food court? Wanna grab one? I've got just enough time if—"

"Nope. Don't want a burger."

We pulled out into traffic and Kenny wiped his forehead with the back of his arm.

"All right. Look. If this is about the tits, I didn't mean to—"

"Not about my boobs."

"Well, it's about *something*. That's for sure." Alarm bells screeched in my head the further we drove, and while Kenny made for a good robber, his poker face needed a lot of work. The sweat on his skin wasn't just from the mask, and his troubled eyes almost seemed to vibrate in their sockets. "What's going on?" I asked. An anchor of fear plunged into my stomach. "Kenny, what have you done?"

"Huh? I haven't done nothin', Joey. Just...yeah, the tits got me all wrong in the head. I'll drop you at your Pop's and take this shit to my place, okay? We'll drive it out to the brothers tomorrow mornin'."

A PENNY FOR YOUR THOUGHTS

"All right," I said, more to avoid an argument than anything, and eased back into my seat.

Something's wrong.

When we reached Briarwood, Kenny let me out two doors shy of my Pop's and I walked the rest, watching his angry red taillights disappear in a cloud of sharp exhaust fumes. Maybe his newly acquired chest *was* responsible for his mood. Hell, I wouldn't dare leave the house, but something told me it wasn't that. I'd known Kenny many years, and the only time he shut his motormouth was when—

"He had a plan," I muttered, and broke into a run across the lawn. My heart slammed as I burst inside the house and made for my room, no longer caring if I woke Pop or not.

My window stood open.

Dirty footprints stained the carpet.

I planted my hands on my hips, eyed the ceiling and shook my head as I whispered, "You absolute *motherfucker...*" and then I punched the wall.

The jar was gone.

CHAPTER SEVEN

"YOU FUCKER."

I clenched my jaw and gritted my teeth. A memory flashed of me grinding my teeth, going through withdrawal, and was gone.

"You *motherfucker*." I squeezed my hands into fists and forced myself to take a deep breath before letting it out slowly. I didn't hear Pop stirring in the hallway, so the dent I left in the drywall hadn't disturbed him.

"You *dumb* fucking motherfucker!" I hissed the words instead of what I wanted to do, which was *scream* them at the top of my lungs.

I shut my eyes and sucked in another controlled breath, then I checked the time. I had five minutes until curfew, and baby wasn't ready for bed.

Nope. That wouldn't do. Not at all. Not right fucking now.

I barged into the hallway and stopped, listening to Pop's deep, even breathing as he slept.

I had to get to Kenny's place before the idiot wished for a second dick, or to fly, or be married to Prince Charming.

"Kenny, you dumb fuck," I whispered, stalking toward the kitchen. The bottle of McClelland was a good deal lower than I'd seen it yesterday but I didn't blame Pop.

Hell, he'd earned the right to have more than a snort full of top-shelf.

I eased open the kitchen door and gently put it back in place. The cold night air tickled my skin, but my blood ran hot. I was pissed and I was scared. It was *not* a good combination.

Kenny's living room light spilled a piss-yellow glow across his lawn. I took my time, stepping carefully and quietly, as I approached his porch and peeked inside. There he sat, in his dirty tank top, on that dirty green couch of his, tilting a beer into his gullet.

On the coffee table separating him and the TV, sat my jar, surrounded by an overflowing ashtray, empty packs of cigarettes, beer cans, and a grease-stained pizza box.

I tested the front door, twisting the handle. Locked.

From my past experience here, this was not a problem. Staring through the window at the moron himself, I gripped the knob and did a slow upward *shrug*—over to the right, up again, back to the left—and the door lock popped open in my hands. I froze in place, watching Kenny bathe in the neon glow of the TV. Nothing. No recognition or awareness of me. With his gaze still on the screen, Kenny reached for the lid of the jar.

That would not do.

Something I learned on the inside is if you're going to do something, then do it fast and hard and don't let up until you've achieved your goal.

I swung the door open so hard it slammed off the cheap paneling, and Kenny's gaze spun toward me, bug-eyed and stunned at the intrusion. I took two short strides from the front door toward his living room and launched myself at him.

A PENNY FOR YOUR THOUGHTS

Kenny managed a throaty squeak before I landed on him and the couch overturned on us. The edge of the coffee table skidded and the penny jar fell and rolled against the wall. We tumbled to the carpet and even in the chaos, I had a moment of pure disgust as I noticed several of Kenny's socks had been stuffed beneath the sofa. I didn't ever want to know what foul secrets they were privy to.

"Joe, what the—"

I jammed my hand against his wet face, covering his mouth with my palm and turning his words into a garbled mess. I was pissed at Kenny, *super-atomic-Godzilla-level* pissed, but I didn't want to actually *hurt* him.

Except Kenny didn't know that.

He grabbed a handful of hair and *yanked*, twisting me away. On instinct, I reached out and jammed a finger in both of his eyes. He let loose a scream and grabbed for his face. And though I think it was by accident, he brought his right knee square into my balls. "Asshole!"

The wind left my lungs, and a dull, aching gut-punch rolled through me. I rolled off him onto my back and lay on the carpet, clutching my pulsating crotch.

"The fuck, Joe? How come you done that?"

I squinted my eyes, my vision doubling, as Kenny backed up against the living room wall. He breathed heavily as his ample bosom rose and fell like a tide in an oncoming storm. Both of his eyes were bloodshot.

I gritted my teeth against the agony in my balls—*Jesus!*—and tried to speak. I rested my head on his dirty carpet. "You stole the jar, Kenny." My words came out in a pained whisper.

"Joe, I..." Kenny cleared his throat. "I didn't *really* steal it. I just wanted to—"

"You took it out of my goddamn *bedroom,* Kenny, so yeah, I'd call that stealing." I turned onto my side and forced myself to sit upright. The pain finally started to ease. Christ, he got me good. I felt like I was going to throw up for a moment.

Kenny sat there, looking ashamed of himself. He got to his feet and lumbered to the fridge, coming back with two cold beers. "Here." He offered one to me, and I took it.

"Look, Joe. I'm sorry, okay? I'm *sorry* I stole it, but can you fuckin' blame me? You got a brand new bike and I look like Dolly *goddamned* Parton!"

I cracked the beer and took a swallow. Cheap swill, but right then it tasted damned good. "Kenny...in all honesty, I don't think Dolly Parton's tits are nearly as nice as y—"

"Joe!" His face scrunched with emotion.

"I, uh...I kinda touched 'em, actually."

"What?"

His attention snapped to me but I refused to meet his eyes.

"When we were, y'know, fightin'. My hand accidentally landed on one of 'em and—"

"Joe!"

"I'm sorry! It's..." In hindsight, maybe I should have kept this to myself, but at that moment, it held some sort of fucked-up logic to make Kenny feel better. "Felt kind of nice, actually. Firm, y'know, but not—"

"Jesus *Christ,* Joe!"

"I'm just sayin'—"

"Well *don't,* okay? *Don't* fuckin' say!"

I finally looked up. Tears glistened in Kenny's glassy eyes, but I couldn't blame it on my *Three Stooges* finger defense. He stared at me, his face, for all the world, looking like a toddler upset over a scraped knee. But I couldn't help myself. My focus was drawn to his chest like a goddamn magnet.

"Kenny, you, uh..."

"What?"

"You're having a wardrobe malfunction."

"A what?"

I nodded to his left tit and Kenny's gaze followed my lead. His tank top had stretched askew during the tussle, and there it was, peaking out over the thin cotton fabric—Kenny's nipple, pert, pink and as pretty as anything the fine girls in *Hustler* magazine had to offer me during my time on the inside.

Kenny stared down with his chin doubled. A high-pitched giggle escaped him. Then another. A third, and I joined him and then it was, well, it was *lunacy*. It turned into that howling, insane, tear-inducing laughter that dances on a fine line of a good memory and booking a room with padded walls.

But eventually our fits eased, and both Kenny and I wiped the tears from our faces.

"Ahhhh shit. *Whewww.*" I took a swig of beer and set the bottle down on the coffee table. Thankfully, we hadn't broken the damn thing.

"Kenny, we'll figure this out, all right? But these *things*... Look, man, I don't know what's going on, but we can't afford to be dumb. What if that little girl wasn't only envious of another girl's tits, huh? What if she wished to be a big girl like some teenage cheerleader she was jealous of? You want to read that out loud and start having your period, too? Every 28 days, *bleeding from your dick?*"

Kenny blew a sigh and snatched his beer before taking a slow pull. He nodded agreement and burped. Poor fuck still looked sick about the whole thing.

"So what now, Joe?"

The pain in my crotch had thankfully dialed down to nothing but a dull sensation. Truth was, I had no idea how to answer. It was a fucked up situation. I glanced at him, then to the penny jar. It had rolled against the far wall, bottom end pointed at me like we'd been playing *spin the bottle*. That's when I saw it, standing out like a bit of sea glass on a beach. I crawled closer to the jar, squinting.

On the bottom, stuck to the inside, was a small sticker. A sticker about the size of a postage stamp. In faded type, it read: **CARRINGTON'S GENERAL GOODS.**

"Kenny, who's the oldest person you know?"

"Why?"

I held up the jar. "Because tomorrow, we're going to find out what to do next."

I knew there was no way in hell I'd get busted for curfew but it still made my heart race a little on the walk home. I didn't like the idea of getting pinched for something as stupid as being out this late and going back to prison.

What're you in for, killing a man? Right on. Me? Nah. I was caught outside after nappy time.

The crickets sang a chorus and my mind raced. The jar somehow felt *alive* in my arms; *buzzing* with energy. It dared me to smash it right there on the sidewalk and *read, goddammit, read every last one!*

And I didn't like it one goddamned bit.

I got into the house without waking Pop and eased myself into bed. It was a long time before I fell asleep.

The next morning I woke to the sounds of Pop in the kitchen. I heard him running water into his coffee cup and setting it in the sink before the front door opened and closed.

A PENNY FOR YOUR THOUGHTS

Stifling a yawn, I texted Kenny and Ava to meet me at the Lowback Post Office. I figured it was a good point to start asking about Carrington General Goods. Everyone who's everyone uses the Post Office and over time it had become the hub of gossip in Lowback.

I remembered Pop talking about Carrington's from time to time, but the place had been closed since before I was born. I didn't even know where it used to be. To avoid Pop hovering over my every move, I needed to upturn some new rocks.

Kenny and I got there just after 9:30 and Ava showed up a few minutes later. She was carrying her dog in her arms and I noticed it had a red canvas collar around its neck.

"How's the pooch?"

Her face broke into a grin and she used her free hand to pet his head.

Kenny looked to the dog and then back to Ava. "Wait, your wish came true, too? You got a dog?"

Ava's smile widened. "He's the best, I swear. He's so smart, he—"

"I bet he is and that's just great and all." I cut her off as Kenny crossed his arms in front of his chest. He was wearing a hoodie despite the heat, hiding his chest blessings. I recalled my brush with those funbags and shuddered. "Look, I found something on the bottom of the jar. Start asking around and see if anyone knows where Carrington's General Goods used to be. It's the only thing we've got, but it's something."

In a town as small as Lowback, everyone knows everyone. Sometimes you can't let a fart slip without a neighbor three houses down knowing what you ate for dinner. I knew it was a matter of time before we found what we were looking for and I couldn't have been more right. As it turned out, it was Ava who got the information from an old woman headed into hip surgery later that day.

Carrington's General Goods once sold everything from Levi's jeans and plugs of chewing tobacco to homemade jams and canned goods from local farmers. Though the store had shut down more than thirty years ago, people still remembered it, and the Carrington family never moved from Lowback. Ava got an address and we all piled into Kenny's car and headed out.

The farmhouse sat back from the road, but at one time it must've been a glorious sight. Now it was little more than faded gray clapboard siding and overgrown weeds. Sycamore trees lined the drive, and I noticed things on their thick trunks of peeling bark—foot high carvings—strange symbols I didn't recognize at all. A row of hosta plants edged the porch, and out of control rose bushes bookended the house.

The dog whined from the backseat as Ava shushed it and rubbed its head. Kenny pulled into the gravel drive and we rumbled up the dirt path to the front porch. He killed the engine.

"Looks like a great place to be murdered and eaten."

I wanted to argue but didn't say anything. The place *did* look pretty rough. The only thing indicating any life at all was a thin patch of garden off to the right. Several rows of corn and overloaded tomato vines rose from the swath of dirt, though it looked as if the gardener hadn't pulled weeds in quite some time. A single row of cantaloupes ended the vegetable patch and the sickly sweet smell of their rotting flesh filled the air.

We climbed from the car as the screen door opened. A thin black woman walked out onto the porch. She stepped from the weathered landing as her gaze ran us over. She paused on Kenny, tilted her head in a questioning expression, but didn't comment. She carried a dishtowel and wiped her hands as she cut across the grass. "What can I do you all for?"

Ava and Kenny turned at me, and in that moment, I suppose I took the lead. "Sorry to bother you, ma'am, but are you related to the Carringtons?"

"I'm Sadie Carrington." She folded the towel in half and half again, then slung it across her shoulder. "Now, I'll ask again. How can I help you?"

I walked closer. She looked tired. Worn. Her hair was kempt and pulled back in a loose ponytail but shadows drooped beneath her eyes. "I was hoping you could help us out with some things."

She put her hands on her hips and stared at us a moment longer, then waved us on as she returned to the porch. I reached into the car and got the penny jar and the three of us followed suit. The old woman settled onto a porch swing with a blanket folded up as padding and I sat down in a reed-backed chair on the other side of the front door. Ava sat on the porch and Kenny crossed his arms over his chest, finding stones to push around with his sneakered feet.

"Miss, we, um..."

I realized how insane this was right then and there. Tracking down an old woman on her farm to ask about a penny jar that granted decades-old wishes written from some young girl. Christ, she was likely to call the cops. But we had no choice—it was the only damned thing we had to go on.

"I found something that seems to have been bought from your family's store years ago and I was hoping you could... tell me anything about it. Anything at all."

I held out the jar and Sadie's eyes widened. Her hands shot to the edge of the swing and gripped the wood. "Shouldn't ought be messin' with them things. You get them right up on out of here, now."

I left the jar between us, confused.

"You hard of hearin', white boy? I said get 'em on out of here, *now*."

Ava looked from the jar to Sadie. "It's just a jar of pennies. What's—"

The old woman's attention snapped to Ava. Her expression was a mixture of fear and anger. "You shut your damned disrespectful mouth, lil girl. You don't know what the hell you're talkin' about."

To Ava's credit, I could tell she had some smartass comment on the edge of her lips, but she clammed up. She took the jar from me, almost looking ashamed of herself. As she walked back to Kenny's car, Sadie watched until Ava set the jar into the backseat. Her expression softened a little and her white-knuckled grip on the swing loosened some.

"Where'd you find them, boy?"

"Out in the woods, up on the Lowback Trail."

Sadie nodded. "Knew me a woman once, used to make things just like them. Helped out my daughter Lily more 'n a few times..." She looked at some long ago memory, invisible to us. "Did some good things from time to time, that woman. But doin' good things don't necessarily make you a good person."

Something in her voice grated against me, shifted things inside my head. "Is she, is that woman, still around?"

Sadie's eyes shot to the gravel driveway. Her focus shifted from tree to tree as her voice fell soft. "I'd say it was the Devil's work, but no, that ain't rightly true. The hand that helped make all of that mess is much older than that poor fallen angel all the Christians love to hate. I'd take it back if I could, but I'm not the one who rightly did it..."

My brow creased. I had no idea what she spoke of, but I leaned forward with the chair creaking beneath my weight. "Miss, can you tell me that woman's name? We'd really like to ask her about—"

There was a momentary swirling of expression as the woman turned back to me, like watching thunderheads in a smoked mirror. Her eyes grew dark as her fears vanished, leaving nothing but hot anger.

"Not my place to be telling you all this." She glared at Ava. "If your grandmamma wanted you to hear it, then the words would pass between her lips and not mine." She pushed from the porch swing, leaving the seat swaying. "Ought not to be messin' with this kinda thing. Only a fool plays with a loaded gun." Her voice grew louder as the rage flowed through her speech. I noticed she glanced at her dress, seeing something I couldn't. I was reminded of war Vets having flashbacks. "It'll leave a stain on you!"

Clearly, it was time for us to fucking leave. I glanced at Ava, who was nodding at me, and Kenny, who was already fishing for his keys.

"It'll leave a stain on your *soul*, y'hear me?" Sadie trembled as she screamed at us. Her hands were clenched fists of burned driftwood by her sides. The dishtowel fell from her shoulder to a heap on the porch.

We backed off quickly, bee-lining for the car. Kenny jumped into the driver's seat, started the engine, and was already pulling away as Ava and I yanked the doors open and got inside the car.

Sadie's words slammed us as we left her drive in a cloud of dust.

"You all leave it be, y'hear me? *Leave it alone!*"

CHAPTER EIGHT

WE PULLED INTO the Quarry Overlook just as the first droplets tapped the windshield. This spot was another old 'Lowback secret', well-known by the youths as a place for boozin' and neckin' and sticking your fingers where they don't belong. A thicket lined either side of the trail, and should one floor the pedal and drive on ahead, they'd smash through the guardrail and plummet fifty feet to the brackish waters below. Kenny's bumper sat a foot away from that guardrail, with the engine ticking as the torrent outside our windows swelled. Our collective mood darkened alongside that weather. *Raining rats and frogs*, Pop would've put it.

"She knew my Grandma," Ava said. She scratched the sleeping puppy's ears while staring out the fogged-up window, her expression unreadable. "Looked me right in the eye and said she knew Grandma."

I drew my finger across the cold glass, a little awkward and not knowing how to approach the fragile subject. I'd brought Ava to that woman, after all, placed her in this position. It was my fault. I went to speak when she surprised me with a sad chuckle. "She was always flat-chested. Grandma. It's starting to make sense."

I turned in my seat. "You think it's hers, then? The jar?"

"I'm pretty damn certain, Joey. Wanting a puppy, big tits, the foul-mouthed attitude." She laughed. "Trust me, if you met the woman, you'd know."

"And she's in the Woman's Correctional Facility?"

"She's in *prison*, Joe, yes."

"Do you think...any of her wishes came true? For her, I mean?"

I only asked because a woman with murder on her mind and a magic jar could surely get out of a pickle if needs be. A simple *'don't send me to jail',* would've sufficed. *Something had gone wrong.*

"Unless one of 'em said, *'send me to prison for murder',* then I very much fuckin' doubt it. Plus my Gramma never had the biggest chest, Joey. Always sneered at the catalog models. That all but confirms it." The puppy's head shot up and Ava shushed the dog, some of the redness in her cheeks dissipating. She sighed. "Sorry, Joe, I'm just sick of explaining to folks that, *yes,* Grandma went to jail for murder. And I know as much as squat because she wouldn't tell me nothin'." Tears rose in her eyes as she avoided my gaze.

"I'm sorry," I offered. "I just got to thinking that if the jar *does* belong to her, then we can get some answers from her directly. I...didn't mean to stir the waters."

"Who cares if we *do* get answers?" Ava spat, and for the first time, I saw her age—young and frightened, her defensive wall crumbling.

I rubbed my forehead against a swelling pressure headache. "Because I had you take one, Ava, that's why. Kenny took one...*Pop* took one. If there's anything else to this 'mojo', as Kenny puts it, then we need to know. Everything has a price. I'm not prepared to have my Pop pay for something he didn't ask for. I *need* to know what I've done. This sure as shit ain't God we're dealing with. Sadie said as much."

Ava remained silent at that, stroking the dog some more. "I have papers," she mumbled. "Old receipts, journals...stuff like that. I can check out her handwriting... confirm, y'know, if it does belong to her."

"Would you do that?"

She finally raised her head, misty-eyed, and nodded.

"Thank you."

"I'd like to go home now. Be alone."

"Sure thing," I said, and Kenny keyed the ignition without another word. As we backed from the quarry and drove through the downpour, I wondered what, exactly, I'd unleashed on Lowback. See, Ollie, my old pusher, sometimes threw me a nickel bag on lay. 'Another time,' he'd tell me, but he *always* collected. Once broke my back molar with the business end of a screwdriver over twenty bucks. *Twenty fuckin' bucks*, man. So what would a dream-come-true cost to a deity, if one such existed?

More than a penny, that's for sure.

We pulled up to a sidewalk on the far side of Leeds Mill Road where a lone trailer sat by a fat pine and a full garbage can. An untreated wooden fence surrounded the property of overgrown grass, and Ava was quick to climb from the car. A crooked slab of concrete jutted from the rest of her drive and caught her shoe. She tripped and cussed.

"Get that fixed," I called out. "For yourself, and that pup. Don't want you breakin' a—"

She didn't listen, just hunkered against the rain and trotted through the yard with that puppy hot on her heels. Together, they slipped inside the trailer and Kenny and I sat a moment as a melancholic cloud settled around us.

Kenny's lighter clicked as he sparked a smoke and rolled his window down a crack. A draft caught the cloud and pulled it from the vehicle. "Lily Carrington," he said with a lungful, and tipped ash into the tray. "Just came to me."

"What did?" I asked.

"Hooker out on R56."

"Excuse me?"

He sniffled, wiped his nose with the back of his arm, tapped the wheel. "Decade ago, remember the Denny brothers had a nickname for me, stuck about as long as their memory lasted, they called me–"

"Cottage Cheese," I finished. "How could I forget?"

"Well," he said, "Remember our 'poker' nights? They were a sham, Joe...It's why you were never invited. We told you we didn't like Angie and that sure as shit was true, but the real reason was..."

"Hold up," I said. "You've been cussin' Angie like she killed your family since I got out. Now I know you two never liked each other, but what in the blue fuck happened that night?"

In the cinema of my mind, I remembered Kenny bursting through the living room door with his face strained and a vein fat enough to be called a sausage throbbing over his right eye. Luckily, Pop hadn't been home, and, as per usual, I had no idea where Angie was. Kenny roared through the house like King Kong, yelling, *'where is she, huh? Where the fuck is she? I'll kill her!'* before stalking out. Angie and I went away after that and I never did find out what the hell happened.

"My...my comic books."

"Huh?"

For a moment, I thought Kenny had changed the subject, but as he twiddled his fingers and licked at his lips, I waited for the words to come. "Fuckin' *Uncanny X-Men*..." he whined. "Issue 94, Joe...*Incredible Hulk*, Issue 181..."

"*No comprende, Padre*," I said. "You're speakin' Double Dutch here."

He sighed as he eyed the roof and shook his head. "She stole my goddamn comic book collection."

I took a beat, waiting for the punchline. It never came. "Wait, *that's* what this has all been about?"

His eyes bulged as he gave a throaty '*guffaw*'. "That's *all?* Dude, *X-Men* 94 could've netted me ten grand. Ten grand! You know how long I kept those in pristine condition, huh? Know how *hard* that was for me to do? That was a *lifetime* of effort! A lifetime! She snagged it that night you tied-off watchin' *Wayne's World 2.* We were havin' beers and she didn't shoot, 'member?"

"She had the flu," I said, almost defensively.

"Like *fuck.* She was waitin' for me to pass out and, goddammit, I did, sure as shit. I came back over yellin' and screamin' and—"

"—and you're damn lucky Pop wasn't home."

"Yeah...yeah, you're right there. Look. Anyway. Now you know. Can I just get back to what I was sayin'?"

"Sure thing," I said, and just about suppressed a laugh. Damn maniac wanted to string a girl's neck for almost a decade over *comic books.*

"Okay, look, our *poker nights* were just named that as a joke." He arched his eyebrows, waiting for the bell to ring. "*Poker,*" he said. "*Poke her* nights. Joe, we were hitting up the R56 brothel."

"There's no brothel on R56, man. It's a forest trail. Only house out there is old Miss Cramm's cottage, falling apart by the...*wait.*"

"Yup." Kenny looked out the window, his forefinger drumming the wheel. "Making sense now?"

"Miss Cramm did *not* run a brothel."

"Nah, calling that place a brothel is like calling my home a mansion. She had two girls out there, it was fifty apiece, and—"

"Jesus Christ, Kenny..."

"And she'd, y'know, let you in after she screwed a red bulb into the living room for *ambiance*...used to light up her porcelain miniatures like a downtown district. The funniest part was when she made you take off your shoes before entering. *The house*, I mean. That's old ladies for ya."

"I used to bag her groceries when I was a teenager."

"Man, an extra fifty and you could even bag *her* if you—"

I raised a palm. "Stop. Just stop. Please. What the hell are you getting at?"

"Well...one of the girls...it was Lily Carrington. That cranky lady's daughter. Look, if Sadie wouldn't tell us about the General Store, maybe Lily will. I was out there just six months ago, it's like an annual trip for me. Don't look at me like that, dude. Your palm must be asking for marriage the amount you've been rubbin' 'em out in prison. Look, Lily's still living out there with Cramm. And if the price is right, she will talk, I'm sure of it."

I took a moment to absorb the situation. "So...you wanna take me to an old woman's cottage—now a brothel—and pay a lady I don't know for her services? You're serious about Cramm?"

"Swear on my left double-D, Joe."

Jesus.

"What else happens in this town I don't know about, huh? Priests running drugs through the parishioners? School kids selling guns at lunchtime?"

"Just Cramm and her 'toothless twists', that's what she called 'em. Gotta see it, man, she gets down on her—"

"Shut it, Kenny. Just...shut it."

"Right. Well, look. We can go out there and see what we can get outta Lily, but you gotta make a quick stop-off first."

"Yeah? Where to?"

"Well, two stops, really. Remember when we were out at the units?"

"And you stole the jar."

"Well, that's kinda the point. I was with you, *I* didn't steal it. I...I paid the Denny brothers."

"How much?" I gritted my teeth, already imagining a blank space in my room where there'd once been a Gibson guitar. *Kenny, you bastard.*

"Not really a 'money' thing," he said. "I told 'em about the jar, showed 'em my...y'know, *chest*, for proof. And I said...well, I said they could take a wish each, Joe."

"You *what?*"

Fresh, hot anger bloomed in my face and my nails bit into my palms. My jaw worked back and forth.

He raised his hands in defeat. "I said I counted 'em, *lied*, so they'd only take the two. But they *do* got two of 'em now so I *really* think you should get out there if you think we should, y'know, keep this to ourselves."

"Oh, y'think?"

I imagined the Denny brothers yapping to every thug in Lowback about our secret...Hundreds of thieves spying my house day after day...Pop breaking down and kicking me out while Officer Henderson threw me a look of pure disappointment over anger. And wasn't that somehow worse? Then my thoughts turned to *prison*. That much scum around Pop's house would be all it took for Henderson to drag me back.

I cussed and slapped the dash. "Where's the second stop, Kenny?"

"My place, man," he said as he wriggled in his seat. "Gotta switch bras. This one is chaffing the shit outta me."

After leaving Kenny to his wardrobe change, I kick-started the Suzuki and high-tailed it through the hills of Cairn Road with my near-bald tires chewing up and spitting out dirt. Pop hadn't called and I was glad for it. Let him enjoy the respite and the cash before—*if, Joey, if!*—something demanded payment. I zipped past two hatchbacks on the bad bends while thanking the gods I didn't pass a squad car. With no helmet or proper road gear, I was doing a great job of keeping myself on the down-low.

Careful, Joe.

As the farmhouse bobbed on the horizon, I veered into the packed dirt with my back tire blowing out an orange cloud. The usual bathtubs and scorched piles of the Denny's property appeared before me, and I spied a new sight amongst the trash—a dead pony.

I skidded to a stop and kicked the stand before climbing from the bike with my thighs still ghosting from vibrations. I crossed to the animal and planted my hands on my hips.

Flies buzzed off the pony's white flank, and a spider scurried from its mouth. The soil drank the crimson leaking from its neck, and a column of muscle was split wide from what had to be a box cutter. I shook my head and made my way to the decrepit house on foot, watching closely for the brothers in the weeds. They had once shot at the mailman—missed him by an inch—after a night of amphetamines, and Raymond went in for six months on a misdemeanor, claiming intoxication and fire practice. The urine test came back clean. Those brothers were dumb, but they weren't stupid.

"Jerry? Ray?"

I stood at the foot of the porch, greeted by something like chlorine and copper...I climbed the steps. "Hey, you fuckers home?"

With my elbow, I eased open the door, only serving to amplify the stench. A brown stain caked the floorboards, and in the kitchen, a shape shot by the open doorway. "Hey, the fuck is going on here?"

Canned laughter came from the living room as I passed and I crossed my forearm over my face to block the stink. Something shifted in the kitchen again, then a *crash*, and I raced inside.

"Jesus, Jerry!"

His hands glistened in the light, his wild eyes seeming to shake in their sockets. But worst of all was the steak knife rattling in his fists, jabbing at me.

"Back, fucker! Get back!"

"Dude." I raised my palms outward, backing toward the littered table. "It's me. Just Joey. That's all." My breath shook as it reached my lungs but I maintained eye contact—a rule I learned in prison. Break that, you get your neck cut. "S' goin' on here, buddy? You can tell me. Whatever it is, we can fix this." The last word disappeared in a rasp as my saliva dissipated. I licked my lips. "Ain't here to hurt you, Jerry. You know that."

"The fuck have you done to us, Joey?" And this was a new sight: tears from the eyes of a Denny. Had I not seen it for myself, I'd have thought the sight as rare as Bigfoot or a UFO.

"What's the deal with the pony outside, Jerry?" I asked. "You need help getting rid of that thing?"

He laughed, pushed his palms into his eye sockets with that knife pointing toward the open door as if telling me to *run*. Red gunk was stuck beneath his fingernails despite his clean and shining arms, and I suddenly understood the 'swimming pool' scent: bleach. "You got blood on you?"

"Fuckin' *pony*," Jerry spat. "White as coke and...not right, Joe. Thing came—came throttlin' through the field like it was—on a *mission*. Went up, up, up on its hind legs and smashed the back porch to shit. Weren't right...I'm all, 'the fuck is a pony doin' out in the dirt here? A circus come close by or somethin'?' And then Raymond, well..." Jerry shook his head again, sniffled. "Raymond's just *gone*, Joe. After the pony, *just* after, like someone hit me with a big ol' one-two."

"The fuck you mean, 'Raymond's just gone'?"

His face hardened, and his voice came as a monotone—slow enough to give me the chills. "Was your damn wishes, man. Kenny said we could have one apiece. Just one."

"And? What did they say?"

Jerry placed the knife by the sink–*thank Christ*–and some tension slipped from my muscles. I only then realized I hadn't been breathing.

"First, wasn't nothin' serious. And, Joe, not to be bad, but it weren't nothin' personal. To be honest, we was just lookin' for *fun*. Didn't want no payment from Kenny, really, juss wanted to get out the house for the night. Have a good time...Mine said..." He cleared his throat as if reciting a verse for school: "How 'bout a pony then, you sumbitch? No puppy, no luck, no fair. It's not fair! A pony."

"And you got your pony," I said, more to myself. The room seemed to spin and I pressed against the table for support.

"'Cept it weren't *right*." He smiled without a trace of humor. "That thing was all kinds of *off*, Joe. I had to grab it and cut it before it left the property. Couldn't have the police comin' down here and snoopin' around if it hurt someone, y'know? Ain't another house for miles. They'd come here first. Caught it by the Cairn hills just in time. Had to take it down."

"And what about the other wish, then? Raymond's wish?"

"Handwritin' was clearer on that one. Hold on." He pulled the note from his pocket and threw it my way. It spiraled to the dusty floor, light as a feather. *Too* light, I thought. I scooped it before unraveling the page. The penny was missing. It simply read: I want to disappear.

"Where's the penny?" I asked.

"Huh?"

"The *penny*, Jerry. Each one of these had a penny taped to it. An old Lincoln wheat penny."

Jerry scratched his head, scrunched his face. "Took 'em off, of course. Thought I could get somethin' for 'em. Looked old, like."

"Before you read the wishes?"

"Before I..." He licked his lips, appearing aggravated once more. "Yeah, what of it, fuckface?"

"Listen to me, Jerry. You're messing with something you don't understand, man. I don't know if it'll work, but you find me those pennies right now. Let's see if we can fix this. Before you *balls* things up any worse. And Ray, is he...*around?*"

The definition of 'disappear' could vary, and without payment for the wish, my imagination went straight to a dark place. Though when another tear slipped down Jerry's cheek, he didn't need to say a word. The simple sight confirmed my worst fears.

And yet, he spoke anyway. "In the walls," he whispered. "Been hearin' him all mornin' long...cryin' out in the walls, in the attic. He's here. But *not* here. Just...disappeared."

Someone groaned from overhead and we both faced the stained ceiling. The peach fuzz on the back of my neck rose and a beat passed as my pulse drummed my ears.

"Shouldn't have taken 'em, Jerry. You fucked up *real* bad."

"I swear I won't take nothin' from you no more!" His eyes widened—*pleading*. "Look, look, I'll even make good with you right here, wait."

As he fished about in his pocket, alarm bells blared in my brain. "Jerry, what are you—"

He pulled another piece of paper (*fucking seriously!*), this one ripped from where he'd yanked off the coin. "Here, I didn't mean to take an extra one, it just popped free with the other two and I couldn't get it back in. I haven't read it, not after the pony and Raymond and—"

He shook the paper between us, *begging* me to take it, but then his excitement slowed as his expression neutralized.

"What?" I asked. "Jerry, what is it?"

"Could be a way out," he said, and his tone raked fresh fear up my spine. "*Could* be, man. Could be...anything."

"Don't you dare read that paper, Jerry."

But he didn't listen. Like a cornered fox biting off its own leg to escape a hunter's snare, he raised that wish to his face and his eyes shot from left to right, left to right, his mouth moving soundlessly.

A PENNY FOR YOUR THOUGHTS

I spoke in a whisper. "Well? What's it say?"

As Jerry lowered the page, his eyes found mine. A solitary tear slipped down his pocked face, then another, as he hitched, once, twice, and his lower lip quivered. "No, Joe, no..."

"What? What does it say?"

The page slipped from his open hand, and I swear: I never saw anything so pathetic or pitiful in all my years. A grown man wearing a backward baseball cap with blood on his hands, stinking of bleach, and alone. *Terrified.* My mind turned to the brothers many moons ago, listening (but not listening) to our principal's words at their fallen brother's funeral. *Jerry had snickered.* But he wasn't snickering now. No, sir.

He looked me straight in the eye and said, "Reads, 'I just wanna die', Joe. That's what it reads. That's all."

Then he fell.

And from some place out of sight—perhaps out of this world—I swear, I heard Raymond screaming.

CHAPTER NINE

"JERRY'S DEAD?"

"Deader than dog shit, Kenny. Fell to the floor like someone flicked a switch."

Kenny took a drag from his cigarette and stared at the ground. Despite the chilly air, he stood on his porch in a pair of striped boxer shorts and his usual white tank top. He didn't much care about the cold.

"We're gonna need a new fence."

I stared at him. "A what?"

"A fence. You know, someone who buys stolen stuff off us."

"A new fen—what, did you just step off the set of *Goodfellas* or something? Yeah, okay, we'll need that, but right now, there's bigger shit we have to deal with, don't you think?"

Kenny took a longer drag, finishing his smoke, and flicked the butt into the yard. "*I* did this, Joe. I mean, the Dennys weren't fuckin' saints or anything, but goddammit, I didn't mean—"

"Stop." I gritted my teeth. I was still pissed at Kenny for the setup, having the brothers steal the damn jar and offer them wishes as payment. But what's done is done and I

103

couldn't have Kenny wallowing around in self-pity. This was a shitstorm and I needed him focused. "*You* didn't do this. Whatever this fuckin' jar is, whatever controls it... *that's* what did it."

"I'm the one who told 'em—"

"Doesn't matter. What *does* matter is your idea of talking to Lily Carrington. We need some answers and maybe, hopefully, she's the start."

Cramm's brothel wasn't elegant.

I still had a hard time wrapping my head around the fact that the sweet old lady I used to bag lemon blueberry muffins and wheat bread for, ran a whorehouse since before I ever put a needle in my arm. What goes on behind closed doors, I guess. Just another Lowback secret.

A moss-patched roof topped the dirty gray single-level rancher sitting beneath a copse of tall pines. Splashed mud shaded the bottom edge of the siding, and the untreated wood of the front deck bulged like Kenny's belly.

A Honda Civic sat in the driveway, but the lack of light from the rancher made me question our timing.

"Kenny, you sure the place is even still in business?"

"I'm sure." He opened his door and I joined him as we walked to the front of the rancher. I felt like some dumb kid, going trick or treating to a house that didn't want visitors.

Kenny knocked on the door—two raps, a beat, then three, like Morse code. After a shuffle of feet from inside, the lock clicked, and Miss Cramm appeared.

I'm not sure what I expected, maybe her in a sheer gown or something, but she was dressed like she was headed to church—brown slacks and a dark green sweater, with the same short gray curls she'd had years before. Miss Cramm had a few more wrinkles in her face, but otherwise age had treated her well. She glanced at me and held eye contact for a moment, then turned to Kenny with a smile.

"Hello, Kenny, it's been a while!" She stepped forward and gave him a hug, though it didn't last long and I could tell it was just pleasantries. She released him and gave an odd look at his chest, then smiled at me. I thought there was a flash of recognition but I wasn't positive. "Come on in, boys."

She led us to the living room where *Days of Our Lives* boomed from the television. I looked around and it felt like I was in some grandma's living room. Hell, I *was* in some grandma's living room. Hummel statues lined the shelves. Framed photos on the walls. A bad painting of a covered bridge and a waterfall. Brick fireplace and mantel with a little cast iron horse. It smelled like cinnamon and hand lotion. It felt like death's waiting room.

A darkened hallway led away from the living room and rap music played in the distance.

An uneasy feeling hit my stomach. What the hell were we doing here? *Goddammit, Kenny.* It felt *wrong*. Like the first time you go snooping in your parents' bedroom and find porn.

Miss Cramm plopped on the sofa while Kenny and I stood, hands in our pockets, looking like idiots. "You boys looking for a twirl? Tuesdays are always slow and we run a special. Half and half is thirty dollars. Ass to mou—"

Kenny put his hands up and cut her off. "No, no, Miss Cramm. We, uh..." He cleared his throat, looked at me with that 'lost kid' expression.

"Miss Cramm." I nodded to her out of respect. "We're not, uh...exactly looking for *entertainment* today."

She stiffened, her expression less soft.

"Oh, we're willing to pay the same as if we were," I said, "But we just want to talk."

She mulled my words over like a hard-boiled candy. "Boys, if you're paying, you can walk in here with a bag of produce and a snare drum duct-taped to your ass. What you do on your time is yours, as long as you're not causing problems." She settled back into the couch cushion, folded her arms. "Fifty dollars an hour though, slow Tuesdays or not."

I pulled a fifty spot from my wallet and handed it over. Miss Cramm folded the bill and slid it under a lace doily on the end table beside her. "Lily's alone right now, so you boys can head on back. Second door on the left. Just follow the music. I hear trouble and I take out the pistol. Kenny, you know the deal."

The wood paneling of the hallway mirrored the living room, but nothing adorned the dark tunnel. A plastic runner covered the carpeted floor wall-to-wall. The rap music swelled as we moved, Chuck D and Public Enemy tearing up the microphone. My heart mimicked the intense beat.

Kenny was in front of me and he paused at the door before giving two knocks. Someone rose from a creaking bedspring, and then the music was lowered but not turned off. The door swung open to reveal Lily.

She wore a short-brimmed Stetson, an unbuttoned brown suede vest with nothing beneath, pink satin panties, and fishnets. A pair of black cowboy boots ended her ensemble. I think it's safe to say Kenny and I both lost our breath as we stood there with open mouths. Lily smiled at our reaction (I guess she was used to it) and stepped back. "Come in, fellas. Have a seat."

As we followed the light-skinned, knockout beauty into her chambers, my mouth dried and my palms sweated. I felt like a teenager who was just about to cup his first breast. The wonder crossed my mind as to why in the hell she was here, in this one-floor rancher, selling her body, when she could walk into any modeling studio in the world and get a contract on the spot. Then I took a good look at her face. High cheekbones and full glossy lips. Skin the texture of fresh porcelain. But her eyes. *Jesus H. Christ, her eyes.*

I didn't know what this girl had been through in life, but there was no way in hell she could hide the sadness and pain living there, no matter how much makeup she put on. It oozed from every pore, thick as oil...Should she have gotten too close, I feared I'd have caught depression like an STD.

The sparsely decorated room was small but functional. Lily eased back on the springboard mattress, leaning against the pillows propped on the headboard. She kept one foot on the floor and stretched the other down, down, down. "It's been a while since I've had...*two* handsome boys visit me at the same time. What'd you fellas have in mind?" Her vest spread open to reveal the curving swells of her breasts, and Lily trailed a hand from her stomach down to her thigh.

Kenny swallowed hard enough to hear as he turned to me. "We've got time. I mean, maybe we could—"

"Kenny, no, we...that's not..." I won't lie, the thought crossed my mind for a moment. Well, maybe *two* moments. It...had been a while for me since I'd enjoyed the company of anyone but my own Rosy Palm. But that's not why we were there. Even though sweat broke on my scalp.

I took a deep breath, let it out slowly. "Lily, we're just here to talk to you."

Unfortunately.

"Talk?" She gave a soft smile as she leaned her head back and exhaled. Her vest slid open a bit more, showcasing the edge of one beautiful nipple. "Talk is so...boring."

Christ Almighty.

"Yeah, that's...um..." I pulled my gaze from her and sat in a chair at the end of the bed. "We wanted to ask you some questions. We're in deep with somethin', and—"

"Drugs?" she asked, no intonation, no sweat.

"Nah, nothing like that. See, we talked to your mother and—"

"Fuck you say?" Lily bounced upright. Her expression changed from sultry to serious.

"I said we talked to your mother and, I mean, she told us some—"

She reached toward her right boot and a silver shimmer caught my eye, like a minnow swimming in a clear stream. Next thing, a blade pressed my throat as she snatched a handful of my hair, holding me still. Even on the inside, I had never seen anyone move that fast. She straddled me in the chair, pinning me in place.

"Say it again, white boy! Tell me again how you talked to my mom!"

I put my arms out to the side, palms up in surrender, swallowed as the edge of her knife kissed my Adam's Apple.

Kenny stepped back and opened the bedroom door. "Miss Cramm!"

Hurried footsteps came down the hall and the old woman stepped into the room, a look of stern protection on her face. "What's going on here, boys? Lily?"

A PENNY FOR YOUR THOUGHTS

"These fuckers come in here tryin' to start some shit. Talkin' about my mom and—"

Miss Cramm eased closer, rested a gentle hand on Lily's shoulder. "Honey, look at them. Take a good look." Her voice softened even more. "Do they look like troublemakers to you? No. Look in their eyes."

Lily's face remained a twist of anger and pain as she stared at me. For a moment, I thought for sure she'd slit my damned throat right then and there. The pressure of the steel against my skin worsened before she pulled it away and crawled off me. She lowered the knife as she backed toward her mattress. There, she tossed the blade onto the bed and sat. She looked up at me, at Kenny, and then stared at the blanket of her bed. "You're telling the truth."

"These boys don't mean you any harm." Miss Cramm scooped the knife from the girl's mattress. I didn't know what Kenny had done in the past to make Cramm take his side so easily, and perhaps I didn't want to know, either.

I finally moved my arms and rubbed the skin at my throat. My fingertips came away dotted with blood but I figured I'd live. *Goddamn.* I nodded at the girl and spoke in as calm a voice as I could. "We just wanted to ask some questions about something we found. A jar of pennies. That's all."

At that, Lily's eyes widened. That sharp edge returned to her voice as her eyes grew red and brimmed with tears. "Pennies? Yeah..." She sniffed, cocked her head at Miss Cramm. "I could use a...could you..."

The old woman simply nodded and left the room as we remained in silence. I glanced at Kenny and he shrugged slightly. Lily kept her focus on the spiral print of her blanket. Miss Cramm returned with a glass tumbler filled with amber liquid. She handed it to the girl, who took a steady swallow, eyes closed, then another, before she propped the half-drained glass on her nightstand.

"Yeah, the goddamn pennies." Lily sniffed as she looked up at me. "Years back, I had a man. Thought he was a good one." She faced her bedroom window and the dim light shining through. "I was in love, oh my, *so* much in love. He talked to me about gettin' married and what kind of house we were gonna live in. All that."

She took up her glass again, sipped, and cradled it in both hands. "We'd been together 'bout a year or so when I got pregnant. Seventeen years old but I didn't care. We were in love. The world was..." A pause as she angrily wiped her eyes. "That...*man*, that man I thought was *soooo* good, my knight in shining armor, up and left me. Just...gone. Moved off and didn't even stay in Lowback. So there I was, six months pregnant, not knowing what I was gonna do. Hell, I had the sonogram taped up on the fridge. I was gonna have a little—"

She turned away as tears spilled down her cheeks. With a cough, she lifted the glass to her lips. "I cried. Oh my, did I cry. And then my momma helped me. Said she knew a woman who had a *reputation*, but she was a woman who could *fix* things."

I leaned forward, my breathing quickening. "How? How did she fix things?"

Lily's gaze landed on me and I noticed again the depths of her eyes. "I told her what I wanted, that I wished I'd never gotten pregnant at all." She sat up straighter against the pillows, took a deep breath, and then let it out slowly. "Few days later, I got an envelope in the mail. Wasn't nothin' but a piece of paper, 'bout the size of a fortune from Chinese takeout. Had a penny stuck to it.

Words on the paper written in pencil, shaky handwritin' like the person who wrote it was sick or somethin'. One sentence on it, and just what I asked for. *I wish I had never gotten pregnant.* I peeled that penny off and read the words out loud."

"What...what happened after that?" Kenny pulled his hands from his pockets and crossed his arms beneath his breasts.

"Next mornin' I woke up to the worst cramps I've ever had. Bleedin' so awful I thought I was hemorrhaging. I screamed out for Momma and she took me to the hospital. Doctors checked me over." Lily's glossed lips shook as she continued. "That woman fixed it."

Kenny nodded. "Miscarriage?"

Lily shook her head as more tears spilled. "Naww. My baby boy wasn't there anymore. I was having my period. Floodgates opening after carrying a baby for months. My womb was as empty and hollow as the Lowback quarry." She raised her glass and drank two final swallows. "It was like it never happened, like I had never been pregnant at all."

I let loose a breath I didn't realize I'd been holding.

"Thing is..." Lily wiped her cheeks. "That night, next day, every day after...I hear him."

"Who?" My throat was dry as pocket lint, and my hands felt sweaty, like I was jonesing all over again.

"My baby boy. I hear him cryin' all the time." She closed her eyes and crossed her arms as if she was trying to cradle the invisible infant. "Wailin' for me." Her eyes snapped open, full of fear and fire. "I can't...stop...hearing him cry."

I don't think anyone knew what to say after that. The room felt like a funeral parlor and the only sound was Lily's old-school rap. Public Enemy turned over to Eric B

111

and Rakim. Lily's gaze remained on me, but she wasn't seeing me. That poor girl was looking at something beyond the room.

Miss Cramm stepped forward and patted her shoulder. She gently picked up the almost empty tumbler, paused, and then set it back on the nightstand. "You rest for a bit, honey." She nodded at us, motioning to leave and I followed Kenny down the hallway back to the living room. The rap music got louder as we walked away and the thump of the bass felt like a beating heart as we left her behind.

Days of Our Lives still roared from the television.

Miss Cramm didn't take a seat on the couch again and her expression wasn't angry, but worried. "You boys...I know you didn't mean no harm, but that girl's been through enough. You understand I'll have to ban you from—"

"Miss Cramm, I've been a loyal—"

"From seeing Lily, Kenny." She gave him a disapproving look. "I've got a new girl coming in, about two weeks or so. She's from the Ukraine and..." Miss Cramm's gaze landed on Kenny's chest. "She's pretty *open-minded*, from what I hear."

Kenny nodded but kept quiet. I wondered whether he had been coming here more often than a yearly visit.

"Lily sometimes talks in her sleep. Mostly every damned night, really. Sometimes I go in to check on her when she gets really bad." She plucked the TV remote from the sofa, glanced down the hallway, then turned up the volume a bit. "I don't know what you boys are mixed up in, and I really don't want to know. Whether it'll help or not, I don't know, but on the nights it's really bad for her, Lily keeps screaming about...about the Crimson Sisters."

A PENNY FOR YOUR THOUGHTS

"Hell's that mean?" Kenny shifted and shoved his hands in his pockets.

Miss Cramm shook her head. "I don't know, but it's all I've got. I'm worried some biker gang full of boozy ladies is gonna come crashing through my door to find her, and I don't want the trouble, as you know. You find out who these *Crimson Sisters* are, and you'd be doing me a favor, too."

From the hallway, Lily's door opened. I instinctively glanced to the Hummel statues, wondering if I could smash her head in quick enough should that blade reappear. It didn't. She stalked to the living room and stood on the threshold. "When?" she asked.

"What?"

She sniffled as she approached me. Once again, I was struck by the girl's natural beauty, but now, all I felt like doing was holding her and trying to take some of her pain away.

"You said you talked to my momma. When? How long ago?"

Kenny and I glanced at each other. "Drove out to her farm yesterday morning? Just talked to her on the porch for a little while."

I held back from adding, '*oh, and she yelled at us as if I'd pissed on her dog or something.*'

Lily started shaking her head, staring a hole through me. "No. No, no, no." She turned to Cramm. "Told you these boys was comin' here to start some shit, didn't I?" She balled her hands into fists at her sides. "No, you didn't. You lyin'..." She broke into sobs as she ran back to her room, slamming the door shut. We all cringed at the boom.

I turned to Miss Cramm. "I don't understand what—"

"Boys..." She sighed. "I've seen enough johns in my life come in and out of here with dents on their ring fingers and no golden bands to show. I can spot a liar at fifty yards out, so I know you're telling the truth. At least you *believe* you are."

Kenny shrugged. "It *is* the truth. We spoke to Sadie Carrington yesterday morning out at her farm. I don't understand why Lily—"

"Boys..." Miss Cramm clasped her weathered hands together. "Sadie Carrington's been dead for three, maybe four months now. Postman found her lying in her vegetable garden."

CHAPTER TEN

ANOTHER FIFTY BUCKS got me a knock on Lily's door with the added stipulation of 'no promises'. Cramm jacked the volume on the TV, and, like a true granny, made tea for her and Kenny while they busied themselves with some soaps.

"Lily?" I knocked again. "I just wanna talk, so... please don't pull a knife on me or anything."

The door swung wide and there she stood, wrapped now in a hand-me-down bathrobe. I finally saw the real woman, a sad individual, defending herself against the world with a puckered smile and a wink, the exact opposite of this brothel disguised as a cottage.

"Can I come in?" I asked.

She stepped aside and dabbed at her face before easing the door shut behind us and returning to her well-made bed. "The floor will do you just fine," she said, and so I sat, cross-legged and embarrassed.

"Make it quick."

"I didn't lie."

Those words came as fast as her blade, and she simply nodded before answering, "I know."

"And you've got that wish around here someplace, don't you?"

Her mouth opened as if to respond, but she quickly closed it and took a moment. Her gaze fell to the window. "I didn't really think it would, y'know, work."

"Can I see it? The wish?"

She mulled over my request, and after a breathy sigh, pulled open her nightstand and withdrew a slip of paper. Torn from a notebook, I noticed, and heavier than it should be, by the looks of it. She passed the page my way and confirmed my suspicions: a vintage Lincoln wheat penny sat taped next to the scrawl.

"This was your old penny, right?" I traced my finger across the coin. "The one you used the night you—"

"Don't," she warned as her muscles tensed. Her eyes fluttered shut, shaking beneath the lids. "Don't say it. Yeah, that's the same coin. The strange woman gave it to me. I just missed my mom...figured the penny could be reused..."

I passed the page back, but as her fingers found it, I held a moment longer. "Lily, whatever you do, do not take that penny off. Do you hear me?"

She slipped the wish from my hand and placed it on her lap before asking, "Why?"

Because he's in the walls, he...disappeared.

"Because," I said, "I've seen what happens when there's no payment to be made. Kenny calls it 'bad mojo'. And, stupid as he is, I'm apt to agree."

She looked someplace beyond the pane, to a place for her eyes only. Another tear worked its way down her high cheek. "You really did speak to my mother, huh? She's out there? At the old house?"

"She is," I said. "And as long as that penny stays in place, then I think you got your wish. But, believe me, I don't think a penny will be the final cost."

"What makes you say that?"

"I've seen dealers give out shit on layaway before. Always a, 'yeah, pay me next week, it's fine,' but they'll always ask for interest. And 'next week' suddenly becomes 'three days', and next thing you know, you're getting your pinky snapped by some brute named Bubba. Experience, Lily. That penny's just the start."

Her vision snapped to the page before she grabbed it and stuffed it back in the nightstand. Her eyes vibrated and I could almost see those wild thoughts race through her head. "I'm gonna need a lock for this, make sure it stays safe."

And as she spoke, something came to me, and I said aloud, "Or bury it beneath a tree, where no one will find it."

"That's a good idea." She gave a smile before she stood. "I could do that."

"I better get." I got to my feet, too, and made for the door. "Look, I'm sorry if we riled you up. Really, I am."

But her mind was elsewhere, possibly on the idea of walking the driveway to her old home as her mother answered the door just like old times. Perhaps with a pie resting in the oven and a warm hug as good as any glass of Cramm's whiskey.

"Thank you," she whispered, and so, I left. She startled me when she called out, "Becky Barrows...Rebecca."

"Huh?"

I turned on the threshold. She held herself and sniffled. "The Crimson Sisters. They...look, I don't want them here. The woman who helped me, she gave a warning with her note. I've no reason to disbelieve her. Now I don't know why she helped me in the first place, but she did. I'm just a Lowback down 'n out who had a wish. And she warned me. Rebecca Barrows. Take this."

She handed me a piece of paper that, for a moment, I thought was another wish until I read it. "Directions?"

"Understand?"

I nodded and let her be, though my mind and heart raced. I took the hallway without pause and returned to the cozy living room.

"Kenny, up. We gotta move."

He stuffed a custard cream into his mouth and gulped a mouthful of tea. "But, Joe, Francisco is just about to confess his love for—"

"Up, Double D."

His face soured as he crunched the cookie. "Goodbye, Cramm. Tell me what happens."

She nodded she would, though her attention remained on the Vaseline-glow of the soap. "See ya, boys."

And so, we left. Left with a stinging neck, a belly full of cookies, and a single lead: a woman named Rebecca Barrows.

"Shit, Kenny, shit!"

As we rounded the corner into Briarwood Estates, my stomach lurched at the sight of the squad car in Pop's drive.

"Stop here, just *stop*."

Kenny jammed the brakes and I braced against the dash. Without further explanation, I stepped from his car and caught the attention of Pop and Officer Henderson on the lawn. I waved and forced a smile as I slammed the car door and crossed the street and Kenny—*goddammit*—honked as he took off.

"That the slow boy?" Henderson asked.

"Yeah."

"Driving a car?"

"Yeah."

He thought it over as Kenny's car rumbled up the street. "Is that safe?"

"Automatic. Would never let him near a stick-shift."

"Right." He looked to my father as if for confirmation, but the old man had (thankfully) polished off the Scotch before the callout. He just stood with a stupid smile on his face, probably planning more fun with his newfound riches. Not that I could blame him.

"Your neck," Henderson said, and my mouth dried at the words. "What happened?"

"Shaving," I lied, and left it there. He studied my throat a moment longer but appeared satisfied. "Mind if we talk?"

"Sure."

He led me toward the cruiser as Pop ducked back inside, and for the briefest moment, I had a flashback of being shoved against a similar grill while out of my mind on White China all those years ago. "Something the matter?" I asked.

"Any circuses ever come through Lowback, Joe?"

"Sorry?"

He looked to the mountain that was our namesake, at the high-up trees that looked like toothpicks. "Old friend of mine found a dead pony, not six miles from here, in a pasture. Was talkin' to your Pop about it."

"Oh?"

"You know the owners of the farm. One of them was also found. Dead as the pony."

Again, I said, "Oh?"

He's in the walls...

"Jerry Denny." Henderson turned back to me. "And we think his brother Raymond is on the run, Joey. Murder."

"Shit."

"Yeah. *Shit* is right." Henderson looked me in the eye, as if searching for some misstep. Anything. He spoke slowly. "Darren Williams, *Officer* Williams, is an old friend of mine. He's in over his head. Now I'm not saying you've got info, I'm *not*, but I do know that you and the Denny brothers go back a ways. I guess I'm just asking... if you have any leads, any at all, I'd greatly appreciate it. And I'd make it worth your while."

I kept my surprise hidden, and instead nodded. "How do you mean?"

"I like you, Joe, the courts like you. You know me and your Pop are shootin' the shit...Well, the courts can see when a good man's caught up with bad people. See them all the time, in fact. Now that Angie girl? She, they did *not* like. It's pretty clear that robbery was not your idea."

I can be one hell of an actor, Henderson, I thought, but studied the car instead.

"I keep out of your hair as much as possible. I think I've been pretty fair. But if you're lying to me...I'll come down harder on you than this cruiser from a skyscraper. Understand me, Joe?"

"I understand."

"Good." He smiled, shifted the mood. "Still chipping away at the donut place?"

"Huh?" For a moment I'd completely forgotten about our cover story. "Yeah. Oh, yeah. Ava's fit to open on Friday. Throwing some local event."

"I might just have to be there myself."

"Oh," I said again. *Oh, shit...*

If Henderson noted my shock, he didn't mention it. "Look, just the usual call today, kid. Give me a vial and I'll be gone."

He withdrew the cup and I glanced at him. "Need me to do the deed in front of you again?"

He shook his head and waved me off so I slipped into the bathroom and did my business to the sound of Pop singing a duet with Hank Williams. Finished, I returned the cup to Henderson's open palm. He thanked me and went on his merry way. As the police cruiser exited Briarwood, a panicked thought struck me: he'd come back Friday. To the shop we had *zero intention* of opening. They'd find my bike trail out at the Denny's place. And Henderson might not realize the connection at first, but he'd make it sooner or later. I was on borrowed time.

I'm going to jail, I'm going to fucking jail.

Unless I pulled a magic get-out-of-jail-free card.

"Can't. Nope. Stupid idea." I mumbled out loud and paced the yard, running a hand through my hair. "Need a penny for that, dumbass. Don't got one."

But I did. I had more pennies than I knew what to do with. I had wishes that needed retracting, too. Kenny's, for instance.

"Kenny's..."

But what if pulling the payment caused more trouble? Lily peeled her coin, and and look what it got her? The girl was a hollowed out version of a woman. It lead to pain. Raymond Denny was somewhere no man was ever meant to go. *In the walls...*So, if I pulled Kenny's coin...Could I really put him through something...bad? *Would* it lead to something bad? I pulled that penny from the 'bike' wish, after all, and no harm had come to me so far...For whoever answered these prays, I decided, the moral compass of 'right' and 'wrong' did not apply.

"He *did* steal my jar. I could risk it."

And in a way, didn't that lead to Henderson snooping at the Denny's? Wasn't this all *Kenny's* fault at the end of the day?

"In a way."

I looked up and saw Mrs. Boden watching me with wide eyes, her limp hose dribbling onto her petunias. I gave a wave before rushing back inside, and then I slipped past Pop's personal concert and locked myself in my room.

I could take Kenny's wish away. *I could.* Pretty simple procedure. And he couldn't afford surgery, anyway. Any old coin might not work, but the Lincoln wheat pennies seemed to do the trick. Maybe they'd been *blessed*, put through some kind of procedure? I could revert Kenny's chest to its former flabby glory. But at what cost?

Just a coin...just a matter of peeling a penny. Quick as a Band-Aid, Joe.

My old jeans lay crumpled on the floor and I dropped to my knees and fished in the pockets. I found the two folded sheets of paper. After putting Ava's on my dresser, I read Kenny's over and over. It suddenly didn't seem very funny. Not funny at all.

"But I can't go to jail. I can't."

I took a deep breath before I did it...and I was right all along: it was just like ripping a Band-Aid.

I held the penny for a moment. I don't know what I expected, a *bang*, perhaps? A *scream*? But nothing followed, and so I pulled a notebook from the dresser and snatched a pen. The notebook had come as a present from Pop during the 'sick time', as he called it. I was to keep a daily track of my mood, and, as he said, make my progression *tangible*. I flicked past blocks of hastily scrawled entries, my stomach knotting with each passage. The words 'vomit', 'shiver' and 'headache' became a motif, and I shook my head before finally tearing the nearest blank page free. Then I blew a breath before I scribbled: *make Officer Henderson forget about Friday, make—"*

I stopped. 'Forget about Friday' could be misconstrued. I was reminded of scholars squabbling over the meaning of the Bible. How there were hundreds of interpretations of Nostradamus. My wording had to be...*specific.* Henderson could easily forget *every* Friday in history, and if his wedding or birthday landed on the day, I was to blame. I pulled a new sheet, started fresh.

*Please make Officer Henderson forget we were to meet this Friday. Make him think Hole in the Dough is doing great business. Get rid of any evidence of me ever being at the Denny brother's home. And...*I grunted before adding, *let them find Raymond.*

Look, the brother was a bastard, I admit, but I wouldn't wish disappearing from time as we know it on my worst enemy. It was the least I could do.

Satisfied, I took Kenny's wheat penny and taped it next to my words. The weight and look just *felt* right, like a smartly tied bow on a birthday present. Then I found myself wondering if that's all there was to this. I hadn't made a wish before—not like this—but from Ava's grandmother's work, I assumed that's all that needed doing. I pushed everything into the dresser before joining Pop for a sing-along as we prepared dinner.

When he suggested a chicken *breast*, I almost vomited.

I rapped on Ava's door before stuffing my hands inside my pockets. Soft light glowed from the windows, and the pup yapped as she unlocked the door.

"Hey."

"Hey yourself. I see you still didn't fix that slab?"

I nodded toward the crooked slate in the drive where the weeds shook in the wind. She glanced out, her expression unreadable, and shrugged. "Just one more thing broken, I guess."

The bags beneath her eyes told me she'd been crying, a world away from the girl I'd met not so long ago. "Um, can I come in?"

She sniffled and stepped aside, but then—almost as an afterthought—her hand shot out and slammed my chest. "Maybe we, uh, can go to the diner? I...I haven't cleaned."

"It's all right." I cocked my head, surprised by her worry of what I might think. We were both Lowback true-bloods, after all. It wasn't like I came from money. The most cash I ever saw at one time came from a robbery, and if the crooked slab in her yard was anything to go by, I didn't expect much, anyway. "Really, I don't mind a mess, Ava."

She hesitated for a moment and then nodded slightly. "All right."

Her hand fell away and I stepped inside, greeted by the scent of freshly brewed coffee.

"You wanna mug?" she asked.

"Sure."

Before closing the door, she motioned to a booth in the small kitchen and I eased myself down as instructed. The place wasn't messy, not by a long shot, save for a scattering of papers on the bed. A neat kitchenette sat opposite, and I had to admit, the place was roomy, genuinely nice, and not at all what I expected. Then again, I didn't claim to know Ava much, but first impressions made me think of taped-up rock posters and ashtrays—not a far cry from the squatter dives I used to frequent.

"Thanks." I accepted the fresh brew and took a sip. Strong and sweet, and although I didn't take sugar (another habit from prison) I remained silent. "Planning on staying up late tonight, huh?"

She followed my gaze to the mess of pages before sitting opposite me. "I've been reading them all afternoon. Old diaries, journals, some as old as the late 50's, Joe. So much...so much *life* right there."

Her lip quivered and I almost reached across but thought better. I didn't want her thinking I saw her in 'that' way.

"You know she won three marathons back in the 60s? Ran one alongside a *real* athlete, too." She wiped her face and gave me a smile. "Two newspaper clippings and three diary entries. She nursed a little dog in '64. Found it by the quarry after a swim. Gave it a home in the city with a couple she said were 'lovely'. She did *all these things*, Joe. And I'm just...sittin' here in a trailer, thinkin'...well, I don't know what I'm thinkin', exactly. But it don't feel good."

I nodded and maintained eye contact, wanting her to know I was listening. My damn heart broke for the girl.

"Haven't read *much* yet, at least with everything that's there, but she had a boyfriend. They were both fifteen. Were crazy in love, Joe. Can you believe, he brought her a sugar-glazed after his family went to the fair, dropped it off at the trailer, and that sent my Great Granddaddy into a fit. He ate the damn thing himself, told the boy not to call no more. But my Grandma, Joe, she said 'donuts were love' from that day forward, and I just sat here laughing my ass off at that. Think Gomez thought I'd lost it."

"Gomez?"

"He needs a name, don't he?" She clicked her tongue and the sleeping pooch leaped from the bed before plopping down by her leg. She scratched his ear. "Anyway, there's so much here to get through, so much of this woman to finally *know*. She was a closed person, not *brooding* now, just...secretive. Loving, though. That, too."

"I brought what you asked."

I pulled her wish from my pocket and slid it across the table. For a moment, it looked as if she'd forgotten about the request. "Oh, thanks. Hold on."

She grabbed a whitened notebook from the bed and returned while flicking open the first page. "See here? Now, this is the earliest one. Must've been about twelve when she started keeping journals, at least that I know of. But right...here." She dabbed at the letter 'y' in 'yesterday'. "See how the bottom curls around and hooks back up? Look at the wish."

Sure enough, the 'y' in 'puppy' did the same, although 'older' Grandma had a cleaner script.

Ava slid her fingertip along several words to demonstrate. "The d's and a's are all identical, too. Just better written. But that's her, all right. Sadie wasn't lyin'. Much as I hate to admit...That jar belonged to my Gramma."

Ava caught my look as she spoke the "dead" woman's name. The corpse who was probably, at that moment, watching television and knitting a new hat. Waiting for her daughter to call.

"What is it?"

"Nothing," I eased down the diary from her hands. "Um, I've got a story of my own, Ava. Better get us both a fresh coffee."

I recounted the trip to Cramm's cottage, and of my run-in with Jerry. After I mentioned Officer Henderson, I paused as a ball of guilt tightened in my chest. Then I forced myself to tell her of robbing Kenny of his wish.

"*Fixing* his wish," I added in defense, "I *fixed* his wish."

"Jesus, Joe!" She jumped to her feet and looked at me as if I'd just suggested we eat a live cat. "You don't know that, you *can't* know that!"

"Right, okay." I held my palms out. "But, we *will* know that, right?" I licked my lips as sweat beaded my forehead. "We'll see Kenny soon. If not tonight, then tomorrow. And then we'll know."

"Then we'll know." She planted her hands on her hips, thinking. "And what's your bright idea now?"

"Well," I said, "We don't need Kenny for this part. It's—"

"You're a coward."

I bit my lip and stared into the depths of my coffee cup. "I deserve that, you're absolutely right. But hear me out. I've been thinking about all these wishes. From your Grandma, from Lily, now this lead on Rebecca Barrows... and I think she might prefer women visitors. The name I heard was *The Crimson Sisters*, after all."

"So you want me to speak with Rebecca Barrows and say I need help so I can see how she puts together these wishes, don't you? You want me to infiltrate a damn, what, a *cult* or something?"

Hearing Ava say it out loud back to me made it seem insane, but then, the waters we'd been swimming in lately were all a bit murky when it came to defining crazy. "That's kinda what I'm thinking, yeah."

"And how do we find her?"

"Lily Carrington gave me this."

I handed her the directions and braced for more yelling or a possible slap. Instead, Ava's tension slipped, and she stared me dead in the eyes. "Fine. I'll go and talk to this Barrows lady. Make up some shtick of how I wish I had a new home. A new drive where the slabs aren't crooked. Of how I'm tired of living with nothing in a trailer park and have no one and my life's going nowhere."

Ouch.

"But there's no way I'm going alone. We're *all* going, Joe. That includes getting Kenny and seeing what the hell you've done."

"Now?"

"Well I don't plan on sitting here drinking fuckin' coffee with you for the whole damn night, now do I?"

There she was, the return of the fiery little demon I knew.

"That a deal?"

"That's a deal," I agreed, though as I studied Ava's eyes and thought of her pain, I began to wonder if she'd ditch us and make her wish come true instead. I didn't much like the odds of Kenny and I fighting our way free of whatever the hell a 'Crimson Sister' was, especially not one with Ava at her side.

CHAPTER ELEVEN

"**S**HE LIVE IN some kinda shack in the woods or something?" Kenny hadn't spoken much on the drive. I think he was running through the events of the past few days in his head, trying to sort things out the best he could. I couldn't blame him. I hadn't slept the night before myself, and now the early morning sun ached my eyes.

"From Lily's directions, I don't think so." I held the sheet of notebook paper in front of me. "Woodmount Crossing sound *trailer park* to you?"

We were on the far side of Lowback, away from what was familiar. I wouldn't go so far as to say there was an *upper crust* area of town, but this damned sure wasn't from our side of the tracks. Farmhouses and sprawling pastures gave way to thick forests and I wondered if it wasn't some sort of age-old barrier left in place.

Ava leaned forward between the seats. "Briarwood Estates doesn't sound trailer park either, but well, there I am, living among the great unwashed."

"You have a point." I glanced at the directions again. "Up here on the left should be Cranbrook."

"She's not gonna turn us into a goat or some shit, is she? Isn't this bad enough?" Kenny glanced down at his breasts.

I'd checked his chest a number of times myself, but not out of any kind of sexual desire. Guilt gripped my stomach every few seconds, but so far, Kenny showed no visible signs of his torn-penny taking effect. Ava hadn't mentioned my doings, either. I think she was giving me room to step up and admit it myself. I wasn't quite ready.

"Just don't say anything to piss her off." Ava grinned as she spoke. "Though, a goat with tits would *truuuuullly* be—"

"Ava!" Kenny took the turn, and open fields stretching out to groves of trees surrounded us. We crested a slow rising hill, and on the other side, to the right, lay Woodmount Crossing.

Two stone columns bracketed the entrance of the development with a stacked stone wall and brass lettering showcasing the name.

Kenny gave a soft whistle as he brought the car to a stop.

"Not an old shack in sight," Ava whispered.

The immense houses sat a respectable distance from one another, each unique in their own way. An English-style Tudor mansion stood off to the left. A Spanish homestead with terra cotta roof tiles and cobblestone driveway to the right. In the distance, a home with tall white columns reaching to the rooftop sat like a public judicial building.

Ava looked as if she were standing at the edge of Oz, the way her eyes glittered, and I had that uneasy thought once again she could just run with her wish of leaving her old life behind and throw us to the wolves. I pushed the feeling away and cleared my throat. "Nothin' to it but to do it. Keep driving 'til 430 Woodmount."

A PENNY FOR YOUR THOUGHTS

As Kenny gave a nod and eased his car between the stone column entrance, we officially entered Woodmount Crossing.

The house at 430 Woodmount was two stories of gray fieldstone with a burgundy metal roof and matching shutters at each window. I could tell by looking at it that there'd been additions built through the years, compounding the glory of the main structure itself. Kenny continued up the blacktop drive before parking in front of a three-car garage. Four other cars dotted the circular drive. Mercedes. Cadillac Escalade. Some sloped nose Acura and a silver Hummer.

"Ava, why don't you go—"

"You can knock that shit right outta your head. I told you last night, we're all in this together, *especially* considering what you did with Ke—"

"Okay, all right." *Fuck*. Being here matched my unease at pulling up to Miss Cramm's brothel. Ava's constant glare didn't help the sickness in my gut.

"Okay, fellas. Pull up your big boy pants." As Ava's door popped, Kenny and I followed suit.

The front door opened the moment I set foot on the pavement and four women walked from the house—all of them dressed well. I noticed one of them held a bright crimson length of cloth folded over one arm. Smiles stretched their faces as they glanced at us and walked toward the parked cars.

A *cult*, I thought. *An actual goddamn cult.*

The front door remained open as they got into their cars and a flicker of movement caught my eye. A woman stood there in the frame, a red robe draped over her body. She pulled the cloth closed and tied the belt around her waist, though it was still loose enough to expose a generous area of her cleavage. She appeared to be in her forties at most. Her auburn hair was pulled back in a messy bun and loose strands stuck to her sweaty temples. She scanned the three of us.

"Hi, miss—"

She cut me off with a wave of the hand, seemingly amused at our unease. I wondered how many visitors she got here, and judging by the four cars currently filing out the driveway, I understood Lowback had a lot more going on than I suspected.

"What a...*delicious* morning." She smiled, took a deep breath and let it out with gratification.

"Um, we're here for—"

Again, cut off. "I know why you're here," she said, her expression reading: *obviously* as she shook her head. "The hard part is over. Come in, please." She stepped aside and though Ava paused for a moment, she led the way inside the house and the woman closed the door behind us.

She looked at Kenny and I. "Take your shoes off." Then she took Ava's hand and led her into the living space.

In many ways, the living room appeared normal, but in so many others, it was *anything* but. A wide stone fireplace sat at the far side, and in front of it, on the hardwood floor, was what looked to be a chalk circle drawn on the planks. Symbols written around the edges. And in the middle of the circle, splayed out in a dark puddle—I swear—lay a white goat.

Christ, Almighty. What in the blue fuck have we done? Why are we here? Last week I was trying to stay clean and get a job at the Dollar General or something and now we're—

Its slit stomach seeped entrails onto the polished hardwood, its beard soaked in its own blood. Vacant eyes stared at the great beyond, and five silver chalices sat lined at the edge of the fireplace.

"Sorry about the mess. We were trying something new today."

The woman, *Becky*, smirked. Then her focus landed on me and my throat dried up. She cocked her head, moved on to Kenny, and slowly circled him. One of Pop's nature documentaries came to mind, something about predators and hunting habits.

"You're certainly an interesting...*offering*, aren't you?" She trailed a finger over his shoulder, down his arm, and though he remained quiet, I could tell Kenny was squirming inside. She leaned into him, sniffed. "But not...natural. You stink of...blood. Of...*copper*." She smirked as she slipped behind him—*inspecting*.

I figured Kenny had been through enough lately and I wanted to draw her attention away from him. For a split second, I wondered if *this* could be the result of my penny-pulling.

I cleared my throat. "You, uh...you have a lovely home."

Various statues mounted on metal stands were showcased around the room in inset shelves beneath lamplights. I stepped toward one to pull focus away from Kenny. The statue was roughly two feet high, and looked like sandstone. Tall and thin, the winged figure was only the upper half of a body, with wide teeth and bulging eyes, its right hand held upward in a semi-salute. "This is...uh...interesting."

Becky's smile grew as she stepped farther into the living room area (much to Kenny's delight). She paused at a coffee table and shook a cigarette free from a pack before lighting up. Smoke curled from the cherry toward a gleaming chandelier overhead.

"I'm a fan of ancient things," she said. "That's Pazuzu."

She glided across the room and caressed the statue's head like a pet. "He was a demon king in Syria and Babylonia cultures." She leaned closer to the sculpture, appearing to sniff the stone. "Such an...*immature* being." She dragged on her cigarette, breathing dragon-breath as she spoke. "But revered, oh, yes. Even for being so young. He still has a following, did you know that?"

I shook my head.

"Still an immature *prick* of a..." She paused, exhaled smoke and smiled at me. "Useful, in his own way, I suppose." She motioned with her cigarette to another statue. "Hun-Came. From the underworld. His name means *One Death* and he's...simple-minded. Easily harnessed." She pointed to another on a pedestal near a bookshelf: a misshapen dog-like baboon. "That's In-Tep from Egypt. Still has a quite a few worshippers, even today." Her gaze swept across us. "Does this *amuse* you?"

We nodded.

"Good...delightful." Another pull of the cigarette as she motioned to yet more statuettes. "Azathoth, Balor, Ob, Phobos, Aypep...all saplings compared to the true one."

"*True* one?" Kenny's face said he regretted speaking aloud.

"The true one, yes." Becky smirked. "These...'gods' are but infants. The true one's age is infinite." She moved to a beige loveseat, stretching out to let the robe fall and expose a smooth, slender leg. Her gaze fell on Ava. "Would you like something to drink, dear?"

Kenny spoke up. "I'd...I'd like some water if you—"

Her focus snapped to him. I swear, in that instance, her hatred was as visible as her cigarette smoke. "In the interest of teaching you social etiquette, if someone's eyes are focused on *you*, that means they're talking to *you*, if they're not, then...*they're not*." She let her granite stare linger a moment longer, then returned to Ava.

"No thank you, ma'am," Ava said, her voice small. "I'm fine."

"Then, please, tell me, what brings you *fine* folk to visit me on a beautiful day like today?" She tilted her head back, her slender neck moving with her words. "It's been a *delightful* but busy morning, and the rest of my day will be busier still...so get on with it."

The three of us remained frozen in a Mexican standoff. Thankfully (after an audible swallow) Ava stepped forward. She took a seat on the matching sofa. "Ma'am, I've come to ask...I'm tired of the way I've been living. See, life just ain't—"

Becky laughed out loud, the *suddenness* giving me a jolt. She leaned her head against the cushions and slowly shook her head. Her eyes closed. "I'm sorry, little flower, but so many are. Go on, continue."

"I've been living in a trailer park as long as I can remember and...I feel like it's all I'll ever be. Just trailer trash." She leaned forward. Brave. "No matter what I do, I can't seem to find someone I'm meant to be with and—"

Becky sat up in a fluid motion and waved her hand. "Stop. Please stop." She glared at Ava, then to me, and then to Kenny, who couldn't seem to look at her directly anymore. Her ash-tipped cigarette bobbed as she continued. "Life is...*can be*...short. There's truly no use in wasting time."

Her legs spread, and my gaze snapped to her posture. Becky caught me. "You both stink of...something *familiar*. But you come into my house and..." Then, as if remembering something, turned back to Ava. "You're not exactly telling the truth, but then, your words aren't necessarily...*untrue* either, are they?" She smiled as she brought her cigarette to her lips. "But you stink of debt."

Ava shifted in her seat. "Ma'am, I'm just...I just want to change the way my life is going. I'm tired of—"

Becky uncurled from the loveseat. Her voice rose as she spoke and her expression grew serious and stern. "What did I *just* say to you?" She muttered as she stalked to the chalk circle and flicked her cigarette butt into the fire. And then—

Oh, man...

—her hands dove into that goat's intestines.

"Jesus, lady..." Kenny's hand shot to his nose as he scrunched his face. But like Ava, I didn't dare move.

She grabbed the slick ropes, hung them like a banner across her bare arms as she rose to her feet. Viscous liquid dribbled through her fingers and onto the floor. "You come into *my* home with false words?" She flung the entrails to the side with a wet *splash*. Her maroon-stained hands worked the liquid into her skin of her forearms and wrists. "Leave and don't come back. Not until you have something worth trading."

"And what would we get out of this trade?" The words tumbled out of me even though my insides were shaking.

Her eyes bored into mine. "Freedom from *it*. You know what I mean. That...particular god is a...let's call him an acquaintance. I can clear a debt. Set the books straight."

I'd heard stories of swindler fortune-tellers making broad, general statements that could apply to anyone in order to trick gullible clients. The goat, the get-up, the statues, was it all for show? Did Rebecca Barrows *really* know anything of value about the jar? Or was this 'freedom from *it*' just another con artist's bluff?

"Jarring," she said with a smile. "Isn't it, Petal?"

Petal?

Even Kenny caught that—an old pet name from Angie. No one knew that name outside us. No one. I stammered for a response.

"Hush," she warned. "You can't even begin to imagine how that works..." Then, to Ava, "*You* can stay if you like... your wish is *half* true at the very least. The Crimson Sisters would happily welcome you into the fold, little flower. I just need to know *where* you would like to live your wish. A big, *exciting* city, bursting with life? The islands, maybe? Water so clear you can see your past as you splash your feet?

"You'll find the first *true* home you've ever had." She raised her bloody hands again, presenting the room. "Look around you. You think I was *born* into wealth? Oh, no, little flower, I was raised in a clapboard shack with swamp rats crawling through the house when we all went to sleep in the cold. Late night knocks from a stepfather looking to quench a thirst..." She paused. "You know the like...Join the fold, dear girl, and leave all that behind. Become what you...*could* be. What you *wish* to be, Ava."

As a junkie, you pay attention to detail. And I knew *damned well* Ava hadn't mentioned her name the entire time we had been here. None of us had. Yet Becky knew it. She knew my nickname from Angie. Knew our purpose before we ever opened our mouths.

I had no doubt she knew I had the jar.

There was a long pause of silence.

I wanted to signal to Kenny to run. Just run like a bat out of hell to the outside and get away from this woman and her living room, stinking of goat guts. *Fuck* our shoes, *fuck everything*. Just run and get in the car and haul ass out of here. I doubted Ava would be coming behind us. *Why the fuck would she?*

And then...that sweet fiery demon of a girl, spoke.

"Thank you, ma'am, but I...I'm sorry...I have things I need to do. I..." Ava sputtered the words with a level-eyed gaze as she stood from the sofa.

Becky took a deep breath as she stared at the hardwood floor. Then she let it loose and nodded. "It's a shame, but I understand. But you think about it, little flower. Think about it long and hard. We'll be here. Waiting to welcome you."

Ava stood in place for a long moment, and I thought again of Pop's nature documentaries, the way a cobra could freeze a bird in place with fear.

Then she turned and Kenny broke free of his frozen position. I followed after him, forcing myself to not shove him forward.

"Don't come back 'til you have my jar. Or something else worth trading."

When Kenny opened the door, we damned near *ran* from the house.

I felt more lost than I had the day before.

CHAPTER TWELVE

KENNY PULLED OVER just outside Woodmount Crossing and vomited. He coughed and spat and stood upright, facing the heavens with his hands planted on his hips as he sucked in breath after heaving breath. After a wet belch, he climbed back behind the wheel.

"All good?" I asked.

"Ain't like the movies, huh? The fuckin' smell and the *sound*. That was a real goat, Joe, not a prop."

"I know."

"She was playing with its guts like a goddamn Slinky." Kenny looked on the verge of throwing up all over again.

"I know. I was there."

Kenny's frail constitution shocked me, though I supposed adrenaline was the only factor keeping Ava and me from joining him at the roadside. My heart still jackhammered, kicking my ribs like a feral critter.

"Ever think the police show up there?" Ava asked.

"After everything I've seen lately, I somehow doubt that."

"She can work anyone into anything," Kenny added. "I ain't *never* been intimidated like that before."

I agreed. The way the Barrows woman stalked us like a tiger around fresh steak...

Don't come back 'til you have my jar. Or something else worth trading.

Kenny wiped his mouth with the back of his hand. "I'll say one thing, there's big money in goat guts n' bad mojo. That's for sure."

He gunned the accelerator, leaving Woodmount Crossing in our wake with his 'present of the gut' drying by the columned entrance. In the rearview, two birds flapped down and dug in.

"*My jar,*" Ava said. "That's how she phrased it. *Hers.* She just bein' over-confident she'll get it?"

"Hell if I know," I said. "What else do you think she wants?"

"A new goat?" Kenny replied. "A maid to mop that hardwood tonight? Fuck. And I'll tell you one thing, ain't no way in hell I'm going back to find out."

"Don't think we should trust her?"

"No, *Petal.* No, I don't think we should trust the crazy lady who put her hands inside a dead goat."

"Fair point."

"Man, she *knows* about it. Knows what those coins can do. She—"

"—can also clear our debt. Just remember that, Kenny. Because a damn penny ain't the full price here. And we've all made a purchase."

A little while later, we passed the quarry before hooking a right for Briarwood. My muscles eased as we closed in on home, and I imagined the other two felt much the same. If I never set sight on the mansions and pastures of Woodmount Crossing again, I wouldn't waste tears. Though something told me it wouldn't be the last I saw of the place.

A PENNY FOR YOUR THOUGHTS

"Hey, I don't know what *she'd* do with the coins," Ava spoke up, "But I know someone who might. And if we're considerin' her deal, then I suggest we do a little background check on the psycho."

We pulled over at the sidewalk two houses from Pop's, something of a routine by now, and Kenny and I turned in our seats.

"You're talking about your Grandma, huh?"

Ava looked to the orange-pink sky. "I am. Haven't been to see her in a year, she's a stone when it comes to talking these days, and she said she 'didn't want to be a hassle.' Last I called for a visitation, the guard told me she didn't want no visitors. I respected her wishes, but tried again at Christmas. She doesn't wanna talk to me. Probably out of shame. But that's my Gramma. Still, we need to know what we'd be getting into if we give her that jar. We can try."

"I have an in," I said, throwing the thought out loud before I second-guessed myself. "Angie."

"Jesus, Joe." Kenny cocked his head and scoffed. "Really?"

"Look, I haven't been to see her. I've...I've been meaning to."

And I had, though I kept the idea locked tight in the attic of my mind. And even with all this proverbial shit slopping off my plate, that intention still banged and banged. It was time.

"I can drive you," Kenny said, and the genuine care in his voice hurt me something fierce. His betrayal with the jar was nothing new—shit, I should've *expected* it—and I'd backstabbed him by pulling his damn wish.

Can always put the penny back, Joe, eat a nice slice of humble pie and let Henderson catch you...

I shook the thought before saying, "You've done enough for me already, man. Can't have you do that. Besides, I haven't spent much time with Pop lately. I better ask him and make a day of it."

"You sure?"

"Yeah, man."

"She your girl?" Ava asked.

I turned in my seat and struggled for a response. *Was Angie still my girlfriend? Despite it all, did we ever truly break up?*

"Kenny told me when we were waiting for you after the hospital. I didn't do no stalker shit, don't worry."

"Sorry," Kenny offered. "Small talk, y'know?"

I sighed, rubbing at the tension forming behind my eyes. "Look. They're in the same building. I can ask Angie to be our middleman. After I...talk things over with her. But if your Grandma is as tight-lipped as you think she is, it might not be easy. But I can try. I'll talk to Pop tonight. Two one-hour visits every month was what I got, I imagine Angie's in the same situation. And, believe me, I doubt anyone's been out to see her lately."

"She bad?" Ava asked.

"Oh, she's bad." I laughed at that, recalling raunchy nights with that ghoul of a lady, witching hours spent by the neon glow of a broken TV surrounded by passed out strangers as people yelled upstairs and warm honey pounded through my veins.

"Joe?"

"Huh?"

"Phased out a bit there, buddy."

"Sorry. Long day." And that wasn't entirely untrue, it wasn't every day you got to see a woman dip into the stomach of a goat like moistened clay on a potter's wheel.

A PENNY FOR YOUR THOUGHTS

"Look, I can get out there tomorrow, it's Saturday and they'll be accepting visitors. I just don't know what kinda mood she'll be in. But I can try. See what Angie can get from your Grandma. Learn what that Barrows lady wants."

"After seeing those damn statues on her shelves, it ain't nothing good," Kenny said, and I agreed whole-heartedly. Anyone chummy with a deity who accepted payment for a wish was someone I wanted no dealings with. If possible.

A shiver ran through me at how easily I'd accepted this bizarre new world as fact. Reality had been flipped on its head, but not for the first time. Going from high school into Angie's arms and onto the needle was like slipping into Oz, then falling back to the dire pits of sobriety in a prison cell was like passing on to another dimension. Getting out of jail and finding a magic jar wasn't too strange a concept for me to process, even with a trickster god in the mix. Reality had always been splitting at the seams for me.

"I'll talk to her," I said, and when Ava cleared her throat, both Kenny and I turned.

"Guys, I just wanna say, you don't gotta worry about me leaving...okay?"

Kenny threw me a glance.

"Seriously. I was in the pits, all right? But the way I see it, I ain't never been caught up with something so... *important* before. This could answer a lot for me, and with my Gramma? I want...no, I *need* those answers." She laughed then. "A secret of the universe unraveled by trailer trash, how could I pass this ride up?"

"Yeah, but you gotta stop thinking yourself trash," I said, and popped the door. Cold air tickled my skin. "You're better than that, Ava."

Kenny grabbed my sleeve. "Wait, wait, what are *we* gonna do while you visit Angie?"

I thought of Ava's puppy at her trailer and couldn't help but think I'd found my own. Granted, Ava's dog was much cuter and didn't have a chest to rival a pornstar. "You get working on finding us a new buyer," I said. "Can't have our original plan slipping because of this jar, man. We still need the cash coming in. And Ava's almost got the shop all set up to process the...dough."

The bad joke got a smile from him—Hell, I never said Kenny was a man of taste.

"Right," he said, "I got a guy out on the Susquehanna I can talk to. Move our load by next week. Get the cash flowing."

"Good. I don't need a name."

Having a job seemed to calm Kenny, and I attempted to pull from his grasp. "You can let go now, big guy. Get a good—"

But that's as far as I got. Liquid blossomed through the pits of his shirt. I jerked myhand free. "Kenny, the fuck?"

He craned his neck down as his brow creased. Then he yelped. He spread his arms and the stain crept across his chest to meet in the middle like a wet t-shirt contest. He batted at the door handle before climbing out and pulling the shirt off over his head. His stomach caught in the soaked fabric before flopping free and he balked again. The black sports bra struggled with keeping those jugs clutched, but their strain was slackening by the second.

"They're deflating!" he yelled, and the Boden's trailer light popped to life. "What the hell is happening?"

Ava and I watched in astonishment as Kenny's chest sagged and more liquid, the texture of bacon grease, oozed down his sides before pooling at his feet. He wailed like a wounded mule and only drew more attention from far off homes. I rushed to his side. "Kenny, calm down, lift your arms. *Lift.*"

I held up his forearm as I pulled him beneath a streetlight. A tiny hole, not much larger than a pea—or a wheatback penny—pulsed liquid. "Other side, turn."

He did as instructed and I found an identical leak.

"Am I dying?" he asked, sweat glistening on his brow. "Joe, what the hell?"

"Off with the bra, man. Come on, take it off."

He shuffled free of the item before flinging it across Mrs. Boden's flowers where it bobbed on a bush. By this stage, his nipples pointed to the pavement.

"I...I think it's stopping," he managed in a shaky voice. "I can feel it seepin' out, but...I think it's stopping. Check for me, Joe, please."

He raised his arms again and, yes, the liquid had slowed to a thin trickle, turning pinkish as it ceased. "It's done, man. I—I think that's it."

"They're gone?" Kenny grabbed hold of one flabby mound, pulled it out, let it slap back against his stomach. My guts roiled at the action. *The sound.*

"What the fuck was in 'em, Joe? Like the stuff that's in a *blister?*"

"Might've been just that," I said, but, of course, I knew better. Whatever had been inside him turned to something else the moment I pulled his wheat penny. "They're gone, Kenny."

"Popped like damn balloons!" he cried, then, "What am I supposed to do with saggy tiddies, man?" A tear cascaded his cheek—an actual fucking tear. "How am I supposed to get with a lady when I got deflated sandbags on my chest?"

He kept idly slapping the excess skin against his stomach and I grabbed his hand. "Stop doing that. Look, man, I don't know how to tell you this, but you weren't exactly Mister Universe to begin with, okay? I don't think your love life prospects are changing much, either way."

"Oh, fuck you, Joe." He sniffled before arching an eyebrow. "You *did* something."

"I did not."

"The wish changed. You *did* something, man. I'm not a fucking idiot."

Ava's voice made me jump. "Tell him, Joe." She stood with her arms crossed, leaning against the car. "Just say it. Or I will."

"Say what, Joe?"

Man, there are some days you just wanna seep through a crater right in the ground, know what I mean? Wind up on a beach in Australia with a beer and the sun and leave every loved one behind. I could lie with the best of 'em, I knew that, but Kenny *had* done a lot for me, we'd really bonded lately—and as for the jar stealing, well, you can't teach an old fart new tricks. I should've known better. And I said as much.

"I'm really sorry, Kenny."

"What did you do?"

Again, that uncut, genuine honesty of his tone sent guilt pummeling though me. I couldn't meet his gaze. And so, I told him.

"You...you could've killed me, Joe."

"Yeah, well, I didn't, all right?" I spread my arms in defense while my face heated with embarrassment. "*You* could've killed us *all* by giving the damn jar to the Denny brothers in the first place! Ever consider that?

Jerry and Raymond with supernatural powers? Think about that for a moment."

"I made sure they only took two wishes."

"Oh, like the Denny brothers have their morals in check."

"*Had.* They're dead now. At least one of 'em is."

"Because of you, Kenny."

"Oh, don't act like this is all *my* fucking fault." He snarled now, but his lower lip still quivered. "How about you take responsibility for once, Joe? This is you and your fucking jar. You started everything. Look at the damn *mess* of me. I shoulda never asked you for help."

"Fuck you and your saggy tits, man."

I stalked toward home, leaving Ava and Kenny by the car. I shoved my hands in my pockets as I overheard Mrs. Boden yell at Kenny to '*put a fucking shirt on, you sick pig!*' before I opened the door and, without realizing, slammed it shut. I *knew* I was moping, I did, and I *knew* I was wrong, but right then I didn't care. I made my mind up. I was going to give Rebecca Barrows the damn jar and be done with it. Damn the consequences. I'd get a normal job and ignore Kenny and Ava and let it all be damned. That's what I was going to do.

Then I faced my Pop.

"You did *what?*"

I fell onto the couch as pressure pulsated behind my eyes. Working my palms into my sockets, I watched blind spots dance on my inner lids. I just wanted the damn day to end.

"I hid it," Pop said. "Hid it where you'll never find it. Don't think I haven't noticed things getting *strange* around here, Joe. I'm your damn father, I pay attention."

"Oh, yeah?" I laughed. "But you're happy to take two and a half grand without question, huh? Apple doesn't fall far from the tree, man."

His forehead knotted and he pointed at me. "Look, I don't know how you did it. I don't know how that thing works, but you're getting yourself into something that's beyond you and I'm here to put a stop to it. Whatever's going on, it's not...natural."

"It's beyond anyone," I said in a monotone. "You've gotta realize that?"

Pop eased himself into his armchair, gave me that trademark steely gaze. "Why do you think I've been in the bottle again? Enjoyment?" The anger fell from his voice, leaving a vulnerable tone in its wake. "I'm terrified, Joe," he said. "I can't explain how that damn thing works, but whatever I read came true. Your mother was the superstitious one, and her...her voice won't leave my head this week. This whole thing not remind you of anything, kid?"

"What, you think this is a like a fucking addiction?"

"You seem pretty high-strung about me hiding it, that's all I'll say."

"Because it's not *yours* to take, Pop!" Before I knew it, I was up and jabbing a finger in *his* face. I saw my opportunity to get out, dissolving like painkillers in cold water. "It's *mine*, this has *nothing* to do with you!"

His lip quivered but his eyes remained locked. "Really, Joe? You going to do this to me again?"

"Ah, fuck." I ran a hand through my hair, took a deep breath as ice-cold shame hit me. I couldn't tell him about Barrows or the Sisters. I didn't want him more involved than he was. For both our sakes. I let out a long exhale. "Fuck, I'm—I'm sorry..."

"I know. We've been here before. We'll get through it again."

"Whatever *this* is, it's not like *that*." I took a knee, held his dry hand in mine. "Pop, I swear. It's not like the junk."

"So you can stop this?"

"Yes."

"You won't ask where I put it? You'll just get on with your life? I heard you and Kenny yelling outside with that girl. Whole of Briarwood heard, most likely. You getting mixed up with him again?"

"No." I lied.

"And who's that lady? She's a little young for you."

"It's not like that, Pop. Ava's a friend."

He thought my words over. "I'll trust *you*. If you trust *me*."

"I do."

"Then, please, tell me if you had anything to do with Raymond Denny."

"What?"

His question hit like a bullet, though I kept it from showing.

"You haven't listened to the news at all today, have you?"

He grunted as he pulled his phone and then jabbed the screen a few times before handing it my way. The glare ached my eyes.

Police investigate after man's body found inside of farmhouse wall.

The room seemed to spin, and I folded my legs beneath me, squinted at the text.

Raymond Denny (40) of Cairn Plains was found dead yesterday in his farmhouse, officials confirmed. Police say the 40-year-old was pulled from the walls of the home he shared with his brother, Jerry, who was also found dead at the scene. Although forensics have yet to confirm the cause of death, foul play is "still a possibility," says Officer Darren Williams of the Lowback Police Department. Investigations are ongoing, and anyone with information is asked to...

The accompanying photo caught my eye. A shabby bedroom wall with a hole about the size of a washing machine punched right through the plaster and lathe.

"Raymond Denny was found *inside* the wall," Pop said. "That, alongside my *bite of luck,* has me questioning damn near everything I've ever believed in right now, Joe. And I'm scared. I'm really fucking scared, kid. Promise me one thing?"

"What's that?"

"That Henderson or Williams will not find any trace of you out at that farmhouse. Promise me."

"I promise on my life, Pop. They will find no trace of me out there."

He eyed me a moment longer. "Okay, then."

"I need a favor from you," I said, and cleared my throat. "This weekend, I was wondering if—"

"You want to go visit her?" he finished.

I shrugged, studying his tired expression. "Yeah."

He sighed, the conversation and day wearing on him as much as myself. "I expected as much. Granted, I thought you would've asked much sooner, if I'm honest. This damned *day,* kid. Will it ever end? Yeah, I'll do it. But you're not thinking of *waiting* for her, are you? Tell me that much. Give me *some* peace of mind so I get some sleep tonight."

"Of course not." I answered only to balm his fears, though I didn't know if I was being entirely truthful. My lies, it seemed, could fool even me some days.

"Something the matter?"

My headache was a bundle of road flares, and I rubbed my temples. "Just a long day. Pop, you're right. Kenny and Ava are pissed at me. And, to tell the truth, I'm just worried about seeing her."

"Then start making right. Start there. I don't need to know the details."

"Yeah, Pop. That sounds like a good plan."

He stood then, his back cracking. Sitting on the floor, if I didn't look up, I could imagine myself a kid with Mom asleep in the next room, Pop and I just having finished watching a late night Sci-Fi classic on the tube. "Get some rest," he said. "Sounds like you've had a day as bad as me."

"I will," I said, and got to my feet. "Thanks, Pop."

"Of course." He smiled a sad smile. "You're my son, stupid. I'd do anything for you."

Frost glistened on the rooftops that Saturday as we passed through neighborhoods much prettier than Briarwood, though the homes began to decline in quality the further we went. Eventually, we reached the industrial side of town, and the prison walls loomed on the horizon. I'd called the jail at seven and, luckily, Angie agreed to my visit.

"You okay?" Pop asked. The heater struggled to keep us warm, and his gloved hands steadied the wheel firmly at ten and two.

"Heading to prison on the weekend, not my idea of a good way to spend time."

"Not any man's idea of a good day, believe me." He sniffled. "Did this enough myself. If you've been inside or not, it's never fun driving to a prison."

"True." I blew a breath through my hands and relished the warmth. A cellophane bag of butterscotch candy rested on the center console of the car and I cocked my head. "Thought you didn't eat them anymore?"

"Yeah, well," he said, "After this week, I'm indulging. What would your mom have said, huh?"

The matriarch's rule of the house: *no candy within my walls.* Diabetes. I wondered if my needle-use hurt Pop that much more on account of Mom's condition. Needles, forever in our home. *Needles, needles everywhere, and not a vein to prick.* I noticed the bottles of insulin in our bathroom medicine cabinet more than once, but I never had the heart to tell the old man to throw 'em away. He wasn't the most attentive person to what lay in the drawers and cabinets of the house, anyway. I once found a two-year out-of-date box of crackers next to a five-month-old jar of jelly. Let him have his damn sweets. I unwrapped one and popped it in my mouth, giving him a sideways grin.

"Here we are." Pop turned into the mostly full parking lot and it made me wonder about all the lives thrown into chaos by the people behind these walls. The closer we got, the more my stomach fluttered with apprehension. We remained silent as we stepped into the crisp morning and speed-walked to the entrance, both probably thinking the same thing: *I'd rather be anywhere else right now.*

I held the door for Pop and we made our way to the reception. The guard behind the desk stared us down with cold eyes and I half expected him to tell me I was going back inside, that Pop had pranked me to get me in front of an officer and it was all 'for my own good'. Instead, the guard asked for our inmate's name and buzzed us in. That sharp sound gave me a jolt—*eeeerrrkk!*—old habits and all. We made our way through detectors and stern looks and all the while I tried my damnedest not to throw up my meager candy breakfast.

Eventually, we reached a waiting room and Pop sat next to a couple holding hands on a steel bench. "You go on ahead," he said in a hushed voice. "I'll be right here."

I followed the guard through to the phone lines we've all seen a thousand times before in the movies. Being on the opposite side of the plexiglass didn't make matters easier. And when a lady in an orange jumpsuit was led through and seated herself on the far side with a grin, her hands in cuffs, I hardly recognized her. My heart still punched, all the same.

I raised the receiver to my ear. "Angie."

Those sad green eyes I used to adore now chilled me. I hadn't noticed the cunning watchfulness before, like a coyote ready to pounce on a carcass. Nor did I notice how her lips seemed to be frozen in an arrogant smirk, like she knew all about me from a single glance. Her brunette hair showed the first strands of white—a new development—and hung limply around her shoulders. She'd lost weight she couldn't afford to.

"About time you showed up." Her voice raked fingernails down my spine.

Hearing her speak, I was transported back to *those* days, and I didn't like it one bit. I didn't like *her*. And I downright hated myself.

"How's it feel to walk free?" she asked, but I had no response. "How's it feel to *rat* me, Petal?"

There it was: *Petal.* '*Put my head on your lap, Petal...got a five, Petal? Ollie's down at the docks with a new batch...It's just a grocery store, Petal. Just sit in the car. In and out, easy as pie...*'

"You did this to yourself."

Her grin widened as her eyes became slits. "Oh, did I? That what you keep telling yourself? What you told the board?"

"If they didn't believe me, I wouldn't be on this side of the glass, Angie."

"You always did have a way of making people believe you."

The plexiglass suddenly didn't seem like enough of a barrier between us. I wanted a damn shock collar on this tiger. Her very presence felt like it could seep through the phone line and coat me, pull me back down to the pits I'd crawled from. Angie read my expression like a psychic.

"If you're not happy to see me, baby, then what's this all about? You need something, don't you?"

I sucked a breath and thought, *oh, here we fucking go.*

CHAPTER THIRTEEN

I **ONCE SAW** a man in the chow line, three spots in front of me, get slashed from forehead to chin over a chocolate chip muffin. You wouldn't think a melted toothbrush sharpened to a fine-edged blade would do the sort of damage it can do, but that man's face opened up like a goddamn Christmas present. It's a different kind of world you're livin' in when a man damn near gets killed over a fucking *muffin*. But that's prison.

When you're doing a stretch on the inside, the easiest way to deal with things is to accept the idea that prison is its own ecosystem. It's rude and wrong and royally fucked up, but you have to accept it in order to survive. Prison is a closed society with an incredibly strict pecking order, social status, levels of employment, and economy. You learn.

Angie's dirty emerald eyes sparkled as she waited for my answer. That coyote grin slid back in place and the crow's feet at the corners of her eyes deepened.

"Look, Angie..." I focused my eyes on the Formica countertop. "I know I should've come to see you before now, okay?"

"Well, *Petal,* guilt has a real funny way of keepin' people apart."

"You would have done the same fuckin' thing to me if—" My blood thrummed as my voice rose and I hated her at that moment, talking to me with that calm, controlled voice behind her barely concealed smile. I hated her but hated myself even more for letting my emotions barrel ahead and allowing her to manipulate me. I took a breath, reeled myself back in. "Yeah, Angie. I need something, okay? But...it's more than that. I really *did* want to make sure you were okay." I slumped, my lies sounding as effective as a broken whoopee cushion. "I mean, y'know, as okay as you *can* be."

"No matter what, it's good to see you, Joey." She moved the receiver to tuck hair behind her ear, and then moved the phone back in place. "You remember the first time we tied off and shot?" Angie's gaze turned downward as her smile softened. *Acting,* I reminded myself. *She's a politician with this shit.* "Up at Laurel Ridge. Those pine trees up there hiding that moss on the ground beneath them, so thick it looked magical, like the Emerald City or something."

"Yeah, I remember." She was right about that—it *did* look magical, from another planet. We had sat beneath the cover of the pine branches and had our own magic hut for most of the afternoon, eventually rolling around naked on the soft moss.

"If I could go back to any moment in my life and just... stay there...that would be it for me. Just the feel of that cold, dewy moss against my back and that very first needle pop against my skin, the two of us floating on clouds. Both of us together, that very first time." She licked her lips as her eyes became glassy. Then her gaze found me again. "Magic."

Her memory made my stomach flip as I recalled the details from a lifetime ago. To go back and make another choice instead of shooting up. I gritted my teeth.

"Do you remember the *last* time we shot up?" I leaned onto the counter and clenched the receiver. "In the brick warehouse over in Darlington, close to the old fairgrounds. Whatever that dealer sold us was cut with so much fuckin' baking soda it should have had an Arm & Hammer logo on the baggies. Wasn't strong enough to get *either* of us right, let alone *one* of us. And I ended up throwing my guts up later that night because we couldn't score."

Angie's expression hardened as she gave a slight nod. The dreaminess vanished from her eyes. "All this sappy shit aside, what do you need from me?"

I cleared my throat. "There's an inmate here, an old lady, in for a long haul prison sentence."

"Murder?"

I nodded. "Thing is, she did it when she was a young woman. Didn't get busted for it 'til a few years back."

Her eyes narrowed again. "Petal—"

"I really wish you'd stop calling me—"

"Joey—"

"You're using your *Mommy-means-it-tone* and I *really* don't—"

"Fuck sakes!" Angie jerked the phone away from her face and glared through the plexiglass.

I put my hands up in an apology and she eased the receiver back to her ear. *Jesus fucking Christ, how did she keep pushing my buttons like that?* But a part of me enjoyed the realization I could rile her up as well.

She stared at me with the phone in her hand for a moment, before easing it back to her ear. "I know who you mean. The ol' lady, yeah. I know."

"Just like that?"

"Sweetie, she's a haggard ol' witch in for murder. Ain't a lot of dainty Gramma's with that kinda reputation. I know the chick."

"You talk to her before?"

"*No one* fuckin' talks to her but I know her celly, well, *ex*-celly. She was only in there with the ol' lady for a month before she begged for a cell transfer."

"How'd she transfer out so fast?"

Angie sat back in her chair and gave a disgusted look at me. "You been a free man so long you done forgot how shit works in here? She fucked someone. Blew someone. Ate someone out. Fuck's it matter, Joey? She got transferred."

"Why?"

Angie jutted her lip and shrugged. "Talks in her sleep about all kinds of whacko shit. 'Dead men walkin',' that's what Darla, her ex-celly said. Mental disorder, but no judge saw it that way. Gives people the creeps, talkin' like that in her sleep. Even the guards don't fuck with her much."

I looked away from her and sighed. "Yeah, okay. Well, I need you to get word to the woman that she *needs* to talk to her granddaughter."

Angie cocked her head. "She needs to talk to her so fuckin' bad, how come she didn't come herself? How come you're talkin' for her?"

"It's a long story."

Her '*I knoooow you*' smile returned. "Bangin' her, Petal? That why you ain't been to see me? Got some trailer split-bottom on your arm?"

She shot to her feet and jammed the phone receiver back into the cradle so hard I winced.

Fucking hell. It was here. I was right here and it was all coming together and—

I hammered the plexiglass, begging for her attention now, despising my desperation. Angie took a step, then another. Her shoulders rose and fell. A beat passed.

She turned and scuffed back to the chair, sat, and grabbed the receiver. I breathed a sigh of relief even though her eyes didn't meet mine. "I'll do what you want, Joe. I'll try, at least."

There's a catch. There's always a catch...and the award for best actress of the fuckin' year goes to...

"But..." A pause hung in the air as her white-streaked hair fell across her face. She gazed through the strings. "*But* I'll need things from you. You know how it works in this fuckin' place. Barter. Trade."

"What can I do? What do you need?"

Her melancholy sadness vanished, a flip of the switch. A little threat of rain clouds on her face and a pooched out, pouty lip and she had me wrapped around her finger. This felt no different. She was playing me, yeah, but I had no choice but to ride along.

For Pop, I reminded myself. *Gotta learn what I owe, for Pop's sake. And my own.*

"Get me a little taste, Petal. Just a little. Oh, God, it would be so good to float away in here. I'll be *soooo* good to you when I get out." She licked her lips and cocked her head. Those dusty emeralds gleamed as her acting skills resurfaced. I could *see* the dirty thoughts floating behind them. Just like she wanted. "You don't know what they want for a taste in here. It's—"

"I'm not smuggling smack." I popped that bubble before it floated off with me inside. "I can't be around that shit anymore, Angie. If that's what you want, then fuck—"

She growled behind gritted teeth and her silky tone changed to a hard-edged voice. "Then bring me some *fuckin'* cigarettes, Joey." She jammed the phone back in place before I could react, and stood before I even had my mouth open. A corrections officer approached and escorted her away without a single glance back. And she was gone. The air seemed lighter.

Cigarettes would always be a currency in prison—useful for everything from playing chess and poker to getting a requested library book. It was the base monetary system. What the walled-up yards were founded on. I only then realized I was still holding the damn phone. As I stood, I placed the receiver back in the cradle. It was a start, at least. I let go of a breath I'd been holding and started for the exit.

"Joey?"

My brain shuffled through its old files for a voice match. Then I noticed the corrections officer leaning against the wall, arms folded and wearing a smirk on his face. A chuckle escaped me.

"*Niiiiice* mustache. You look like you oughta be in here with the kiddie diddlers."

"Shut your ass. The wife likes it, y'know what I mean?" He gave me a wink and his face broke into a smile. "Son of a bitch, it's good to see you. Didn't expect you within five hundred miles of this place."

Corrections Officer Nelson Novotny. *Sonuvabitch*. He was different than other officers—older and not full of raging bull testosterone. No power trips here. He treated everyone fairly unless they brought shit down on their own heads. A real friend. And in here, that meant the world.

He put his hand out and we shook. I couldn't bring my smile down.

"Well, I hadn't planned on it, but..." I cocked a thumb to the empty phone block.

"Oh yeah." Nelson nodded. "Your girl. Damn shame, but yeah, I get it, I get it."

"What...what are you doing here?"

Nelson looked around sheepishly and shrugged. "Saw too many assholes doing too many things and tried to run it up the ladder. Didn't work. I gave a shit but nobody else did, so they transferred me to the women's prison." He blew a breath as he slapped his arms down. "Same shit, different place. Got eight years left to retire...So, yeah, I don't give a good goddamn."

I grinned. What a treat to see the one man who gave me, and so many others, hope on the inside.

"Good for you, man," I said. "Eight years? You *got* this. Ain't shit."

He clapped his hands and barked a laugh. *'Ain't shit'* was one of his mottoes for the convicts, no matter how long their term was. *You got this. Ain't shit.*

I was enjoying the company, felt like I'd just rose from the deep sea for air, but then Nelson stepped closer and lowered his voice. "Look, Joe. I know she was your girl and all, but you watch it, all right? Get on with your life, man. Be what you wanted to be before all this shit. I don't want to see you back on this side of things."

"Oh, that's not gonna happen, but I can't cut ties with her just yet. Some things going on right now that I need her help for a bit. But I need to get her some...stuff."

Nelson raised an eyebrow.

"No, no. Not like that. Just some cigarettes, y'know? Make things easier for her."

As he chewed his lip, he glanced around at the other visitors on their phones. "Yeah, I can help you with that. No serious contraband. I'm not risking that shit, but smokes, yeah...I can help. Fifty dollars per delivery."

"Seriously?"

Nelson shrugged. "Business is business, Joe. I'm giving you the friends and family discount, if that means anything."

"Yeah, okay."

"Bring it to Corrections Officer Stapleton out front. He'll know what to do and I'll get it where it needs to be."

I shook his hand again. "You got it." I took a step away and stopped, whispering, "Hey, Nelson? How many deliveries like this you do a week?"

He thought it over and shrugged. "Twenty, maybe thirty. What, you thought I could afford to retire on this shitty salary?" He scoffed. "Ain't shit. I'll see ya, kid."

I walked back through the visiting room doors as Pop rose from the bench with a newspaper in hand. He looked pained, and I knew a part of him despised being back in a prison. It was an ache I'd probably never fully understand. And it made my heart hurt.

"Hey, Pop."

"Go okay?"

I nodded. "As okay as it could, I guess. You mind running a quick errand with me?"

Three cartons of Winstons later, I was back at the prison, walking down the drab gray hall to the visitor's desk. My eyes scanned the man sitting behind the plexiglass and read his badge. Stapleton. He looked up from his desk, glanced at the three cartons and nodded.

"These are for—"

"I know. You got the seventy dollars?"

"Seventy? Nelson told me..." Yep, the prison economy

is alive and well, folks. Don't ever doubt it. I chewed my lip and nodded acceptance. "Yeah. I got it."

I shoved my hand into my pocket. A hundred and fifty dollars in cigarettes and seventy to deliver them inside. At this fuckin' rate, I hoped they were the best damn cigarettes on the planet. I put a fifty and a twenty on top of the cartons and Stapleton pulled them inside his cage and tucked them beneath the desk. "All good. Have a nice day." He turned back to his paperwork.

Nothing to do but turn and leave. Transaction complete. Yeah, there was no way I was *ever* fuckin' going back inside again.

We got home just before one o'clock. An entire day dedicated to nothing. It felt wasted but I knew it wasn't. No, actually I *didn't* know...I *hoped*. Angie could just take the smokes and barter her way to anything she wanted. There was barely a reason to trust her *before* she went inside and not one single damn reason for me to trust her now.

I thought about calling Kenny, making shit right. I thought about trying to search the goddamn house and find out where Pop hid the penny jar and driving out to Woodmount Crossing.

I thought about Raymond.

And finally, weariness found me and I slept.

CHAPTER FOURTEEN

ONCE, WHEN I was fourteen, I woke to Pop sobbing at the kitchen table. His best friend, Peter Ashley, had been killed by a drunk driver just two hours prior. Mom was still asleep, and as his bleary eyes found me standing in the doorway, he forced a smile and called me over for a hug. I did as instructed, but his shaking—like a damn *jackhammer*—made me nervous. My father was made of sturdy stuff, see? Yet, as he pressed his cheek to my forehead, hot tears found my skin. I didn't move. I didn't speak. And I hadn't thought of that moment until today, when that haunting and unforgettable sound crept through the house and woke me once more. It was five a.m.

"Pop?"

Those bleary eyes, a blast from the past. "Hey, Joe." He cleared his throat and spoke without looking directly at me. "You want something to eat?"

"Everything all right?" I crept over and placed a hand on his shoulder, an awkward sign of affection he knew took a lot on my part. We were never a 'touchy-feely' family. Even when Mom died, I don't think we hugged. I gave his shirt a squeeze. "What's up?"

His calloused hand worked over mine, tightened. "You know, I remember when the rotary switched to a landline, Joey. Monumental time, true advancement. Then when your mother got that cordless digital thing, 'member that? We both agreed we were livin' in the future. I had the same feeling the day she got that old computer with a dial-up connection that sounded like a scalded cat when it was workin', remember? And then along came broad...*broadband*. I didn't quite understand how things could move at such a clip, just *firing* along into the unknown whether we liked it or not. Things I didn't understand. Still don't. But I've been feeling a lot like that again lately."

"What are you talking about?"

Pop sighed and released my hand, and then he fished about in the pocket of his jeans. He removed a sheet of paper, and the sight made a lump form in my throat.

"It's that *wish*, Joey."

I knew that much, but what I really wanted to know was where had the penny gone.

"Pop, what did you do?"

He gave me a sad smile, his red-rimmed eyes glistening. "It's like the phones and the Internet, things just *evolving*. Right when I think I've got a grasp on how it works, it just shoots off and leaves me in the dark. The penny was a wheaty, did you know that?"

"A what? Pop, I don't understand what's going on."

"A *wheaty*. Used to collect 'em as a boy. Whole lot of folk did. Mint stopped pressin' 'em in '59, but up until then, the penny coin had two wheat stalks on the back. I took the coin off the wish to see if it *was* a wheaty. It was. I hadn't seen one since I was a boy."

The bare wish gripped me with horror. It looked *wrong*, like a suit missing a shirt or a clown without make-up. I took the page from Pop's hand. "Where's the coin?"

"I got it here." He pulled the money from his shirt and twisted it in his palm. Sure enough, two wheat stalks framed the shiny back. "A wheaty, just like I thought."

"And what's happened? Tell me what happened, Pop."

He tapped the coin against the table, taking a moment that stretched out forever. "Someone stole the car last night, Joe. They—"

"They *what?*"

"Kids. Just kids. They took it for a joyride. Smashed the damn thing into the quarry at 3:30 in the morning and popped the windows with a pistol. Police want me to swing by the station and give a statement around 7:30 this morning. No one's dead. But the car's gone, and I... well the car was never mine. I borrowed it from Henry Fisher at the mill. He said it could be mine if I wanted it. Him and the wife upgraded and weren't in a rush for the money, knowing I was good for it. Guess how much I owe Henry Fisher now, Joe?"

I swallowed hard. "About two and a half grand?"

"Two and a half thousand on the nose. Not a penny less."

I stared down at the coin in his hand. "Give me that penny, Pop."

"You put that penny back on that paper and I'll throw you out this door just like I've done before." His eyes, full of flame, found mine, and I actually took a step back from the fury I saw. "It's like the phones and the Internet," he repeated. "I don't know how it changes, but somehow, I got a feeling I got off lucky. Like a bullet whizzed by my ear and it could've been a lot worse. I'll pay my dues, Joe, but I want no more part in this... *whatever* it is. I got off by the skin of my teeth. Do you understand me?"

"I do," I said, though I doubted Pop was completely out of the forest. Something told me when you signed up with this *bastard* of a deity, there was no going AWOL.

"Good." He flattened the penny on the table, sighed, and eased himself from the chair. "I'm going back to bed. I *loved* that damn car."

"I know, Pop. I'm sorry."

"I'm burning that wish, Joe. And I wanna hear no more about it. Don't mention it to me again, don't ask where I put the jar, don't try and tell me how it—whatever *it* is—works. I just want out, and I want you out, too. There's no more of these things floating around, right?"

"No, Pop."

He studied me a moment longer—a routine I knew well. "Good. Now get some sleep, too."

And as Pop left, Abe Lincoln's immortalized stare pulled my gaze back to the kitchen table, his confidence and honesty forever frozen in aged-brown copper. I envied the man's integrity. Pop called from the doorway and asked, "You promise me you won't do anything else with that jar, Joey? It's a clean slate now, let whatever it is rest. Don't poke a sleeping dog."

I crossed my fingers and said, "I promise, Pop. A clean slate."

I listened to him stalk away to his bedroom before the door clicked shut. And as the dawn broke and hazy light reached the window, I reached out and swiped the penny and stuffed it in my jeans pocket. A penny was a proven commodity now, just like Angie's cigarettes: a *get-out-of-jail-free* card. I couldn't let it go. I'd tell Pop I tossed it out back, up in the river, and that he'd need not worry. Unlike Abraham Lincoln, my integrity was slanted and I *would* lie. Shit, it's the only thing I was good at. And that was the truth.

I exploded from a nightmare in the pale morning. My heart slammed as cold sweat trickled down my skin. I ran a shaking palm across my face as the door opened and Pop stepped inside, his brow furrowed. "Joe? All right?"

"Yeah...yeah, Pop."

For all of his anger earlier, the undeniable worry now etched on his face comforted me. He shuffled over and rubbed my shoulder and my muscles relaxed some. "Bad dream?"

"The worst."

He laughed at that. "No, the worst was when you woke up and projectile vomited across the room like the damn *Exorcist*, 'member that? I still owe Mrs. Boden a new pot 'cause I borrowed her gumbo bowl for you to sick in."

I never imagined such a dark time could be looked back on with humor, and the fact fascinated me. I wondered if we'd ever look back on these times and chuckle, but somehow I doubted it. Some things you just know.

"Your mom was always good with nightmares. I'm a little rusty."

"You're doing a good job, Pop. Thanks."

"Yeah." He stayed there a moment in that comfortable silence only known to family and friends. "I miss her."

"Me, too, Pop."

"Even the routine hurts sometimes, you know? Expecting to wake up and ask her if she took her shot while I put on breakfast. Not that I'd help her, either way.

Those damn insulin injections always weirded me out. But I'd watch her stick herself a billion times over just for one more day, that's for sure."

He smiled before the tears came. "Heading out to work," he said with a sniffle. "Jim Blevins is swinging by to pick me up but I've got to pop by the station first and give a statement. I'll leave you some bacon. Get some rest."

When he left my room, I collapsed back on my pillow and drew slow breaths. If Pop could shrug off everything I put him through, everything the blender of *life* put him through, then I could shake away a bad dream.

Even if in that dream I watched my dead father shuffle back home from a graveyard covered in dirt.

"Stop, Joe..."

His cataract eyes seeking the door as he shambled up the drive, knocking...calling my name...a sound like a clogged drainpipe. Jooooeeyy...

"Just a dream. Just a dream."

Though I once thought a child's wishes were nothing more than hope, too.

I drifted off as Pop hummed along to Hank Williams with strips of bacon popping in the skillet. In my dream, that sound warped to an image of melting flesh.

"You look like shit."

"Well, fuck you very much, Ava."

She ran a towel across the countertop before dropping it into a mop bucket. The sharp scent of lemon cleaner filled the shop, and in the afternoon sunlight, the place looked great. I'd brought us coffee from downtown, and—almost as a joke—jelly donuts.

A PENNY FOR YOUR THOUGHTS

After untying her apron, Ava snatched one of the desserts from the wax paper bag on the counter and bit in. She chewed like I thought she would, mouth smacking to give a full view of the doughy glop. "God, these are good. Why don't we just go clean and run the damn shop, Joe? Stop it with the stupid stolen shit. Donuts for breakfast every mornin', huh?"

I took a glazed one from the bag myself. Despite Pop leaving me food, I didn't much feel like eating when I woke up. The glaring sun chased off my morbid nightmares, and now that my appetite had returned, I bit in. "Maybe we will soon," I said. "But do you know the first thing about filing taxes and ordering materials and health inspections and all the other hundred things that go with *actually* running a place? Because you're talking to a guy who spent half his adult life junked out of his brain and the other half throwing up behind bars."

"Can't be any harder than getting away with robbing."

"Robbing, I know. Business, I do not. And going into an actual partnership with Kenny would be like letting the marble-eating kids run the school, know what I mean?"

She smiled at that, popped the last of her donut into her gob. "You're too hard on yourself, man. You've got a good head on your shoulders, despite it now looking like you just put it through a washing machine."

"That awful, huh?"

"Yeah." She hopped on the countertop, legs swinging. "I doubt I look much better, don't get me wrong. It's hard getting on with the day when you know about...new stuff. Does that make sense?"

"Most definitely does."

"It's like we know how the sausage is made now. And, frankly, I ain't in no rush to get cookin'. I tried a normal penny after that first night, almost as a joke, you know?"

"You what?"

"Well, I wanted to *see*. Wished for a chocolate malt, something specific, was my thinkin'."

"And?"

"And I got no malt. They must've done something to the pennies first. The Crimson Sisters. And I just can't stop thinking about them and that Barrows woman. How do they go about their normal day, knowing...*secrets*. How do *we* do that?"

"We seem to be doing okay," I offered, though I didn't trust my answer. "People have been getting by while believing in different gods forever. It's a cornerstone of our species."

She shifted on the counter and crossed her arms. "Well, whatever this is, it doesn't feel like a *god* to me, more like—"

"—a pusher," I finished.

"How so?"

I swallowed the last of my donut, suddenly wishing I hadn't eaten. My guts roiled. "This all feels *familiar* to me. Whole last few weeks feels like I stepped right back into my old life. Whatever *it* is—it feels like a pusher."

I tapped the countertop, wondering how to phrase my thoughts. "Little doses of good to start, just enough. Two and a half grand for Pop, a puppy for you, Kenny gets a set of tits to make a porn star weep... then everything sours. Payment's needed, and if it's not given, then you get a broken finger or a trashed house—for starters. Then you get desperate, get in deeper, making things worse, and before you know it, folks are dead because of you and you're so far gone you don't even care. I've been here before."

"That's why you haven't just wished for everything to go right, huh? You think there'll be one helluva price-tag for it?"

"Of course there would. Pulling Kenny's tit wish, that's small-fry shit. A little pain for him, a lot of leakage, unpleasant but not unbearable. I wish for something bigger, I'm thinking I'll owe a lot more. At least, that's how I'm thinking it works."

"But you *did* wish for something bigger, Joe."

My stomach turned like a bad washing machine at her words and all I could answer was, "I know."

If anything ever happened to the penny taped to my *'please don't let me get caught'* wish, I was in deep. I'd owe the pusher money. And although I knew this fear well, that didn't mean I could handle it any better.

"You speak to Kenny?" she asked.

I laughed. "Tried calling him on my way here. He told me to 'suck his fat one' and hung up. I'll let him burn it off. He's pissed. Has every right to be."

My phone rang. I half expected it to be Kenny but I didn't recognize the number. I excused myself.

"Hello?"

An automated voice replied, "*You have a collect call from Angela Sanderson, an inmate at the Lowback Correctional Facility. This call may be monitored, and—*"

"Yes," I yammered. "Yes, yes, yes."

"*To accept this call, please press—*"

I jabbed the '1' and a beat passed.

"*Thank you. Please proceed with your call.*"

"Angie?"

"Got her." Her voice drew nails up my spine. "Old lady's gonna speak with you next Saturday, nine in the morning, no later and no sooner. I got you a half hour."

Ava mouthed *'who?'* but I stalked outside, not wanting her to overhear. A chance to learn about Rebecca Barrows was the starting point of fixing this, and I couldn't afford to lose concentration. Talking to Angie was like playing two simultaneous games of chess. On the phone, she sounded like she was smiling, and I knew why. "The cigarettes weren't the full payment, were they, Angie?"

Just like the damn pusher in the sky.

"Just the beginning, baby."

"And you're going to ruin this for me if I don't play ball, aren't you?"

"You know we're being monitored, Joe. I would *never* do anything to *Ava's* grandmother if you don't do what I say. How could you ever accuse me of something so wrong?"

I took a deep breath. "What do you want, Angie?"

"I *wish* for another visit. I don't like to deal when we're not face-to-face. It's so...impersonal."

She knows! Sweet Christ, she fucking knows!

"Fine," I said. "Just tell me what you want."

And so, she did.

I hung up, bit down on my phone, and yelled.

CHAPTER FIFTEEN

MY STOMACH HURT and the acid burn of a headache flooded the back of my skull. I stuffed my phone back in my pocket as I closed my eyes and leaned against the building, taking even-paced breaths as I forced my heart to slow. The goddamn *thump* in my ears blotted out the world—a world I no longer trusted.

"Mornin' Joe."

I opened my eyes to find Henderson sitting in his cruiser, smiling at me as he raised his foam cup in a 'cheers'.

Fuck me running. The day just kept getting better and better.

"Morning back to you." I walked over with my hands in my pockets, poker-faced.

"Place is looking..." Henderson stared past me at the outside of the building. The exterior called out for a fresh coat of white, the weathered gray clapboard popping through the cracks like sores. "Great, Joe. Seriously. I'm really glad you're part of this. It's good for you." He sipped his coffee before pointing with the cup. "Really classy. And all this just for donuts? Even the sign looks sturdy as all hell."

His glassy eyes focused on something I—or anyone else—couldn't see. The old sign hung from one rusted eyehook, threatening to break free from the other.

Henderson smiled and nodded in complete sincerity. "Pride in your work, I like that. Gotta say, you've gone above and beyond here."

"Yeah, uh...thanks. It's really coming along."

"Sure looks like it. Hell, I might have to break my diet and lie to the wife when you guys open." He patted his stomach with his free hand and grinned. "Haven't touched a donut in almost seven months now. She was gettin' on me about being healthy and all that shit so I gave them up. Can't find it in myself to stop the beer yet, though." He winked and added, "Or a little whiskey now and again."

"Guess she's just looking out for you."

"Yeah, she knows best, I suppose. I love her, Joe. I do. My son, too, though he's..." A pained expression crossed his face for a moment, then it passed and he refocused. "He's special needs. Always will be, so it's...it's hard at times."

"Oh, I didn't, uh...didn't know that. I'm sure that's tough." I wasn't sure what the hell was going on but Henderson was *off*.

He sighed and nodded. "Sometimes, Joe...I love them. I do. But you ever think back to, you know, when you were a young man? Before things got all..." He waved his hand as his face scrunched. "*Serious* and shit. Before you became an adult, I guess, with responsibilities and bills and..." He looked through the windshield then, off into the distance, but I don't think he was staring at anything in particular. His voice softened, almost wistful. "Ever think back to those days and just...wish you could go back, knowing what you know now?"

"Yeah, I guess...sometimes." My stomach churned at his choice of words and my throat tightened. "But be careful what you wish for. Sometimes things are the way they're supposed to be."

"Yeah." Henderson kept on staring at nothing and everything and there was a too-long pause before he blinked, popping the mood. "Pay no attention to me, Joe. I'm just rambling, I guess. Was up all night working that damned..." He cleared his throat. "You give any thought to the Denny brothers for me? Anything come to mind?"

Here it was. The other fucking shoe about to drop. My junkie ability to bullshit on the fly took the wheel. "You know, I *did* think of something. A name. Maybe nothing, *probably* nothing, but—"

"No, no. Anything at all might help." Henderson excitedly set his cup down and pulled a pen and notebook from his jacket pocket.

"Back when I was...using..." I hated the way that sounded, the way it made me *feel*, but no use avoiding facts. "There was a guy the brothers used to buy from. Marky Gallows."

Henderson mumbled as he scribbled down the name. "Know anything else about him?"

"He was from up north, I think. Philly, maybe. Like I said, it's probably nothing, but you never know."

"You never know." Henderson stuffed his notebook away again. "I'll look into it." With that, he reached for the keys and started the cruiser. "Well, I'm headed home to get some grub. You take care, Joe. And again, place is looking fine. Real fine." He gave the building one final approving look before he pulled away from the curb.

I watched him drive off as the door behind me opened and eased shut.

"Your parole officer drink on the job?"

I ignored Ava's jab as I walked back inside the shop and slid down a wall to sit on the floor. I was shaky. The call from Angie and seeing Henderson had collided together to leave no room for much else. I watched Ava's pup sniff along the counter and I gave a soft whistle as I held out my hand. "C'mere, Geek."

"*Gomez*, not Geek." Ava walked back into the shop and hopped on the counter. "Geeks are circus freaks."

The dog trotted over and I scooped him onto my lap, giving him a good scratch along the back of his soft head. "Circus freaks?"

"Yeah, geeks used to be part of the sideshow. They used to bite the heads off animals and shit."

"Tough way to make a living." The pup closed his eyes as I rubbed his ears, his little tail batting my leg. Angie stayed on my mind like bubblegum on a shoe. I wondered what the hell she was going to angle me for, but didn't think Ava needed to know that part. "So...I have an appointment," I said.

"Kenny getting a tit-tuck? Photo op with *Playboy?*"

Normally, that would have made me snicker, even though I felt bad for the guy about everything. But not today. "Next Saturday morning. Going to talk to your grandma." I stopped petting Gomez and met Ava's wide-eyed stare.

"How? I mean...Joe, what did—"

"Doesn't matter, okay? It just..." Gomez jumped from my lap as I got to my feet. "Saturday morning at nine o'clock."

Ava nodded and stared at the floor. She gripped the edge of the countertop and stayed quiet for a moment. "I've been reading more of her journals, you know."

"Yeah?"

She nodded again, hopped to the floor, and walked to her backpack. I leaned against the wall as she unzipped the bag and withdrew a book the color of burnt cherries. She flipped it open to a playing card used as a bookmark. "I think this was the last one before she went into prison."

She held the book in front of her, and started to read: "Been having strange dreams lately. Dreams mixed with memories, really. I was back along the Lowback Trail, back where the dead pine needles are so thick, it's like walking on carpet. I remember being there when I was a young girl, stripping down bare as a newborn, and wading into the swimming hole where the fallen sycamore trees had made a natural dam. In my dream, I went out into the dark Lowback waters until they reached my chin. So real, I could feel the cool mercury slide over my skin in the hot August sun.

"And then, the blood came. Rushed from inside me like the great flood itself, flowing over my hands and my skin. The loss of innocence, of welcoming sin. I've been waking in cold sweats from it all and though I'd like to say I don't know why, the truth is, I most certainly do.

"I remember, as a girl, when I'd sit among those pines, I'd be still, so very still, watching, waiting for something. The Sisters told me the spaces in between is where it lies. The void. The beyond. If you stay real still and listen, you can hear things whispering. Things older than time itself.

"This isn't the life I wanted, but it's the life I've made. We all make choices, and I've damned well made mine. I've evened out some things, put others to rest back among those pines, but I wonder, for how long will they sleep?

"I wish I could go back before it all. Before everything. Some days, I wish I could be new again."

Ava stopped reading, tears brimming in her eyes. She put the card back in place and closed the journal. After a shake of her head, she returned the book to her backpack. "I can only read a little at a time, y'know? It's just..." She sniffled and raised an unsteady hand to her face.

"Yeah, I know."

She shook in silence as I walked toward her, and rested a hand on her shoulder. She spun around and glared at me, tears trailing down her cheeks. "What're you doing?"

I stepped back. "Nothin'...I just thought you—"

"Well *don't*, okay? Don't think!" She batted at her face. "I'm *fine!* I'm—" Her expression dissolved then as tears came harder and she folded against me. I held her there as she cried. "I'm not trailer trash!"

"I know, hon." I patted her back. "I know."

I had no idea what Ava's comment had to do with it all, but I knew sometimes, you had to be angry and fight back at something, *anything*, even if it's not the right thing at the time.

If you want to measure the true genius of a junkie, take a look at their ability to hide their stash around other junkies. Oh, you hid it under your mattress? *Fuckin' noob.* In a Ziploc baggie floating in your toilet tank? *Could you possibly be less original?* On the top shelf in the back of your closet in an old shoebox? *Give me a fuckin' break.*

The trick to hiding your stash is putting it in plain sight. When shit got bad and we had a hard time gettin' fixed, I'm ashamed to say I held out on Angie. Often. Looking back, that was fuckin' *awful* of me. *Terrible*, really. Selfish and self-centered as hell, but that's what being a junkie is all about: *me, me, me*, all the time.

A PENNY FOR YOUR THOUGHTS

I'd put my stash inside a dirty sock and leave it in a pile of laundry. No way in hell Angie was going to touch that. Or I'd flatten it out in tin foil and stuff it inside a DVD case of some shitty action movie. Chuck Norris and Louis Gossett, Jr., in *Firewalker* or Sho Kosugi in *Ninja III, The Domination*. Any stupid 80's movie she would never bother with.

My favorite was taking a sheet of newspaper or an empty potato chip bag and wrapping my bindle inside it, crumpling it up, and tossing the whole thing into a corner of the room to let it blend in with the other shit strewn about the pigsty.

I tried to take care of her when she was getting dopesick, but *I* never went dry until we were both hurtin' because I knew how to hide shit.

My father, my beloved Pop, would have been a great addict.

I stood in the living room, hands on my hips, sheen of sweat on my face, and studied the room. I'd looked in the kitchen cabinets and his bedroom closet. Under his bed and in the bathroom closet. I pushed up the drop ceiling tiles and peered into those tight, dark cracks. Hell, I'd even popped the closure door on the furnace to see if he'd somehow lodged the jar *there*.

Fuckin' nothin'.

As my meeting with Gramma Greenfield loomed on the horizon, I needed preparation. If she told me Rebecca Barrows could help, I wanted to hightail it to Woodmount with that jar and not lose a single second more. Time was the enemy, if not Barrows herself.

"I don't think it's in the house." I chewed my lip and shook my head. "*Ohhhhhh*, Pop." I turned in a slow circle, scanning the elements in the room. My gaze landed on the bookshelf in the corner and I walked closer, my eyes running over the titles of the paperback thrillers he used to read. Never saw Pop read much anymore but damn, he used to. The spines of the books all lined up together, hardbacks and paperbacks all flush and facing out, no matter their height. I smiled to myself.

"Pop, you clever man, you." I reached over the top of the books until my fingers met the wood backing—and the open space behind. "Bingo."

I pulled a group of the paperbacks and set them aside, ready to grab my jar and race to my room.

But then I paused—and felt like someone smacked my guts with a hammer.

Instead of a jar in the cubby, I found a small rectangular box—one wrapped with Christmas paper. On top of the present, a red foil ribbon was bunched up and coated in dust, and a plain paper tag read: Meg.

For my mother.

I didn't find the penny jar that day, but the long-forgotten Christmas present for my mother brought another lesson—be careful you don't hide things so goddamned well that you hide them from yourself.

CHAPTER SIXTEEN

I NEVER OPENED Mom's present. I never spoke of it. But the entire drive out to the jail that Saturday morning, the horrible feeling of that discovery rose in my throat along with some bile. Pop had rented a car from a place downtown that Wednesday, and although the vehicle was nice, it wasn't *his*. I could tell that bothered him by how his usually immaculate steering was hampered by his grinding of the clutch. But like I said, I didn't mention a damn thing. I just watched as those prison walls grew ever closer, and took deep, slow breaths. To this day, I don't know what's inside that box. I think it's the only time I've ever had any real restraint.

"Wait for you as usual," Pop said. We parked in a free spot and I climbed from the car. His sullen features glared in the morning light, and the sight made my chest tighten. I guess I never thought of him getting old. He'd been drinking that week, and—unusual for him—recreationally rather than celebratory. I wondered if this is what he must've felt like watching me fall off the wagon, and the taste of my own medicine made for a bad breakfast.

"Take all the time you need," he said through the open window, tapping the wheel. "I don't have anywhere to be."

She leaned on the counter mere inches from the glass, her chuckle distorted through the earpiece. "Hey, baby."

"Angie."

She worked me over a moment (needing to set the scene, you know?)—I was the food, and she was the tiger. She wanted me to remember that before she eased back in her chair and crossed one leg over the other. In my pocket, I worked my fingers over my secret weapon as she said, "Tell me about your week, Joe."

My throat clicked but I maintained eye contact. "Why?"

"You're my boyfriend, aren't you? Isn't that what couples do? *How was your day, baby? What's for dinner? Have you fucked that little piece you got on the side yet?* That kinda thing."

"If you're talking about Ava, no, I have not. She's my friend."

"You don't have friends, Petal, you've got beggars and hangers-on, I've told you that before. Don't you remember anything I taught you?"

Oh, the pickaxe was out, alright, chipping away at my ego just like old times. Sickeningly, the familiarity actually comforted me. At least I *knew* this routine and this world. I knew my place here. But, with my plan solidified, I leaned forward and thought of Pop for strength. The man who hid presents behind paperbacks and gave what was needed. "I want you to tell me what you want for today and cut the bullshit, are you hearing me?"

Well, being the theatrical *treat* she was, Angie leaped back in her chair looking like she'd received a blast from the throat of a diseased dragon. A nearby guard grabbed for his belt, his eyes wide. "Joey!" she said, mocking me with that high tone. "Who's a big, bad wolfy wolf, huh? *You are! Yes, you are!*"

"Stop it."

Her face soured and her voice lowered. "Fuck off, dipshit. You ever talk to me like that again and I'll—"

The guard loomed above her, a brick shit-house ready to pounce. "Problem here, ma'am?"

"No, sir," she said in a voice as soft as butter, her neck craned back for a full hit of those wild emeralds. "Not a one, sir. I swear it. Not a one..."

He gave me a knowing look before repositioning himself by the wall—a lion tamer scared by his own animals. Angie arched a brow. "We need to have a big talk about your attitude when I get out of here, big boy."

"Not gonna happen."

"No?" Her clownish smile returned, ready to deliver the blow. "I got an old lady comin' to talk to you in half an hour. I can put a stop to that right now by makin' it so her mouth don't work so good. You don't think I'll do it? Try me, Petal."

I feigned nervousness, tightening my grip on the item in my pocket. The cold surface gave me comfort. "You wouldn't."

"Then don't test me and do what I say."

Her *check-and-mate* expression almost made me laugh. For the first time, I was one step ahead of her.

"You got what I asked for on you?" she said.

I cradled the earpiece between my shoulder and neck and pulled out the pen and paper.

"Good," she said, leaning forward with an open mouth. "You must've known something that piques your interest would pique mine, honey. I just *had* to know...and now...I don't fully believe this bullshit, but if it doesn't work? Then what harm? I still had a laugh. But here's what I'm thinking..." She leaned forward, her gaze tight on my face. "I'm thinking if it *does* work, Joe? Oh, baby, we're gonna have us some fun."

"Just tell me what to write."

She licked her lips as a chuckle rattled from her throat. "Write...Angie gets out of prison and the police never come looking for her, never find it odd that she leaves... and neither will Joe's father."

I stopped writing. "Don't you bring Pop into this."

Her mouth opened into a wide 'O'—the kinda face you just wanna squeeze in a vice. "Write what I want, baby."

I thought of the thing in my pocket, and then I wrote as requested. I dotted a period and dropped the pen.

"It's actually kinda fun," she said. "Even if it ain't true, it's some damn good entertainment, huh?"

"This what you call fun, I'd hate to see you at a circus."

"Shut up and get on with it," she said. "Add the penny."

Here it is...

I pulled the pre-taped coin from my jeans, slow and deliberate. I stuck it right next to the words, working out the kinks with my thumb. Satisfied, I lifted the wish and showed her my work. She smiled, leaned back in her chair, and gave a giggle. "Good," she said. "Very good. Except for...one little thing."

My stomach knotted. "What?"

"Pull that penny and stick the *real* one down."

"*What?*"

No, no, no!

A PENNY FOR YOUR THOUGHTS

"I said...pull that penny. Stick the real one down. You didn't think I'd comb the finer print with the old bitch? We were always good with details, Joe. You've gotta remember that much."

My shoulders sagged. It was a losing battle. Useless. And right then, I knew my place. I understood why Angie was always the one to make decisions. No matter how far ahead I *thought* I was, no matter how hard I pushed, I was only as far as she allowed me to be. I ripped the fake penny free of the paper and felt something deep inside me rip, too.

She said, "Just let me see first. Oh, I *gotta* see what you tried."

I flipped the coin and she laughed, clapping one hand on her knee. "No wheat stalks! I fuckin' *knew* it, you cheapskate. You absolute fuckin' try-hard."

I pocketed the penny from '05 and withdrew the real one, the one from Pop's *bite* wish. Somewhere in the back of my mind, I knew she'd one-up me. Shit, when *hadn't* she?

I switched the coins without thought. To fester on it would only delay the inevitable. And at that point, I just wanted the ordeal over like wanting to be out of a dentist's chair. Her eager eyes bulged as I fastened the real deal. Job done, I flashed my work.

"I'm ready for Ava's grandmother. I think we're done here, Angie."

"I think so, too, Petal." She couldn't contain herself—her laughter popped like kernels in hot oil. "I'll be waiting for you out front then, huh?"

Did she believe her own words, or the ritual for that matter? It was hard to tell. Right then, I think she simply got a kick out of one-upping me; sheer entertainment. But as she stood and placed the earpiece back into the cradle, she clapped her hands and laughed soundlessly as the guard led her off and I think she *did* believe. I wondered if that guard took a wrong turn at the end of the hallway... would anyone bat an eye at the jumpsuit-wearing lunatic with the ability to size up a bear, being ushered out the gate? I hoped so, but I diverted my attention to the vacant seat behind the plexiglass. I had another appointment that morning, and the woman herself had just entered the room.

Her swollen eye glistened like a wet plum. Her white hair was thick as cotton. Her skin (around the scratches and scuffs) remained wrinkle-free despite the harsh years. I recognized Ava in her stoic glare, a look that made me feel small, like she knew things about me even I didn't know, without a word passing between us. But that was about to change.

"Joe," she said, and flashed a smile that belonged on Ava's lips.

"Miss Greenfield, I am so sorry."

The apology came unannounced, a *need* from my core. I imagined this was how religious folk felt in front of the Pope. She had *presence*. Even the guards appeared uneasy. Her expression remained unchanged, my words bouncing off her rough skin much like Angie's beating.

"I've taken fists," she said, "I've taken boots, I've even taken a baton. And I'm still here." Ever hear an elderly person talk with such clarity and wish you reached that age with even *half* of their grit intact? Yeah, she was one of *those*.

"She shouldn't have touched you," I said. "That's my fault. I shouldn't have gotten her involved."

Miss Greenfield simply blinked, slow and controlled movements. "I'm short on time. By choice. Is my granddaughter okay?"

"Ava's more than okay," I said. "She's one of the best people I know."

Her split lip twitched. "Good."

"Miss Greenfield, I...I don't know how to tackle this conversation. I know you don't want to talk much, but I guess...the only way I can put it is—"

"Your world has turned upside down. Reality revealed itself fickle and frail and that frightens you. Your loved ones' fate lies in your hands." She let her words hang in the air as she studied my reaction. "You found my jar."

"Yes."

Another slow and even breath. "It's too much to keep contained, isn't it, Joe? Like water through your fingers. It has a way of getting out. Of getting *messy*."

"Yes."

"You think, 'just a small help, a hundred dollars to cover the rent. That's all,' don't you? But that comes at a cost. And then people question where that money came from. So you tell a friend. A family member. Well, they need things, too, don't they? And soon enough, it's spiraled beyond your control...It's a mirror to our worst side. Good intentions could overcome it, but we're not built like that. We're hardwired to mess it all up. *He* knows that."

My heart slammed. "What is this?"

"Ever throw a penny in a wishing well?"

"Yes?"

"Then you already know. Does its name matter? What matters is what kinda cheapskate accepts a single *penny* for a wish, Joe? One who knows they'll get much more than a single cent in the end, that's who. He's a dealer. A pusher. That's all you need to know."

My thoughts exactly.

"And how did you come across him?"

She blew a long breath before easing back in her chair. She took her time. And in those moments, the muffled conversations around us faded. The lights seemed to dim. It was just me and Miss Greenfield.

"The Sisters collect deities like companies collect investors. You have to know who I'm talking about."

"I do," I said, and a shiver surfed my spine. "It's why I'm here. I need to know about that woman."

"I was just a girl then. Ten years old. They used me like bait on a hook. I needed an escape, Joe. You must know what I mean. My family have lived in Briarwood for generations. It's a place where dreams are about as useful as wet sticks in a flood. Escapism is necessary."

My veins itched at that. I knew what she meant all too well.

"I used to play up the Lowback Mountain, same as all kids have. It's our little secret, isn't it, that place? And back then, the river was little more than a stream, coming from someplace far away, eating away at the dirt for years and years...and when it arrived, and made what you all now know as the quarry, it was officially titled the Lowback River. The town celebrated by tossing pennies. Wishes."

"When was this?"

"In the winter of 1952. I was eight years old. I stood with my father, all the other parents and children, and we tossed pennies and dreamed big dreams. I even had cocoa that night, back in town at Carrington's, wrapped in a scarf and mittens...Miss Carrington had given us kids the change from her till that morning. All day, we bubbled with excitement, 'til our parents took us up and we all threw those coins, just...splash, splash, splash...

"But someone was watching. A lady. She approached me the next day as I got milk and butter from the store. Said that I wished the hardest. Said she saw it all over my face—just how *bad* I wanted my wish to come true. Do you know what she had me do, Joe?"

I understood rhetoric when I heard it. I remained silent.

"That evening, after I'd done my chores, she had me trek up the mountain with her and *fish* out all those coins... the dreams and prayers of the town. Said I deserved them. That I could turn them into anything I wanted. Said Kelly Armstrong called me names, but I don't know how she knew that. Said Kelly didn't deserve a wish. Said Harry Preston killed the Thompson's cat and it never did get run over by a truck out on R57. *He* was listening to me, she said. I was to wish for whatever I wanted.

"After I waded down the bank with the sun setting through the pines, I came out ten minutes later with my hands dripping and those shiny pennies cupped in my palms. Standing right there on the bank, she asked for them. Even then, I wondered why she never climbed into the river herself.

"Years later, one of the Sisters let a 'rule' slip. She's not around anymore. She told me why Rebecca needed me in the first place. Something about keeping the children's wishes pure. A woman of Rebecca's calibre, of her *age*, she'd ruin it all if she showed her greed and snatched those coins from the waters.

"And even at eight, I was smarter than that, Joe. I was poor, and I knew something of value when I saw it. I said I'd keep them, but she could help me use them. She knew *how* to use them. She said she'd give me paper the following day, and that I was to meet her at Woodmount Crossing and tell no one, *absolutely no one*, what we were doing. This was our secret. And, so, I promised.

"I woke at the crack of dawn and trekked it all the way from Briarwood...she met me by the fields, even gave me two boiled eggs from her basket for breakfast. Carried that wicker basket like the Wicked Witch...and after we'd eaten, she took out a notebook, a pen, and made my first wish with me. Made it like a game, got me all excited. I wished for a warm blanket on my bed that never got cold because November hit hard that year. That was the only thing on my mind. We taped the first penny, and soon after, we made more. I watched carefully, knowing how to do it myself, so once she shooed me off home, I could try my own. She took my wishes I'd already written up, said they'd be safe with her."

"And were they?"

"Well...I ran home expecting to find a new blanket. But my wishes never did come true."

"Why?"

"The bitch had switched the pennies, Joe. Of course she did. I didn't *see* it, but she did it. She kept the pennies at home, ready to turn them into whatever she wanted. All the while, I spent months at home making my own wishes with any old coin I could find. But it never worked. And here's the funny part. In the back of my mind, I remember Woodmount Crossing as a dire place. No better than Briarwood Estates. I see it, almost like a dream, trailers and muddy yards...except it's a prosperous place with gargantuan homes now, isn't it? Isn't that funny?"

"Wait," I said, and at that moment I wanted to vomit. "Are you talking about the Barrows woman? Rebecca?"

Miss Greenfield's good eye narrowed to a slit. "The bitch is older than me, Joe. That can't be the biggest surprise you've gotten?"

Unsurprisingly, it wasn't, and I said so. I also realized what this meant: I wasn't giving the jar to The Sisters. I was back at square one with what to do with the damn things.

"But I got them back," she said. "The real coins. Once I figured my dreams weren't coming true. I knew what she'd done. Us Greenfields have always been cunning. We know a deal from a backstab, and a thief from a savior. So, I was patient and I waited and I broke into her house and stole them when I was fifteen. When I really needed something to come true. And this is why you're here, right? To know *how* it happened?"

"It is now," I said, and my mouth felt very dry. I'd lost my one hope in Rebecca Barrows. No one could help me now. Up shit creek without a boat, let alone a paddle. My hopes were dashed, but I devised a new plan right then and there. I'd learn Miss Greenfield's history with the jar. Learn from her mistakes...and pray I never repeated them.

"Well," she said, "This is it."

And this is what she told me, exactly as she told it...

Chapter Seventeen

THOMAS BENTLEY WORKED at Carrington General Goods, tagging cans and bagging goods. He was seventeen. That was two years older than myself in 1959, but age don't matter much in the ways of romance. I'd just bought two bottles of milk and a twist of tobacco for Pa when Thomas threw me *that* smile. You know the one.

They say love at first sight is bound to fantasy, daydreams for idealists and hopefuls, but me? I never gave love the time of day. I was fifteen years old, kid, and I had school, housework to think of...but right then? Right then I learned what it meant to have my heart stolen. Yes, I did. It would be my first, and my last.

"Anything else?" A smile played on his lips, mirroring the twitch of my own. I fixed my hair without thought, slipping into autopilot as the bag rustled and he placed it aside before ringing up the till. A 'spark' bound us, and we both knew it without a word. It could charge a damn lighthouse and then some.

"Miss?"

"Oh...um, no, that's all. Thank you."

He laughed at that—had I made a good joke? Did I seem cool or like a square? I didn't know, but it made me laugh, too, and as I handed over Pa's ten-dollar bill, I swear I thought I'd puke. Or pass out. Or both.

Thomas gave me change before commenting, "I like your laugh."

Joe, there are things out there that make this life worth living. Rain tapping the window while you read a good book in bed. Christmas as a child. The taste of something warm on a winter's day...and the first honest-to-God compliment that scares the butterflies all across your stomach. I could've floated right out the door and drifted to the moon. Could've taken on the world one asshole at a time and asked for more. But instead, what did I do? I honked a dorky laugh while my face flushed as it reached my ears and I snatched that bag off the counter.

Nobody said love was perfect. It's messy, confusing—and on occasion—just a little more than embarrassing.

"I gotta go."

"Wait." He rounded the counter as he untied that work apron, one with a smiling face logo mocking me. Sadie Carrington had left him alone that day, and I suddenly required adult supervision. Up until that point, I'd never *really* had an ultimatum. Those were for adults. But as he said, "I'm Thomas," we both knew '*it*' had begun, whatever '*it*' was. A rollercoaster, it felt.

"Joyce," I said. "My name's Joyce Greenfield."

And with that, all the songs on the radio suddenly made sense. The world brightened to a point I didn't know possible. I don't remember much of the conversation from there, Joe, but I know that when I left, even the gray sky made me giggle. The birds sounded funny. The air itself smelled sweeter.

A PENNY FOR YOUR THOUGHTS

Thomas was picking me up the next day at 4 p.m. and we were going wherever I wanted. I wanted to go 'anywhere', and that was fine by him. Because he wanted to go anywhere, too. And that's how it all began.

I should've left that store with my good sense intact.

For two weeks, I met Thomas at the base of the Lowback after he finished work and we'd take a hike. For that brief time, everything was right with the world. Chores weren't hard. The cold snaps weren't what I remembered. And I went to bed each night just wanting the hours to speed by to be back outside again, talking about everything and nothing, learning all about his life and his family. Talks of the future, too. The world with Thomas was full of colors I didn't know existed, but back home, our trailer was the same dull gray, and even that didn't bother me. Until it became tinged with Pa's violent red.

"He what?"

I stammered for a response. "Took me up the Lowback a couple of times, that's all. I didn't think—"

"Damn fucking right you didn't think! What if he pulled a *knife*, Joyce, huh? What then?"

"But he didn't," I said, and my answer stood firm. "I like him. And he didn't do that. Nor would he."

Pa fell onto his bed while raking a hand across his haggard face. He looked older in that moment, and though I'd glimpsed this temper before, it'd never been shot *my* way. "You gonna take off with him, that it?"

"I don't know what I plan to do, Pa, I just like him and it feels good. Can't we just leave it at that? Feeling good?"

"You fuckin' him?"

Joe, I felt like someone had dunked ice water over my head. I had *never*, and I mean *never*, heard my father speak *nasty*. I'd never watched him *shake* that way, and all of a sudden it clicked—he was afraid to be alone. He'd lost my mother, and now he was faced with losing me. I'm sure he'd thought of it before, but like most things, he probably tucked it away to deal with 'later'. I loved the man, but I wasn't going to throw away my chance at building something to keep him placated. I had a life to live, too, and I told him as much.

"What you got," he said, and stood, "Is a goddamn *death wish*. That's what you got."

When I asked whether from *Thomas* or from *him*, Pa just gave a 'you know' kinda look and stalked from the trailer, though not before slamming the door so hard my teeth rattled.

And that's when it hit me.

I did not have a death wish. But I had many wishes. And a strange woman named Rebecca Barrows had them all locked away.

Thomas became bolder. When I told him I couldn't meet for our usual stroll, he knocked on the trailer door at 4:30 p.m., and at 4:32, he was on his back with a busted nose and an even stronger constitution. Pa warned him (and in truth, he *did*—for all of two seconds), but that only further solidified my man's goal. And it just made me love him more. Pa took to drinking.

The second time Thomas called 'round, he dodged Pa's punch. He backed from the yard while matching

Pa step for step, and he spoke fast. Even from the trailer, I heard him say he loved me and...and, well, that was the greatest thing I'd ever heard in my whole damn life. Just as time froze for me, it kicked into overdrive when Pa caught up to Thomas at the mailbox and knocked out one of his teeth. That was two for two.

Round three came in the form of donuts. Thomas (being smarter now), left two jam-filled desserts in a paper bag before knocking and taking off. Smart move. Either he could come dressed in riot gear or he could take off before my Pa, the dog, came snarling. See, he'd been at the County Fair the night before with his family. An event he wanted me with him for. Of course, Pa refused. I was beginning to wonder if that man even *really* cared anymore or if this had become a matter of stubbornness. It fit his mold, either way. And that morning after the knock, Pa was first to the door.

"What is it?" I asked. Pa grumbled as he peered inside and tossed the bag into the garbage. Without a further word, he dressed for work and left as I still wiped the sleep from my eyes. I noted he had a donut in his mouth as he buttoned his faded shirt. And right then, I hated that man something fierce, Joey. I hated him more than possible. The cloud of liquor that had begun to follow him made that pretty easy. When he left, I snatched the donut bag from the trash, saw one more inside, and I ain't ashamed to admit, I ate it. I loved every bite. And I needed the energy. I had a long day ahead of me.

But before I tossed the bag away, I noticed Thomas' handwriting. He'd written something to make me smile: *Donuts are love.*

And ain't that the truth.

Joe, this is the part I'll skim over. It's not a day I like to remember.

I broke into Barrows' manor as the sun set. Last time I set eyes on the place, it was nothing more than a shack set off the road. All those homes were. And some part of me remembered that. Doctors and lawyers and stay-at-home pretty moms infest that place now, sure, but it weren't always that way. And, even then, I bet that smart bitch knew there'd be a price. She took a gamble, couldn't help herself. But she was cunning not to use all my pennies up. She was still researching, see. Even now, too. I often wonder what price she'll eventually pay for Woodmount Crossing. Or if she even cares.

From my first meeting with Rebecca to that day, I remembered our first get-together almost as playtime. Like we were playing make-believe. But right then, seeing Woodmount as a paradise with my own eyes, it all snapped back. The bitch had my pennies. Part of me wonders if her comeuppance, her *payment*, was me remembering. I still don't know.

After I found the living room window open—can you believe that?—I hopped inside. I didn't overthink it, just readjusted the hunting knife jabbing my ribs. I found my pennies at the foot of a statue, one sculpted into something with too many eyes and tentacles. I could've fit three of Pa's trailers in that room, but I didn't hang around to take it all in. Didn't overthink what that statue *was*. My mind was still locked in that *get-out-get-out* state, and those pennies were weighing down my hand-me-downs. I had the *real* coins back, though, and that was a comfort. So I sneaked out without a hitch. And when I went home, I...I found Thomas dead in the kitchen, Joe, I'm—I'm sorry, this is hard to talk about.

Pa was nowhere.

Bastard *took off!* Way...the way I pieced it together, Thomas called 'round and wasn't taking no for an answer anymore. Pa'd been drinking, the usual by then, but Pa also had a hammer. That's all there was to it.

I lost my mind, best way I can describe it. Just wanted to *wake up*, y'know? Curled up on the floor and tried to sleep, thinking it'd make things better, hit a reset button, but in the morning light, it was only worse. My clothes soaked through with blood. *His* blood. I never knew the human body could hold so much.

And then...well, then I lost my mind, kid.

I threw open a drawer in the kitchen, flung it to the wall, found a pen and paper, started my wish. It took me five tries on account of my shaking and the blood on the page. I eventually wrote what I wanted, what I *needed* more than anything in the world, and taped a penny to that damn crimson-stained sheet. I wished for Thomas to come back, see? And I wished with all my heart.

As I waited, I spent the day digging out my old useless wishes and taping down the *real* coins. I wanted everything in the world to be good. All the wishes I ever made, I wanted them all true. I *deserved* it. That little girl who got tricked and back-stabbed deserved it. *I* deserved a good life. *I* was a good person. And so, I put them all in a jar for safe keeping. Pa's cookie jar that I was never allowed to touch without permission. It seemed only fitting.

And that evening, my first wish came true.

He sat up at six p.m., his hair a rat's nest and his skin whiter than a cloud. He winced, but kept on smiling, and then he stood. I felt like Doctor Frankenstein in that old black 'n' white, like I was watching a movie, and through choked cries, in the harshest voice I ever heard come from my own throat, I asked if it was him.

"Of course?" he said with a shake of the head, but, Joe, those eyes...it *weren't* him.

He spoke fine, yeah, he looked okay, but that *thing* wasn't my Thomas. Like a *replication*, or just something my brain *wanted* to see, you know? Does that make sense? Whatever electrical wire passed from him to me had been severed, and my heart just knew it. That's the only way I can put it to you. I shattered all over again, my body unable to take no more. It wasn't right, messing with nature this way. Like I'd asked an actor to come and take Thomas's place while I slept. Make me feel right. But none of it was. And right then, I understood those pennies weren't to be messed with. So, with the last of my energy, I made one of my final wishes. I wished that none of my wishes would come true for me. That's how I wrote it, and I remember it clear as day. *'I wish none of the wishes inside that jar will ever come true for me'*. And sitting here in jail, taking my beatings and the rest, I think I've finally paid my cosmic bar tab. Having a little sense, I didn't place that penny-wish in the jar, though. Nah. I put *that* one someplace nobody will find it for a very long time. And then I cleaned my love's blood by hand.

A PENNY FOR YOUR THOUGHTS

I could've wished it all away, sure, gambled it just like Rebecca Barrows. But I decided I'd put together quite a bill already, and as a little of my good sense returned with the manual labor, I knew I couldn't afford the price. Being poor, you know you get nothing for free. This was no different.

It's a good thing I didn't wish it all away. I'd come to learn in time that there are *rules*, Joe. Cancelling out a wish with another is just one of them. Like wishing for a million other wishes on a magic lamp. It doesn't work like that. And if you take one warning away from all this, let it be that.

Thomas, or, whoever he was, helped me clean. How bizarre is that? A man happily mopping his own cranial leakage, only stopping to say, 'Hey, I love you.' I shivered at every word.

Around sunrise, we had the place back to normal. Or at least, what passed for normal. Pa never returned. I didn't expect him to. Joe, I don't want to go over too many details, but I'll put it like this: I kissed my Thomas on the lips, told him I loved him very much—even though I was speaking to *my* Thomas the whole time, not the copy in front of me—and then I made two final wishes. I wished for Thomas's soul to be laid to rest. And as soon as I taped that penny, that very second, he dropped like a sack of wet clothes. I popped that wish into my pocket. And then I wrapped him in a tarp.

Then I wished my father dead.

I buried Thomas out back o' the house. The job took me two days, two blistered hands, and then I reported my father missing. They found him three days later. He'd died of a heart attack, slumped over a bar in York. The trailer became mine. And beyond having to listen to people talk about Thomas up and leaving town (how could he when he had such a nice Mom and sister at home depending on him?) not much was done about it all. This was the start of the sixties, Joe. Time just moved differently back then. Besides, young men leave home every day, wasn't big news. I eventually got a job downtown, met a guy, and in 1969, I had a daughter. The father? Just a guy. Safety wasn't my top priority, I just had needs. He was...just a guy. I raised Kelly, Ava's mom, until she up and left Briarwood the day she turned seventeen. And sometime later—years later—I got a little bundle on the doorstep that led to months of court meetings and paperwork to get my granddaughter into my legal possession. Despite all the hardships, I never once used a wish. I could've. I had two sunk at the bottom of Lowback quarry in a lunchbox and one buried away. But I left those, and that jar, where they belonged. Beneath the dirt and the water where no one would ever find them.

And I raised Ava.

When I finally had enough of a nest egg, I put together my donut shop. Because *donuts are love*, Joe. 'Cept before I could open the damn place, a cold case file lands on a desk in the Lowback Police Department. Some snappy little deputy decided to take a look with all the new tech they have, and they come sniffing around the property and...well, here I am. Fingerprints on a tarp and a hammer, even after all those years. Technology, kid, I could never keep up.

Now don't look at me like that. I think you always suspected my innocence. And there you have it.

I'll just ask that you'll do the right thing with those pennies. Put them where they belong, Joe. Though I know that cunning little bitch has already shook one out of you.

A PENNY FOR YOUR THOUGHTS

And I'm not talking about Rebecca. Angie's been giddy as a schoolgirl all week long. Keep a close eye on her now. I know how she can be. She's leaving this prison today, you mark my words.

You've got a storm coming, Joe. You best be ready for it. Now leave me in peace.

CHAPTER EIGHTEEN

A STRANGE NUMBNESS overcame me as I walked the hallway—detached, like a skyward balloon. The visitors talking in low voices to inmates dissolved to nothing but a murmur around me. The lights became too bright.

"Hey, Joey."

At the sound of my name, I turned in a haze to find Officer Nelson. The smile faded from his face as he reached for my shoulder. "Joe? You doin' okay? You're lookin' a little green." His eyebrows furrowed like a disapproving father. "You still clean?"

I nodded and swallowed hard, the accusation bringing me down some. "Still clean," I said, the weight of his hand keeping me grounded.

"Your, uh..." Nelson glanced around before lowering his voice. "Your delivery got delivered."

"Yeah, I know. I appreciate it, Nelson."

"Need anything else?"

I shook my head at first, and then changed my mind. "Hold up." Kneeling down, I messed with my shoestrings a moment, slid two fifty-dollar bills beneath my right shoe, and then stood up. "As a matter of fact, yeah. This is for the ol' lady. Greenfield. Your delivery fee is in there."

Nelson glanced at the floor as I moved my foot away. He shifted his boot to cover the money, then squatted to pocket the bills. "Consider it done."

"Thanks, Nelson."

He muttered, "No problem," and then I watched something happen in the man's face, a shift behind his eyes. It was like watching a notebook filled with felt-tipped words get rained on—the color dripping and stretching to nothing but an abstract has-been. Nelson blinked, and the moment passed. "She must be some friend to come visit. Didn't think I'd see you within five hundred miles of this place again."

"Well, I won't be visiting her again. Not Angie either if I don't have to."

"Huh?" Genuine confusion clouded Nelson's words. "Angie? The Spanish girl in for assault?"

"What? No, *my* Angie. Well, I mean, not really *my* Angie, but..." I shook my head clear. "Angie *Sanderson*. Armed robbery. Smack junkie."

He pursed his lips. "Model prisoner? She doesn't sound familiar at all, Joe."

"Nelson, I was *just* talking with—" My stomach flipped and I wanted to throw up right there on the polished tile floors of Lowback Prison visitor's hall. "I gotta run," I said. "You take care of yourself, Nelson."

"You, too, Joe."

My heart became rusted gears, grinding to make a labored pulse. I stepped past the front desk attendant, Stapleton, and beyond, shoving the glass doors open to get flooded by the blinding spotlight of day.

I squinted as I cut toward where Pop had parked. As I got closer, Fleetwood Mac's *Gold Dust Woman* drifted to my ears, followed by the sound of Pop laughing, and then... *then...*

A PENNY FOR YOUR THOUGHTS

"*Heyyyyy*, Petal!" The rear passenger door opened as Angie slid from the seat, smiling that exaggerated smile. She wrapped her arms around my neck, warm and genuine. "Wishes *do* come true!"

She wore the same black denim jacket and faded blue jeans she had going into prison, though they sat much looser now. Christ, a trip back in time was *just* what I needed. The snip of a song lyric I'd written in ink adorned her right pant leg:

*THE GIRL BEHIND THE MASK,
SHE'S THE ONE WHO NEVER HAS TO ASK.*

Angie smelled of prison soap and confined, stagnant air. The stink was enough for me to reflexively push her against the car. *Hard.*

"Ooooh, Petal, I *like* it rough now. But your daddy might not wanna see such things." Her tongue flicked across her lips. "Let's wait 'til we get home."

Home? Jesus...

"You got your fuckin' wish," I said, and my nails bit into the soft flesh of my palms.

Pop started the engine and leaned from the window. "C'mon, Joe. Get in so we can get going. You know I hate this place."

"Pop, we don't have—"

"Come on, boy. I've got shit to do. Get in the back with your girl." He jacked the radio and The Steve Miller Band filled my already cluttered head.

Angie grinned and winked and scooted into the back seat as I gritted my teeth and followed.

"Daddy gonna drive us to the movies?" Angie whispered and laughed as she snuggled closer, her leg pressing mine. She leaned into my ear. "C'mon, Petal...let's go somewhere to get a fix and get nekkid like old times. It'd be *soooo gooooood.*" Her hand clamped my leg, slid up my thigh... "You can have me any way you want...*every* way. I don't even *care* about your side piece. Hell, invite her along. Bet she's cute. We can all get—"

"Stop. *Just. Fucking. Stop.*" I hissed the words through clenched teeth. My skin grew hot and, oh, how I wanted to rage on her—let out *all* the hate and kick her to the curb. I'd watch her tumble across the asphalt and leave her where she belonged. The anger pounding through me hadn't been felt since withdrawal, when I wanted to destroy the sun and burn *everything* down to ashes. "You're out. You got what you wanted. We're done."

She pulled back and smiled, that old grin of hers when she knew she was pushing my buttons, antagonizing, just *poke-poke-poke.* "Petal, that ol' cooze in Lowback Prison told me there's a *whooole* big jar of those pennies. After I socked her face right 'n' good. An entire universe of wishes just *waitin'* to be used." She patted my leg like someone reassuring a child. "Whatever makes you think we're done? We're just getting started."

Angie leaned against me, snuggling my shoulder, riling me further. I stared out the window and watched that new and nasty world blur by.

The rest of the drive was silent except for Pop's classic rock on the radio. I seethed and burned from the backseat, wondering what the hell Angie was going to ask of me next. This couldn't go on. I'd have to tell Ava about it. And Kenny.

A PENNY FOR YOUR THOUGHTS

Fuck. *Kenny.* He *did* have every right to be pissed at me, but goddammit, what would *he* have done? I clenched my fists and closed my eyes.

Probably killed her, Joe. He finds Angie on the outside, he's twisting her neck over Uncanny X-Men.

We drove past our house on the way to Angie's mother's place. By that time, she was asleep against my shoulder or doing a damned good job of faking it. Her breath came slow and deep, made me feel as if fresh road kill lay next to me. I rolled the window down to get some air. That harsh prison stink hurt my nose.

Pop braked at an intersection as Angie leaned away from me and yawned. I still didn't trust she'd *actually* slept. As we passed Kenny's place, my stomach jumped. He sat on his front porch, smoking a cigarette. The front of his tank top still bulged like wet sacks of flour were inside it, but at least it was somehow better than before. He took a drag of smoke, squinting at the car.

Fuck...

His gaze moved beyond me. And found Angie. That cigarette fell, sticking to his lower lip, as his face tightened with anger.

Fuck. Fuck. Fuck!

He mouthed the words '*You motherfucker*' before he grabbed his cigarette and slung it to the yard with a jerk of his arm. He slammed the door behind him as he went inside.

Nothin' I could do about that right now. Nothin' at all.

When we pulled up to Angie's mother's house, Pop threw the car in park.

"Sorry I dozed off," Angie said. "It's just so nice to be... free again." She leaned to kiss my cheek but I flinched away. With a smile, she pecked her index finger, then

211

reached out and ran it over my lips before I could pull away. "See you soon, Petal."

As her saliva cooled on my lips, she made a show of opening the door, waving to Pop, and swaying those hips as she took the gravel path like a catwalk. I let out a long breath.

"You movin' up here or you stayin' back there, Miss Daisy?"

I glanced at Pop, unsure of anything at that moment, and climbed out of Angie's open door and into the front passenger seat. As we pulled away, Angie went inside the house to shock her poor mother.

"Joe?"

"Yeah, Pop." I realized my whole body had tensed, tightened like I was going to be in a fight or something. I forced myself to relax.

"I, uh...look, I'm not exactly a spring chicken anymore and..." He cleared his throat and I noticed his worrisome expression. "What exactly...*why* exactly were we..."

I knew strange things rolled around his head, but also knew he couldn't form the words. That gap of memory, the foggy *I-don't-fucking-understand-what's-going-on feeling*. It was the closest my father would ever get to being a junkie.

"It's okay, Pop. We were at the prison so I could visit an old friend of mine." My voice broke. "Travis. You didn't know him, Pop."

He relaxed and nodded. "All right. I'm sorry, I think... think I just need some sleep or something. Day's worn me out."

My heart hurt, but I said, "I know, Pop. I know."

I watched him chew on his lower lip as he tired to shake away the fog.

"I know I've told you about how your mom and I met, but I ever tell you about before we started dating?"

Instead of pursuing that dark road of confusion in his brain, Pop had decided to switch tracks entirely. Relief flooded me. "I don't think so, Pop."

"When I first saw your mother, it was damned fireworks. That's God's honest truth. Loved her so much, right from the get-go, it hurt." He reached out and turned off The Eagles in the middle of *Hotel California*. "But at first, she didn't want a damned thing to do with me. Or so she acted."

"Really?"

"Oh yeah. She was dating this guy, real lunkhead football jock kinda guy. Bart...Bart something. Walder? I don't know. Doesn't matter. But yeah, she was dating this guy and I kept asking her out and she kept saying no."

"So how'd you convince her?" I thought I'd heard everything about my parents. It was good to know Pop still had some tricks left in his pocket.

He laughed. "I was damned persistent, I guess. Stubborn. Anyway, back then, it was common for girls to be...*pure*, you know." He gave me a quick glance. "Not like today. Christ, seems every college girl shows their knockers when they're on camera now."

"Different times, Pop."

"I guess. But back then, it was...pure, I guess. I don't know. But I approached your mother and asked her out, hell, for the twentieth time or so, and she told me no, yet again, and said she had given herself to Bart. Told me to leave her alone."

"Pop, I don't know if I need to hear about Mom giving herself—"

"Shut up and you might learn something." He said that through a smile. Then his face fell. "I told her I didn't care about that. I gave her this long ass spiel about how I would never hurt her and how much I loved her and how it didn't matter what she had done in the past, there was only the now."

I nodded at him. "Damn, Pop, quite the romantic back then."

"Mmmhmmm. I had my moments, I suppose."

"How'd she take it?"

"She walked away from me without saying a word."

"Oh hell."

"Oh hell, nothing. It wasn't a no." He pulled into our driveway, that smile returning. "Couple days later, she broke up with Bart and came to see me when I worked at Jerry's Gas 'Em Up. She told me she lied to me. She had never slept with Bart. She just wanted to see how I'd react. If my words matched my actions."

He put the car in park and killed the engine, the hood ticking.

"And that was the start of it, huh?"

He nodded. "That was the start of it. She took some time telling Bart about her diabetes, see. Guess she trusted me more. Was getting worse at the time, and didn't want to burden anyone else. Didn't want the drain *explainin'* it to someone else. I said I didn't care, of course. Couldn't believe she found that such a big deal, anyway. But that's how it started. Her just wanting to see if my words matched my actions."

"How come you're telling me this now?"

He pulled the keys from the ignition, and paused. "Women always get what they want. That's nothin' new. But there are two kinds of women. Some angle with soft edges, like your mom. She was a clever one. Nothin' on God's green Earth I wouldn't do for her, but she angled just the same, even though it was with a kind heart. Then there's the other kind of woman. The kind that has rough edges like a piece of Lowback granite from the quarry. They angle, too, but you screw around with them enough and you end up getting cut and broken and busted the hell up. Angie's one of them."

I nodded but had no idea how to respond.

"You go on and do what you feel you need to do. I've said my piece and won't say no more." He clapped my leg. "Now let's get inside, boy. That easy chair is calling my name."

I lay in bed, staring at the ceiling as Pop fell asleep in his easy chair with the TV playing old reruns. I half expected Kenny to show up banging on the door in a rage just like he had almost a decade ago. I thought of Angie, welcomed home with open arms by her mother. *Oh, it's a fuckin' Christmas miracle!*

I memorized the cracks in my ceiling tiles. Counted them for the thousandth time, even though I knew there were 132. I thought about scavenging the house, trying to find the penny jar but knew it was useless. Pop had put them somewhere else. Somewhere I couldn't get them.

My skin felt itchy, like someone scrubbed fiberglass across it. The 'junk-sick' comparison refused to let up, and my mind kept flip-flopping over on itself, trying to escape.

Useless.

I sat up and tossed the sheets off with a hour 'til curfew. Creeping on the balls of my feet, I slunk from the house, easing the door shut as Pop continued dozing by the glow of his reruns. Then I set off.

I needed to see Ava.

I figured Ava would be at the shop instead of home. I guessed she didn't want to be in her trailer so much lately and I couldn't blame her. When I rounded the corner to find a stain of yellow light on the grass before the crooked sign, I knew I was right. I stepped inside and found her sitting on the floor, leaning against the wall. Gomez lay curled in her lap as she absently scratched his head. In her other hand, Ava held one of her grandma's journals. She looked up as I shut the door.

"Hey."

"Hey." I eased down beside her, greeted by a yawn of stinky dog breath from Gomez.

"So..." She closed the journal and set it on the floor, repositioned herself. "How'd it go?"

"Well..." A million things to say and not a clue where to start. I leaned my head against the wall, noting the buzz of the overhead lights. "Ava, whatever you read in those journals...whatever she did and didn't do, just know your grandmother didn't do it. She didn't kill that boy."

Ava coughed and swallowed hard, then breathed a harsh breath through her nose. I purposely didn't look her way, not wanting her to be embarrassed about the coming tears.

"We talked," I said. "She and I talked a long time. She told me everything that happened back then. She...your grandmother...she's a good woman that got caught up in all this shit and just—"

Gomez whined as Ava turned and hugged me. Her arms worked around me, tightened, and I reached out and patted her back. "She didn't murder anyone."

"Thank you, Joe." Her words came muffled against my chest. Her throat clicked as she swallowed again, and I let the silence of the shop draw out because I didn't know what to say next because there was so goddamn much.

"My, my."

The voice jolted me, and Ava pushed away, startled. Gomez licked at his lips and worked himself between us. I couldn't blame him.

Angie leaned against the doorframe, her head cocked and her hair still damp from a shower.

"She is *truly* something tasty, isn't she?" Angie shoved off from the door and sauntered into the shop like she owned the fucking place. "I don't blame you, Petal, but I *honestly* didn't think you had the kind of game to get a piece of ass like that."

Chapter Nineteen

"**WHERE IN THE** fuck did you get that, Angie?" The barrel of the Glock drifted from Ava to me, Ava to me. Angie's lips curled. "You don't know me too well if you've gotta ask, baby. The Stover house downtown. You've been there enough times."

The mere mention of that plagued, junkie paradise sent a ripple of gooseflesh through me as old memories surfaced like waterlogged corpses. Ollie Stover could find you anything for the right price, but unlike the Denny Brothers, he'd always had his eye on Angie, too. It's where she'd gotten the gun back when everything changed.

"Your prints are all over that thing," I tried. "Ollie's too lazy to scrape a barrel. Take a shot and you'll be back behind bars before my brains can spray the counter."

"That's just not the way it's gonna happen, Petal. The police won't come for me. The wish guaranteed it. And I'm not one to go doubting what I've seen. Unless this is all some elaborate prank, but I very much doubt that, don't you?"

The gun remained on Ava longer than I cared for. The girl whimpered. "What do you *want*?"

"Shut up." Angie's face fell as a deep fire burned in her eyes. She jabbed the weapon in Ava's direction. "You just *shut the fuck up*, you *skank*, do I make myself clear? This is between my baby and *me*."

"What *do* you want, Angie?" My voice broke on her name.

"I want that damn jar. Gramma Greenfield says there's a whole heap of wishes in that thing. Maybe as many as *forty*. Now I'm not here to fuck around, Petal. You go get me that jar and I'll leave you with this pretty little thing, limbs intact. I promise. For old time's sake."

"That's not going to happen."

"Oh? And why's that?"

"Because I don't know where the jar is. And I'm not lying. I honestly have no clue."

"Well, that's a shame now, isn't it? Because I can pop this bitch's little ankle off and there ain't nothing no one can do about it. I won't even get so much as a slap on the wrist. So you better get hunting. Because I'll do it, and I don't think you doubt me."

Unfortunately, I didn't. Not for a second.

I climbed to my feet—slowly—and raised my hands. "Okay, listen. I'll get you the jar, Angie. But you don't hurt her, okay? I promise you, *I will find it*."

I said that last part more to Ava, and took a step forward. "I will—"

Her aim whipped to my chest. My bladder tightened with the force of a hundred rubber bands. "You're damn right you'll find it," she spat. "And you've got an hour. Not a minute later. One hour."

"An hour," I repeated. "Yeah, that's fine, Angie. I'll do it. Just let me leave now, okay? Let me go."

She nodded but the gun traced my every move. I noted her finger twitching with anticipation. As I reached the door and grabbed the handle, she said, "And, Joe? Just one more thing. The police can't help you. You even so much as try it and I'll get to the jelly filling of this little dessert faster than you can run, okay?"

I eyed Ava an apology, then stepped outside and ran faster than I had in years.

Wherever Pop hid that jar, I'd find it.

I had to.

"Open up, you fat piece of shit!"

I punched, kicked and kneed Kenny's door again and again. He'd done something to fix the door lock inside. A neighbor I didn't recognize threatened to call the cops. I gave them the finger. "Come on, man!"

The door swung wide and Kenny glared at me like a bull spying red. His nostrils flared as he barged from the house, a baseball bat swaying by his side. "You not understand English, Joe? Huh? I'm *pissed* at you, you fuck, and you've got that little whore back traipsing around town, I saw—"

"You don't know what you saw, you knucklehead!"

He raised the bat and I matched him step for step as we moved down onto the lawn. "Kenny, look, you can hate me 'til next Sunday but Ava needs our help. You hearing me?"

My words hit like ice-water and Kenny lowered the weapon. He blinked. "What are you talking about?"

"It's...it's Angie. Look, I didn't get her out, okay? She got herself out. It's a long story. She knows about the wishes. Made me use one. Now you can hate me all you want and mope around the house feeling sorry for yourself but she's got Ava at gunpoint at the store and I...I need your help, man."

"Fucking *gunpoint*, Joe?"

"Fucking gunpoint, yes."

"Jesus."

"Jesus is right. Look, I've got one hour to find this damn jar and—"

"She can't have the jar, man. You kidding?"

"It's either that or Ava gets her head blown off, and trust me, Angie ain't lying." My stomach knotted at what I was about to say. "Kenny, I need you to stake out the Hole in the Dough, can you do that? If I don't make it back in an hour with that jar, you're gonna have to do something."

"But, Joe, she can't have the jar."

"Jesus, Kenny, I've got enough on my plate here. You're just gonna to have to think on your feet now."

"I still fucking hate you, but Joe—"

"We. Don't. Have. Time. To. Argue. Now go!"

I took off running as Kenny shouted after, "Your Pop's is the other way, idiot!"

"Not going to Pop's," I said, and raced for the Suzuki. I prayed to anyone but that asshole pusher god that my plan would work. I left Kenny yelling at my dust.

The Cairn Road hills blurred by as I gunned the bike and the wheels chewed and spit tarmac. My heart jackhammered as the wind whipped my face and my knuckles froze against the sharp air. I rounded a corner and there stood the Denny brother's home, crawling with cops and forensics. Not a single one of them turned at the roar of my bike and I made an involuntary cry of gratitude.

A PENNY FOR YOUR THOUGHTS

See, my plan was simple—I was putting as much stock in my wish as Angie had in hers. No trace of me could be found at the Denny brother's home, and within those walls lay a wish with an old penny I needed more than anything on Earth.

No trace of me could be found...

As those tiny specs bloomed into full-sized people, I yelled, "Hey!", thinking I had enough time to brake and hightail it outta there before they spotted me. But they didn't see me. They didn't hear me. The bike rumbled as I veered off the road and crossed the rough terrain, beelining between stacks of old bathtubs and used cars. I parked beside a cruiser and shoved down the kickstand as a dust cloud billowed past the cruiser's headlights and a single thought occupied my brain: I'm a goddamn ghost to these people.

I decided to test my theory.

A young-looking man wearing a duffle jacket was busy texting on his phone by the tubs. I approached from behind.

"Boo."

He smacked the back of his neck as if feeling a spider, then kept right on texting.

I stepped before him with my breath held, fists clenched, but he didn't so much as glance from his screen. I was in the clear, though that didn't stop my heart from punching my ribs or my legs from shaking. What if someone broke into my room and found my wish while I was here and tore the penny from the page? Would I just *pop* into existence before their very eyes and give the older cops a heart attack? Shit, a young and trigger-happy trainee might blow my brains all over the Denny's front porch. But I couldn't allow the fears to stop me now. I'd come too far.

"Break?" A cop asked, and passed me without so much as a glance. He hopped the porch to where an older cop wearing blue plastic gloves lit a cigar.

"Yeah," the older cop said. "White trash shit makes me depressed. How's about we go downtown? Rookies buy, you know that, right?"

"Ah, fuck you, Brian, come on."

And as they passed me on the porch, I gritted my teeth and squeezed my eyes shut. The older cop's hand brushed my leg but he didn't even turn. I felt like a child playing make-believe, half-expecting one of the cops to sarcastically shout, "*Did you see Joe, anywhere, guys? He's a ghost now, did you know that?*"

But that didn't happen, and so, I entered the house.

As I crossed the threshold, a vice as invisible as myself worked around my gut. I'd been in this house a hundred times before, and the lack of awful rap music blaring from the living room made me dizzy. This home would never see another dodgy deal go down, and, bizarrely, that just wasn't *right*. I needed Jerry to come bounding down the stairs with his lip packed full of tobacco and a cheap chain swinging from his neck. I *knew* that routine. This all felt...alien.

A bald man clutching a camera exited the kitchen and I leaped from his path as he stepped outside. I didn't have to, but I was against over-testing my theory and pressing my luck. They might not find any sign of 'me', but if I bumped someone, they might notice 'something'. I pushed aside my confusion and slipped into the kitchen.

The cops hadn't moved a thing. I imagined they'd lifted Jerry's body some time ago, but the room stood exactly as it had the day I'd last visited. The wall remained intact, save for a jagged crack coming from the ceiling, which meant they'd pulled Raymond from the upstairs. I recalled the newspaper article and couldn't staunch my curiosity. I made my way up. Mumbled voices came from somewhere overhead as I cringed at each groaning step. On the upper landing, a sliver of light seeped from an open door, and I made my way across the hall.

A flash blinded me as someone snapped a photograph, the camera whining as blindspots danced in my vision. "Justin and Brian went to grab some food," one said as I waited for my eyes to adjust. "Wanna get a coffee? Leave George to mind the place? Useless bastard won't get off his phone anyways. I could do with the break."

The other one blew his nose and sniffled. "Yeah. Sounds like a plan. Dust all over this goddamn place, didn't the fuckers ever hear of furniture polish? Have a craving for a burrito anyway, how's about we hit up—"

I pushed open the door and they screamed.

I stood in the doorway, frozen to the spot as if I'd just caught my parents fucking. The two men were frozen just as solid as I was, and stared—right past me—with wild eyes. The one with the camera pushed the other away. "Fucking place is haunted," he yelled. "Swear, I've been hearing weird shit all day."

"All day? Man, we found a redneck *in the walls!* 'Course this place is haunted."

To their left stood the cavity, a six-foot gap of broken plaster and lathe showing an inky maw. In the center of the room stood a halogen floodlight illuminating the excavation, but my eyes went to the beds. Two beds, one room. The brothers shared a damn bedroom. Somehow that hurt, man.

"Come on," the camera guy said. "Feel like someone's watching me. Got the creeps bad. Look at my arms, *look.*"

He raised his right arm to show the gooseflesh making his hair stand on end.

As they left, I darted aside and listened as they bounded down the stairs like cattle. When the front door opened, I crossed the threshold and made my way to a bedside locker. I pulled open the first drawer. One of the men downstairs said, "What was that? You hear something?"

I waited a beat before peering inside. A filthy, old *Playboy* sat next to a half-empty bottle of lube. I brushed them aside and actually chuckled—couldn't help it. I was never one to get something on the first try: the wrong key, the wrong amount of change, and I expected to rip the house apart, yet there lay the page: How 'bout a pony then, you sumbitch?—Jerry's short straw.

I tore the penny from the paper and spun—coming face to face with the cameraman. He blocked the doorway, his mouth a comical, warbling 'O' with his eyes bugging out of his head. He yelled, "There's a goddamn *page* floating up here, Tommy! I swear to fucking God! You want the halogen off? *You're* gettin' up here and doin' it!"

I pushed him aside as he screamed his throat raw, then I leaped down the stairs, out of the farmhouse, and bolted for my bike without so much as a glance behind. As my back tire spat rubble and I shot across the property line, a few heads turned in my direction. I wondered if they saw a bike without a rider. That bastard god had a sick sense of humor.

I didn't have much time.

I parked at Kenny's place and ran to Pop's on foot. I still didn't want him questioning the bike. Not that I needed to worry, though—the old man was out—and I snatched a pen and a scrap of paper from the living room drawer before jotting down: *'let me find the penny jar.'*

For the briefest moment, I thought of writing: *'send Angie back to prison,'* but as I recalled Gramma Greenfield's warning, I refrained. To cancel out a wish was to smear waters I know had endless depts. And I couldn't afford a slip up, not when I stood a chance. As for my wording, I figured my wish solid.

We didn't have any other 'penny jars' around—none that I knew of—and I didn't have time to plan it any better. I grabbed some tape and sealed the deal. And as I got to my feet, there it was—just sitting on Pop's chair as if that's where he'd hid it all along. Some things make you question your sanity. That's the only way I can put it. My skin crawled at the sight, and Kenny's claim of 'bad mojo' worked through my mind, but I had no time to lose. I snatched my wish, shoved it inside my back pocket beside my keys for safe keeping. Then I grabbed the jar and *prayed* Angie hadn't done anything stupid while I was away. Her, or Kenny.

Shit, I hoped *no one* had done anything stupid yet.

But knowing them both, I was asking for a lot.

CHAPTER TWENTY

I KILLED THE Suzuki's engine, coasted toward Hole in the Dough until I was twenty yards or so away, and came to a stop.

Kenny's car was nowhere in sight and I had a feeling it wasn't because he was trying to be inconspicuous.

Goddammit, Kenny! You had one job. One. Fucking. Job.

I hugged the penny jar to my chest as I crept to the shop.

I was so focused on the doors ahead and wondering where Kenny was that I didn't even see Henderson's cruiser until he was behind me.

"Shop's lookin' good, Joe. *Real* good!" He smiled and nodded.

I nodded in return. "Thank ya!" And then I turned to the screams from up ahead. Henderson didn't so much as flinch.

"—fuckin' bash that walking bedroom slipper's head in!"

"I *dare* you to touch him again, bitch! I hope he rips your goddamn throat out!"

Fucking hell.

"Gotta run, Henderson! Have to do the dough thing." I broke into a run as the yelling spilled from inside, praying

Henderson wouldn't step from his vehicle with his weapon drawn. He took off without a care, grinning like he'd won the lottery.

I flung the door open as Angie spun, the pistol leveled at my chest. In her other hand, she gripped the handle of a hammer.

Ava had tucked herself into the far corner with Gomez clutched protectively in her arms. Her eyes were scared but fierce as she glanced at me.

"Okay, all right. Let's all settle—"

"Your *skank* and her *fucking* dog are gonna—"

I held the jar up and, just like that, Angie stopped talking. Her expression warped, and I recognized that shift from before prison—the junkie hunger of spying a fresh bindle. That *oh-fuck-yes* look of salvation. Of escape. It turned my stomach but also gave me leverage. I had bait; a fish on the hook.

"They've got nothing to do with this. With *us*."

She cocked her head and grinned. "*Ohhhh*, Petal. With *us*?" She stepped toward me but I stayed by the door.

"Drop the hammer, Angie."

And just like that, her anger flared, that viper-style mentality of calm and rage shifting like quicksilver. "Seriously?" She adjusted her grip on the Glock. "You're going to play big man now and boss me around?"

I heard the phrase on the inside again and again, from rapists, a few murderers and always, always, *always* from the officers. *Never underestimate a junkie.* We will convince you, break you, sell you. I needed her away from Ava and Gomez.

Fuck it.

I barged through the door as the Glock *barked* behind me. An angry bumblebee whizzed by my head—too goddamn close for comfort—and my mind screamed: *That bitch! That fucking bitch just tried to kill me!*

I leaped across the sidewalk and into the street, popping the jar top free as I moved. I took a knee by the closest sewer grate.

The clear street came as a blessing—not a single resident out for a late-night stroll. I glared at Angie as she burst from the shop, pistol held sideways, *gangsta-style*, pointed square at my eyes.

"I'll dump 'em, Angie. I'll flush the whole goddamn jar into the Lowback sewer. Let the catfish have 'em." I tilted the jar toward the opening and shook it so she could *hear* the rattling coins. Her eyes bulged as her mouth opened like a grounded fish. Just like the time Pop threatened to flush our stash.

"All right." Her voice softened, smooth as ice cream. "Okay, baby." She eased the pistol to her side and released the hammer. It clattered to the cement. "No need to do anything crazy, yeah?"

"The Glock, too. Toss it."

Fear flicked across her face, and then...goddammit all to hell. *Never underestimate a junkie.*

"Joe," she said, "That's not going to happen."

"Every wish you've ever wanted, Angie. *Everything.*" I shook the jar and she took a harsh breath. "Gone. I will dump these things and you'll have to swim through a river of *shit* if you ever want them back." I tilted the jar, *ever so slightly*, and a cluster of pennies slid toward the lip. I smiled at her. "*Petal.*"

Angie grinned back at me, and in that moment, I knew—*I knew*—I was somehow fucked. She pursed her lips and made a *tsk-tsk* noise as she shook her head. "*Nahhhhh*, baby. That's not going to happen. What *is* going to happen is I'm walking back inside. You're gonna follow me with that jar and hand it over. And if you don't? *Ohhh, Petal...if you don't,* then I'm going to unload this fuckin' pistol in your little girlfriend's face. The mutt, too."

She turned and stalked back inside the shop, letting the door slam with me kneeling on the sidewalk. My insides turned to cold cement but I stood and drifted toward the building. No way to argue with the situation. Angie had the upper hand. Same as always. I slowly put the lid back in place. My mind raced with how this was going to play out and *where in the blue fuck was Kenny?*

I went back inside and eased the door closed behind me.

"That's a good boy." Angie waited by the counter with her arms folded, Ava was still glued to her earlier position. The poor girl looked terrified. "Now walk on over here." Angie motioned with the pistol. "*Slowly,* Petal, and set that beautiful jar down on the counter right in front of me."

I stepped forward, but paused. "You remember? Angie, you remember when we first met?"

Her furrowed eyebrows eased a bit. "The party at that jock's house. The rich one whose parents were away in Barbados or some shit."

She leaned against the counter as the start of a smile crossed her face. "You were hittin' the keg pretty hard and threw up in the in-ground pool."

I matched her soft smile, shook my head slowly. "No. That wasn't me, that was the idiot who had the party. Robbie Noble. And his parents were in Cabo."

"Cabo, yeah." Angie's gaze turned down for a moment, then flashed back to me. "That wasn't *you* who threw up?"

I shook my head. "Robbie was hitting on you. Hard. You'd been doin' vodka lemon drops most of the goddamn night and I guess he figured you were an easy target. You and him did three jello shots in a row and then he grabbed your tits. I punched him in the gut and he threw up a rainbow in his swimming pool."

Angie laughed out loud and nodded in agreement, and I noticed Ava tracking the swing of the pistol. It was the first sincere sound from Angie since I visited her in prison. "My knight in shining armor. Then we ended up making out later in his parent's bed."

I let my smile grow, then took a deep breath and let it out slowly, working the moment. "Back then...Angie, back then, did you ever think you'd end up in prison, beating up innocent ol' women to get what you wanted out of life?"

Again, that flip from calm to rage. Behind her, Ava stirred.

I knew the comment about her grandmother would set fire to whatever tinder Ava's soul kept at the ready. I didn't look at her directly, but in my periphery, she eased Gomez from her arms and set him quietly on the floor. She held her hand up, palm out, and the dog sat. As silent and calm as his master.

"Innocent? That ol' split bottom?" Angie released a harsh bark. "*Pleeeeeeese*. That bitch was in for the big 187, Petal. Fuckin' hell, they found the body buried behind her house, fingerprints all over the tarp." She shook her head as if I were just the *stupidest little thang* she ever did see. "Innocent? *Ohhhh, sweetie*. Every convict on the planet's *innocent*. Don't you know that?"

"You think she did it? You really think she murdered that boy?"

"I don't think that ol' cooze was in prison for *jaywalkin'*, that's for sure."

Ava unspooled herself to a standing position, quiet as a church mouse.

I stepped closer—*easy, easy*—and nodded. "Yeah, I suppose. I mean...I guess she was there for a reason, huh?"

"You're goddamn right, she was."

Ava's burning eyes locked on the back of Angie's head as her fingers curled around a push-broom leaning against the wall.

"And by the way," Angie said, "Thank you for *actually* following through with the cigarettes. They were perfect going away presents for me to hand out. I was like goddamn Santa Claus." She cocked her head and smiled. Even her eyes sparkled as she talked. She was *enjoying* this.

"I'm glad I could help out," I said, my heart slamming. *Close. So close.* "Wouldn't want you to have to spread your legs for every little favor you needed inside." *Stay on me, stay on me!* I couldn't resist that insulting barb.

Angie's smile tightened. She scrunched her face up, shaking her head in that mischievous way of hers. Years ago, that same expression might've been over something dirty I said to her in public. "Well, baby, it ain't gonna lick itself."

I came closer, shifting the jar to my left side to keep Angie looking where I wanted. For once, I might actually be a step ahead. *You have no idea what you got comin', Petal...*

I eased the jar onto the counter, *right in front of her*, and watched her eyes glow with excitement. Her tongue flickered over her lips as she waved the Glock. "Step away, Joe. I mean it."

I did as instructed, taking my time, and Angie snatched the jar fast as a striking copperhead. Her eyes darted from the lid to me and back again, her attention off-balance. She popped the lid.

And that's when Ava swung the broom.

234

A PENNY FOR YOUR THOUGHTS

The oak handle sliced the air with a dull *whomp* before cracking against Angie's skull like crisp celery.

Angie grunted and rocked forward, her eyes shocked wide with pain. As Ava drew the broom back, I lurched for the Glock, missed. All I needed to do was *control that fucking pistol*. Ava connected again, and solid wood hammered Angie's forehead with the cracking sound of a homerun. She screamed as her flesh parted in a wide gash. Blood flooded her left eye and trickled from her chin.

I made for the pistol again but she wrenched away before I had a grip.

"You fucking bitch!" Angie's road-gravel voice rose, and to Ava's credit, she didn't even flinch. Instead, she raised the broom for another strike, pistol be damned.

Angie snarled. "I'll fuckin' kill you, skank!"

Never underestimate a junkie, hell no, but never underestimate someone who's been labeled trailer trash their entire life either. Ava dropped to a crouch and rose with the strength of her legs, bringing the handle up like a knight's lance toward Angie's face.

The blunt end caught Angie directly in the mouth, even as she twisted away. Her teeth broke off to the sound of wet pennies grinding against each other.

Then the Glock exploded.

I flinched at the sound, saw a cloud of plaster at the rear of the room as the shop door opened.

"Goddammit, Joe! I told you I'd kick you out of the goddamn—"

The Glock roared again.

Everyone knows the expression 'time stood still'. Well, I learned exactly what it meant in that moment. I think we all did.

Pop stood at the entrance, his words snapped off like cheap plastic. His expression morphed from angry, concerned father to confusion while he peered down at his chest as if he'd just spilled some ketchup.

A dark penny-sized hole opened on his left side, just a few inches below his collarbone. After a quick appraisal of the spreading crimson halo, his gaze landed on us. He smiled and gave a sharp laugh. "Well, shit."

Pop fell straight forward. He smacked the triple-swept floor of Hole in the Dough and didn't move.

And I started screaming.

CHAPTER TWENTY-ONE

"POP? POP!"

My legs carried me forward and I collapsed before his body. Wet crimson bloomed across the shining tiles, seeped into the knees of my jeans—*warm*, I thought. I grabbed his shoulders, grunting with exertion, and forced him over to his back. Then I saw it. A bloodied and crushed nose; an open mouth leaking saliva; a blank open-eyed gaze. I yelled and dropped him to the floor. "Oh God...no, no, no..."

A sharp tang hit my nostrils then—urine—and I understood the implication. I fell back with my mouth open as hot tears dampened my cheeks. A 'tea-kettle' squeal escaped my constricted throat, and two words blared in my brain: *Pop's dead.*

The notion refused to register, bouncing off my skull like hailstones. *Pop's dead, Pop's dead!*

Still, nothing. Yet reality kept trying, forcing the words with all its might. *Pop's dead! Pop's dead!* Pop's dead!

A numbness spread over me then as my mind drifted like a helium blimp. Faintly, I registered a door opening and slamming shut again as cold air swept across me. The sound of Ava's crying drifted to me from someplace far away, possibly underwater, and my brow creased. Beyond that, the only thing retaining focus was the body on the floor, and the tangible *blackness* oozing from every pore of my being. *The body. Pop. The body...*

"Joe."

I yelped as a hand gripped my shoulder, snapping back to the shop. And our situation.

"Joe."

Ava's red eyes studied me, shimmering in their sockets. "She's gone," she said, her voice like 40-grit sandpaper. "She took the jar."

"My Pop..."

"I know, I know..."

She fell to her knees as her shaking arms wrapped around me. Her body hitched as her muffled cries heated my shirt. I don't think I so much as blinked. Across the room, Gomez still pressed himself into the corner, tongue lapping out nervously as he whined and batted his tail. Poor thing was quickly learning the vicious nature of life.

"I can't call the police," I said. "They'll know I'm doing something, I just can't–"

"A robbery. He was here to see you at work and–and we got robbed. I'll call an ambulance. They could catch up to her, she's only out the door, I mean–"

"No. They'll never find her, Ava. She's made sure of that with her wish. We'd be wasting time." A coldness washed over me as my mind coughed back into gear. An idea struck, and as much as it pained me, I removed my hand from Pop's body.

"We just can't," I said. "But I might be able to do... something. I think I might know where she is."

"Joe, she'll kill you."

"Don't. Call. *Anyone.* Do you hear me? No one can know he's here. I can fix this."

"And what about the gunshot? The police are gonna be called, not by me, but a neighbor, *someone*. And that wish might protect Angie, but we're sitting ducks."

"It's Briarwood. We practically fall asleep to people target practicing out on the mountain. No one's calling the damn police."

"Then you gotta go after her. I'm fucking terrified, but if she gets away, this is only the beginning and we both know it."

"I know. Switch off all the lights here. Get Pop away from the door...And, Ava, please be gentle."

She refused to meet my eye as she said, "There's a freezer in the basement. For supplies. I haven't switched it on since I got the power company to—"

"Bring him there. Good. Wrap him up. Clean up, just in case anyone does show up. I'm getting our damn jar."

As I stood, Ava grabbed my shirt, jerking me to a halt. Her eyes shimmered with fear. "*This* is what it wants. *More* wishes. More *blood*. This is the price of it all, Joe, not a fucking penny. Just you remember that."

I eased my shirt free and nodded, but all I saw in my mind was Pop getting back to his feet. Pop's smile returning, just one last time. Wasn't that worth it? I'd pay anything. Just one more. One more wish...

One more hit.

I raced outside and scanned the empty lawn. Beneath the streetlights, blood dried on the pavement, zig-zagging off into the woods. With her face broken seven-ways-to-Sunday, Angie would crawl the Lowback until she found a secluded spot much like Gollum and his precious. She'd hunker in the pines by the moonlight and fish inside that jar, ripping free blessed pennies and scribbling new wishes. A mansion and a pool; a mountain of clean dope that would never make her sick; her looks restored to her early 20s...useless, vapid shit to placate the bitch's ego. I didn't know much, but I knew my Angie.

At the entrance of the thicket, I found a tooth. The white noise of the Lowback River drifted through the pines, and I knew where I'd find her: we'd picked out a stash spot after the grocery store robbery. A hollow in the riverbank about two miles up-slope. Of course she'd be there. Ever a creature of habit was my Angie. I'd find her... and God only knew what I'd do when I did.

Moonlight filtered through the torn umbrella of leaves, bringing shadows to life. The wind hissed through bobbing branches, and, coupled with the river, Angie would never hear me coming—but I heard her. Crying. And after training my ears, I closed in on 'our' spot, keeping my attention ahead and never doubting my footing. One snapped twig was all it took.

She wasn't just crying, no, she was *bawling*. Like a mother who'd lost her son. I traipsed lightly, pressing myself to trunks and rocks as I closed in. And then I saw her: on her knees by the riverbank, head raised to the heavens, shoulders hitching as sobs wracked her body.

Her smashed mouth leaked a sanguine trail that spilled down her shirt, catching the moonlight. Brown-red stains caked her ashen face, her eyes squeezed shut as she shook like a damaged appliance. Her swollen right cheek glistened, probably from Ava's broom-assisted tooth extractions, and her stringy hair clung to her forehead. She looked more monster than human. My Angie. A demon in the night.

A PENNY FOR YOUR THOUGHTS

"Why?" she screamed. Her raspy banshee cry drew gooseflesh across my skin as it echoed across the mountain. I licked my lips and tried to keep from shaking as she suddenly *punched* the earth again and again...and something glistened in her clenched fist. At first, I thought it was a box cutter or a scalpel, a weapon of some kind, but then I saw it clearly: just a pen. A nice one, though. Silver. Angie had gone to some effort.

A torn page trembled in her right hand. A wish. And, as I watched, she crumpled the blood-stained paper, snarled, and tossed it to the waters with a *plonk!*

That sound told me something important—Angie had just tossed a coin-taped wish. *It. Hadn't. Worked.*

"Angie?" I stepped from the trees, palms raised.

Her bulging eyes shot in my direction and she snatched the gun and aimed it to my chest. I froze. "Two bodies in one day? That's rough, even for you."

"I didn't mean to kill your Pop," she stammered through her busted mouth, the words slurring: "*I dinn meenna kih oouurr Paaw...*" Drool slopped to her breast. She winced.

"But you did, Angie. You killed Pop—*Pop!*—and you're getting away with it. You know it. The man who cleaned your *shit* when you passed out in his chair that night, remember? Never even said a word about it to you. *I want you to know how much you've ruined my life.* I hope deep down some part of you knows, can still process what you've done."

"It's not working," she cried ("*izz nooh wuukihhh!*")

"No?" I creased my brow, faked concern, and approached. The gun remained in my peripheral as I kept eye contact. At that moment, Angie just needed someone to fix all of this, it didn't matter who, and it didn't even matter that she'd killed my father—that dark mojo had snagged her as easily as the damn junk.

"Help me," she whined, and extended the shaking piece of paper. "How does it work? Make it work!"

I accepted the page, a bloodstained and torn A4 with simply: 'Loads of Money' printed in a hasty scrawl. *How original.* I tilted the penny into the light and squinted. Something was...off. "You tore this from one of the wishes in the jar, right?"

"Of course I fucking did!" (*"Ahcowwse ah fenneh deh!"*)

"Right. Pass me the wish you took it from."

She flung a scrap of paper at my feet and I scooped it, bringing it to my face. I don't know how to explain what I felt at that moment. My emotions had walled up after Pop, and I felt more like a sleepwalker than anything else. But right then I felt something. Pride? Perhaps. Shock? Oh, definitely. Honored to be the son of the greatest man on Earth? That felt closer to home. See, that page in front of my face? *The page was blank.*

Pop had thrown away all the wishes—probably fucking *burned* them!—and switched the pennies. The one taped to Angie's wish was as common as grass. Just a filthy one-cent piece Pop had grabbed from the dirty back pocket of his overalls. He knew I'd find that jar somehow. He knew I'd one-up him. But the apple doesn't fall far from the tree, does it? That man had always been two steps ahead of my scheming ways.

Pop—you beautiful sonofawhore!

And, as for the real pennies? We're talking about a man who forgot where he once put his wife's Christmas present behind a row of paperbacks. Hadn't found it in over two decades. They could be anywhere. Anywhere at all. And right then my emotional dam exploded and I fell to my knees. I wept, laughed, screamed—just about *everything* I'd ever felt, spilling all over the place.

Pop's dead! Pop's dead! He switched the wishes! No one knows where the real pennies are!

I suddenly found it all simultaneously hysterical and bleak. An inner tug-o-war I had no control over. Yet there was one thing I did know, and through it all, it hit me: I had *no desire* to find those coins! I really did not care—*I was free!* A familiar sensation gave me strength and I opened my mouth to speak—when something *whacked* my jaw. I collapsed as my gums pulsed with fresh pain, and Angie, the tyrant she was, loomed above me and blotted out the moon. "What's so funny?" ("*Whazzo funneh?*")

I stared at this inhuman creature, her *need* for the coins warping her structure, and I actually felt *pity*. Was this the same shadow of a person Pop saw when I fell off the wagon? I suddenly understood his lack of anger, just sheer disappointment...*shame*. A damn fucking shame.

"Don't look at me like that!" Angie jabbed the gun—*gangsta-style*—and that act alone made my chest pang with sorrow. "Stop it!" she cried. ("*Snohpeh!*")

"They're not the pennies," I said with a sniffle. "Fakes. Like baking powder in your dope, huh? No use to you. Just making you worse."

"I have a wish," she said. And right then, her busted lip curled with realization. Through it all, that single revelation was like hot whiskey on a cold night for her. Any semblance of logic had been whisked away as soon as that thought hit home. "I have a wish...My jail wish. I can pull *that* coin. Can have one thing...I can find the real coins."

"But I have no idea where they are, Angie. And you'd want to be very careful about how you word that. The 'real' coins? Every coin is real. The wish would just take you to a bank or the nearest till. 'Find me the coins from

243

the jar'? Well, these *are* the coins from the jar, right here, just not *the* coins. You'd wanna think about this long and hard, Angie. Plus, you'd really sacrifice the cops not knowing you're free for a 1-in-a-100 chance of finding the wheat pennies? That's a small window of time from pulling your penny to finding the jar and setting the wish back, and the cops will be crawling through Briarwood to find you. They'll find you before you find the jar. Don't be stupid." Then I thought: *wait, no, do be stupid!* "It could work," I lied.

She laughed, spittle oozing from her broken lips. "No. You don't understand, honey. *I'm* not going to find them. I don't know where they are, I'm not going to risk wasting time, and you don't know where they are...but your Pop does."

"Pop's dead, Angie. You killed him."

"And I got a wish...I can bring him back...make him talk."

An icy fist squeezed my guts and refused to let up. I stared into the face of a monster. An absolute maniacal demon.

But wasn't this really why I was here? The dark inkling of a thought that propelled me into the forest to stare down the barrel of a gun? Wouldn't I admit I knew she'd do this...and that I wanted her to?

"I'm holding the gun," she said. "So get moving, Petal."

As tears streamed my face and my heart slammed, I hated myself but climbed to my feet and did as instructed.

And all the while, one thought remained: *where the fuck was Kenny?*

CHAPTER TWENTY-TWO

BY THE TIME we reached the donut shop, Angie had practically drilled a hole in my ribs with the barrel of her pistol. She pinned the jar at her side, head whipping side to side as if some jar-stealing ninjas lay hidden within each bush and behind every rock. Paranoid. Just like the good ol' days.

More than a few times, I thought about grabbing for the Glock. Just slam the butt against her nose and let the jar shatter all over the place. Maybe I'd get lucky and Angie would hit her head in the fall. Hell, she might even manage to pop off one final round and hit me square between the eyes—my penance, my *payment* for all of this shit.

But I didn't make a move. I kept steady and endured Angie's rasping breath and jabbing gun until we spilled out of the woods and crossed to the donut shop.

And where in *blue fuck* was Kenny?

Angie shifted the jar close to her bosom like she was protecting a toddler, though we both knew the coins inside were worthless. She stepped to my side and waved the pistol toward the door, the action clear: *move, you idiot, move!*

I raced inside to find Ava sitting on the countertop, now buried in one of her grandmother's journals. For a moment, I saw Ava as a woman struggling, fighting for everything. But more than that, I saw the girl before all this—the innocent girl covered in a thinning white shawl of time. Her head rose and relief flooded her face, but the beginnings of her smile faded when her gaze shifted past me to Angie.

I glanced at the shining floor where Ava had cleaned Pop's blood. Some ghosting of pink still caught the light. My heart ached as I marched forward.

"Hello, Sugarplum." Angie words came garbled through her damaged mouth. *Juicy.* She jabbed me in the back with the pistol. "You two sit down on the floor. Move, and you both die."

We both did as she told us, making our way to the rear of the shop before hunkering down. Gomez crept to Ava's side and let out a low rumble.

After setting the jar on the countertop, Angie slid it aside (begrudgingly) and glared at us. She lay her pistol down before withdrawing a folded slip of paper from her jeans pocket, placing it beside the pistol. She reached for a ballpoint pen next to Ava's backpack and opened the closed journal on the counter, tearing free a blank sheet of paper.

Angie scribbled for a moment, lost to her words, then silently read it over. She crossed some things out with a heavy hand, rewrote. And repeated the process.

I eased my hand onto Gomez' haunches to keep him from attacking, working my fingers into his fur. If he bolted, that poor little brain of his would explode across the floor faster than he could bite. I emitted a barely-audible 'shhhh...'

Finished now, Angie stared at the slip of paper before nodding to herself, apparently satisfied.

"What's she doing?" Ava whispered, but I didn't risk turning my head.

"You don't want to know." My stomach churned at what Angie aimed to do, and though the Lord and I hadn't exactly had a spectacular relationship, I still found myself praying it wouldn't work. For whatever reason. Maybe the penny went bad in her pocket. Maybe she wouldn't speak the words properly. *Any reason at all.*

Angie peeled the wheatback from her old wish, stuck it to the new sheet, and read it aloud through broken teeth, a phrase so jumbled that I couldn't understand. Bloody spittle dribbled down her chin as she mindlessly raised an arm and wiped it with her sleeve.

She released a sigh, set the paper aside, and glared at us again.

"Done," she said. "Let's see what magic this sonofabitch can work, huh? Just think what—"

But her words faded. I think I was the first to hear the noise from the basement.

Just a dull thump, but that was enough.

My mind wouldn't accept the truth. So I just stared at nothingness ahead, and continued to hold Gomez. From the corner of my eye, I noticed Ava slowly turn toward the basement door. Then her gaze settled on me.

Oh, Pop. I'm sorry. I'm so goddamn sorry.

Angie grunted, and I looked up to meet the barrel of the pistol again. Dried blood circled her left eye but the gash on her forehead still glistened at its crusted edges.

I wanted to give her *more* wounds. Hell, I wanted to *end* her for what she'd done. For what she continued to do.

She grunted again and waved the gun for us to stand. She nodded toward the basement door and Ava moved, letting slip a whine. She knew what this meant, though I think she was fighting this reality same as myself. I gripped the doorframe and felt like I was going to throw up.

Angie jabbed me with the pistol, and I followed Ava downstairs as Gomez raced to the far corner of the shop and tried to will himself through it. But through it all, that brave pup didn't leave.

Something smacked against the cooler door, an ancient thing that hummed with a loud electrical whir, kept closed by a simple steel latch. The dim lighting cast from a low-wattage bulb illuminated the metal like some horror movie prop.

At the bottom landing, Ava and I stalled on the dirty cement as Angie made her way to the bottom of the stairs. Ava's face looked ready to break. Her glassy stare refused to leave the cooler and she shook her head. Then she spun on Angie.

"When the cops catch you, bitch, I hope they—"

The pistol whipped up, aimed right at Ava's face. "I can outrun the cops. Can you outrun a 9mm? *Bitch?*" All of Angie's words were slush. A drunkard's words, slurred and moist.

That moment drew out for an eternity. I felt certain Ava was going to rush Angie, pistol or not. And I had no idea what I was going to do if she did. But as a strained groan came from inside the cooler, breaking the silence, our petty arguing was all but forgotten.

"Open it." Angie growled the words.

Ava glided forward on shaking legs, reached for the pin, stalled.

"Open it!"

With a quivering breath, Ava threw back the pin and the door moaned as she pulled it wide.

A dream...It's a goddamn dream...

"Joe?"

I'm dreaming!

I forced myself to look into the corner, to look at my father. Dark red soaked the front of his shirt, and a brown stain smeared his nose, his lips...

Look, I've been dopesick many times. I've felt lower than dog shit when I lied to my father again and again, breaking his trust. I went to prison and did time, disappointed that man and thought about just fucking *ending it all*. But *never* have I felt the mixture of rage and pain and absolute anguish as when I looked into Pop's confused eyes as he sat in the cooler.

Back from the dead.

"What's..." He scanned his shirt and touched fingers to his mouth, pulling them away to study them in the low light. "Joe, where am I? What happened?"

I couldn't speak so I shuffled my numb legs forward, and reached out to help him stand.

"Dreamed I was covered in dirt and walking back home to you." With my help, Pop stepped from the cooler, his movement stiff, and glanced back at the dark container. "I don't know..."

Angie cleared her throat and tried to spit. Though a gob hit the pavement, thin ropes clung to her mouth and she wiped them away. "Let's go, Lazarus." She circled behind the three of us and forced us back upstairs, me holding Pop for stability. Though his clothes were chilled from the cooler, his skin wasn't. I shivered at the implication.

As we reached the shop, Angie again rounded the counter to keep it between us as a barrier.

"We're gonna take a field trip," she said. "If either of you try anything stupid, I'll fuckin' shoot you dead. I don't *need* either of you anymore." She smiled her busted smile at Ava. "And you and I aren't finished dancin' yet, either. I *owe* you, bitch."

Angie picked her wish from the counter, stuffed it in her pocket, and grabbed the jar.

"And you, ol' man, are gonna tell me where you hid those fuckin' pennies."

CHAPTER TWENTY-THREE

A **LONG TIME** ago, Pop dragged Angie and I out of the house when he found us puking in the tub after a rough night. To this day, I can't remember what we'd taken. Either way, something didn't agree, and we vomited our stomachs into the porcelain as Pop rose with the sun and glared at us from the bathroom doorway. He called in sick to work, cleaned the tub with his bare hands while Angie and I sweated and shook in the living room, then gave us two choices as he stood with his arms folded, still wearing those rubber gloves. We could either sit quietly as he called the cops and deal with what may come, or join him on a morning hike up the Lowback, shut our traps, and remain in his supervision until he concocted the next move. Because, he said, we were family, for better or for worse. We chose the latter.

It only struck me then that hiking became my cleanser from that day forth, even led me to the penny jar in the first place. Had Pop not forced us from the house that day, I'd probably still be full of junk.

As Angie shambled behind us with a pistol to our backs and we exited the donut shop into the witching hour, déjà vu overrode my senses. The hike we'd taken all those years ago had a fairytale quality to it. Partly due to the bad shit working its way out of my system, partly due to my lack of sleep and dehydration. Either way, how the clear air tingled my freezing skin and how the three of us together never felt right, it hit me all over again. Except this time, Angie walked behind, and Pop was the one shaking and crying and ashen in the face. *Surreal.* A fantasy. Oh, how things can change on a dime.

"Am I dead?" Pop's panic made me shudder. In all my years, I'd never heard his voice so...*high.*

"You're not dead, Pop," was all I could manage, but I kept face-forward as the tears spilled down my cheeks, my hands working in and out of fists. "You're...you're talking, aren't you?" I forced my voice not to break. "Dead men don't talk."

Pop sniffled. Somehow that hurt worse than any verbal response.

From behind, Angie grunted. "*Juss move, okay?*" She hocked a wad of something and it splashed my heels. "You try anything funny and I'll shoot him again, Joey. Shoot him and raise him, shoot him and raise him. I'll torture you like a captured Marine until I get my fucking pennies. So just you think about that."

"You're not protected anymore, Angie. They'll find you, sooner or later. You can't honestly believe this is gonna work out for you."

"I'll have anything I fuckin' want once I get my coins. Don't you worry about me, Petal. You just keep on walkin'."

I doubted Pop (was he even still *Pop* at this point? I couldn't shake Miss Greenfield's story of her boyfriend) could muster another trick, and only a small window of opportunity existed for Angie's capture. If she got her grubby paws on those wheatbacks, she could blow our brains out and simply wish it all away. She could have anything, anything at all...It was *my* time to act.

I just didn't know how.

We stalked beneath streetlights, passing lit homes and empty lawns. Angie's confidence didn't surprise me. She believed she'd find those pennies before the cops tracked her. And, shit, I believed her, too.

Think, Joe, think!

I could hunker down and trip her, but the risk was too high. That Glock would spit a bullet through my skull faster than I could make a grab. Despite being injured, Angie always had the reflexes of a coked-up cat. I could throw my head back and catch her in the nose, but, again, my brains would paint the sidewalk before I even turned. I could—

"Breathin' heavy, Petal. Getting an adrenaline dump from all that plotting?"

Bitch had me sussed. I said not a word but winced as the barrel pressed my kidney. Her hot breath tickled my neck. "Just move, Sunshine." (*"Jush moo, sushhigh"*)

A porch light popped to life as we entered Briarwood—the Randolph place. June Randolph ran a gardening store out by the Interstate, a nice old lady who brought Pop seeds from time to time. At one point I thought they'd become more than friends, but Pop just flustered and blushed anytime I asked about it. I think his devotion to Mom never budged. June stepped onto her porch.

She pulled a fluffy nightgown across her chest as she squinted, moving fast down the drive. Too fast. "Joey, Is that—"

I screamed at the sudden *boom*. Brain matter exploded from June's skull and splashed her lawn as she collapsed into her Daphnes with a thud. Dogs yapped from miles around and lights blinked on in every direction.

"I say to stop movin', you two?"

The bitch had lost it. She'd absolutely fucking *lost* it.

"Up the pace," she ordered, and nudged my spine with three quick jabs. "You're not fuckin' statues, I just saw those legs workin'. Come on."

A high-pitched cry escaped Pop's lips and I instinctively reached for him but Angie cracked my forearm with the butt of the gun. I couldn't help it, I turned my head to say, 'it's going to be okay, Pop,' but my words froze in my throat when I caught sight of his anemic pallor, his blue lips with spittle connecting one to the other, the sheer fright in the old man's eyes...The *terror.*. The *pain.*

And confusion. So much confusion.

We reached the house without a single door opening on Briarwood. The residents knew better than to take on an armed lunatic. But I guessed the Lowback PD's phone lines were as clogged as winter drainpipes. Hell, I was counting on it.

As we reached the door, a gargantuan gloom settled in my bones. Deep down, I just *knew* I'd completed the last outing with my father. As frightening as it had been, I didn't want it to end. I'd take Angie at our backs, no words passing between us, just to be in his presence eternally. But as he fished his keys from his pocket and struggled to stop shaking long enough to sink them home, shock overrode my brain and switched from manual to auto. The human body can only take so much, and right then I'd been filled up worse than a blind man's gas tank. The lock clicked, and Pop pushed the door wide. He let out a shuddering cry as he overstepped the threshold, and at the far end of the hall I spotted our wooden *Welcome Home* sign and I cried, too. I didn't know what else to do.

Nowhere smells like home. That thought entered my broken mind. That, and, *nowhere feels safer.*

A PENNY FOR YOUR THOUGHTS

Even as Angie pressed the barrel to my spine, I didn't want to be anywhere else.

"Get 'em," she ordered. "Now."

Pop entered the living room as his glistening eyes worked over our bookshelf as if for the first time. He let out a sound of wonder, a subtle 'ohhh...' at the sight of our couch, his armchair, our old TV we'd had since '98. And then he turned. His fingers worked over his bullet wound by their own accord as he said, "I...I don't know where they are."

Angie swallowed. She shook. "Find. Them."

"My—my *brain* doesn't feel right, Miss, I—I can't remember."

'Miss'. Jesus, Pop.

A car screeched to a stop outside. No lights, I noticed. Undercover?

Angie's nostrils flared. Mere seconds now. Could she scribble something faster than the cops could take our driveway?

"*I'll drop* both *your sorry asses right now, old man! Three seconds!*"

The shaking Glock found my face and Pop stuttered, his glazed eyes now widening. "I'm serious, I can't remember where I—"

"Angie!"

The voice echoed through Briarwood. Not a cop, no.

A friend.

Angie swung the gun to the living room door as a shadow crept along the hall. A large man with a large gun and two others in tow.

"I remember now," Pop said, and the dead man laughed. Oh, how that sound warmed my heart. "I gave them to Kenny," he said, just as the sonofabitch stepped into the room carrying the filthiest hack-job of a sawn-off shotgun you ever did see. He pumped a shell into the gun and nodded to my ex.

"Bitch, I've waited for this day for ten years."

Behind him stood Ava, and Rebecca Barrows.

CHAPTER TWENTY-FOUR

ANGIE JUMPED BEHIND me and jammed the Glock against my temple. Hot breath tickled my neck. I knew the threat from her was real and the thought came back to me, *maybe it's what I deserved. Maybe this was payment coming due.*

"I'll kill him, pencil dick. Put a bullet in his head faster than you can—" Her lispy, wet words continued their poor Donald Duck impression, but she was getting the hang of speaking with a ruined mouth.

"Well, well, the gang's all here. Plus...*two.*" Rebecca Barrows eyed the room, pausing on Angie, then on Pop. She smiled as if enjoying the chaos.

"Fuck're you?" Angie took a step backward, pulling me with her. The cold barrel pressed into my head.

"I'm the one who will end you in ways you can't possibly imagine."

Rebecca's smile widened and she took a step closer. She still wore her lounging robe, still commanding attention even in a trailer park. Angie dug the barrel so hard into my neck that the pulse of my blood throbbed against it.

"I'll fuckin' do it!"

Angie was a cornered dog. No, a cornered junkie. I knew she wasn't bluffing at all. She'd squeeze that trigger and my brains would splatter the popcorn ceiling of the house like a Jackson Pollack painting. I glanced at Rebecca. *Just don't call her bluff. Please don't call–*

"And?"

Fuck.

Rebecca stepped within reaching distance and the pressure against my throat vanished. Then the pistol swung outward, trained on the Crimson Sister. Ava's eyes flickered with worry. *Full of fear*, as Kenny gritted his teeth and leveled the shotgun. He looked as pissed off and full of rage as I'd ever seen.

Rebecca's neutral expression never faltered, not even with that Glock facing her chest.

It came down to who'd move first.

Something cut the air with a vicious *whoosh*, followed by a dull *thunk* I felt more than heard. The pistol fired and a new peephole opened in the living room door as my ears rang with needle-like buzz. Angie's grip tightened against me, just for a second, then loosened as she smacked the floor.

Pop held the middle stem of our homemade wooden lamp. Thick as a calf's leg, the heavy mahogany could take down a cage fighter. Pop stared at Angie sprawled on the floor while I worked my jaw to clear my hearing, then Pop let the lamp fall to the floor beside her.

"You okay, Joey?"

I nodded. Kenny trained his shotgun on her prone body, and I swear, his finger tightened on the trigger before letting up. Probably still thinking of *Uncanny X-Men*.

Ava sidestepped Rebecca and closed in on me. She whispered, "You sure you're all right?"

A PENNY FOR YOUR THOUGHTS

I nodded and started to speak but sirens and screeching tires cut through my hampered hearing and stopped me. Red and blue lights strobed through the thin living room curtains.

Rebecca turned to Kenny. "If she's not here when I get back, I'll be smoothing the wrinkles of my face with your blood by nightfall."

Kenny swallowed hard, nodded. Some of the fire had left his face but that sawed-off remained on Angie.

"I'll just be a minute," she said, and drifted from the room.

I crossed to the curtains and peeked outside as she glided down the drive to the single cop car. Henderson got out, one hand on his sidepiece and the other out in a *'stop where you are'* motion. I couldn't hear what they were saying, but I'll be goddamned if Henderson didn't nod and slide right back behind the wheel. He killed the siren and lights, then shut his door as Rebecca walked back inside the house.

"I'll take what's mine now." She folded her arms, and smirked, leaning on the doorframe. I swear she enjoyed every second of this. "What's *owed*."

Kenny nodded. "They're in the trunk."

Rebecca pushed from the doorway and crouched before Angie, cocking her head as a strand of hair fell before her face. She drifted a slim finger along Angie's neck, and I thought of Gramma Greenfield's warnings. But we were out of options. We had to work with this witch.

And I *know* how this is gonna sound, all right? *I fuckin' know*, but that junkie part of me rose up and I spoke without thinking. The leverage of getting 'this for that', always gunning for the better deal.

"You get the pennies and *her*. Fine. What do we get?"

"What do *you* get?" The Crimson Sister reached out to Angie's ruined mouth. She wiped her first two fingers through the patch of blood and then rose—no—she *fucking uncoiled*, to her feet, her gaze directly on me. *Hellfire* shone in her eyes, and for a brief moment, I wondered: *what sort of hell lived within someone who worshipped forgotten gods? What pit of agony awaited them?*

She brought her index finger to her lips and her tongue flicked out as she closed her eyes, savoring the moment. "Mmmmm...the truly sinful always taste...*better*."

Rebecca reached out and wiped two glistening fingers across my cheek. Angie's blood mixed with my sweat.

"How often do you think a fly enters the spider's web and steps free?" Her eyes remained locked with mine. "You get to *live*, little lamb. Embrace it and *rejoice*."

A wave of junk sickness washed through me, as strong and painful as if I'd just broken off the day before, but I couldn't look away.

"*This* man, on the other hand..." She grinned at Kenny. "He brought me what I needed. He'll be...rewarded. In time."

She knelt beside Angie once again and raised her hand. Then Rebecca slapped the girl's face. Smears of blood and an immediate handprint blossomed on Angie's cheek. Her eyes flickered open, and at the sight of Rebecca, and all of us standing around her. She began shaking her head. "No, no, no. This isn't how it's supposed to be." Her expression crumpled like wadded tissue paper as tears streamed down her bruise.

"Hush, girl." Rebecca brushed Angie's hair from her face, she then took her hand, helping the girl to her feet. "It's time to introduce you to...*things*."

A PENNY FOR YOUR THOUGHTS

Angie held none of the cunning of a wild animal I'd seen her wear since going to prison. Now, she looked like a lost puppy, confused and afraid. But she held Rebecca's hand and the two of them walked from the house with Kenny behind them. I raced to the window.

Pausing at the trunk of his car, Kenny handed over a plastic bag of pennies. Rebecca accepted the offering, cradling it to her breast like an infant. She stayed that way for the longest time, smiling like a new mother. Then she motioned for Angie to get into the back of Henderson's patrol car. She herself followed, and Henderson sat at the wheel like a goddamn chauffeur.

The last thing I noticed was Angie's face peering from the rear passenger window. I don't believe she was looking at me, though—not at all. She seemed lost in thought, staring at the great beyond and what the future held.

Kenny came back inside and shut the door. After he lay the sawed-off on the kitchen counter, we looked at each other in silence.

Rebecca Barrows got her pennies.

CHAPTER TWENTY-FIVE

WITHIN MINUTES, CONFUSED neighbors demanded answers outside the house, a gathering of at least twenty-five strong—twenty-five of the bravest, most concerned people in all of Briarwood. I parted the curtains and squinted at their wild eyes. They craned their necks, mouths agape, but dared not step foot on Pop's drive. Even in desperate times, I swear, these folk respected property.

"They want answers," I said, and let the curtains fall back into place. With Angie taken by the Wicked Witch of the West, my reanimated father looking as confused as the day he was born, Kenny with a shotgun, and Ava pale and shaken as myself—there wasn't a single, believable answer I *could* give them.

"The police will be here any minute," Kenny said. "Henderson's one thing, but there'll be more dispatched."

As if on cue, blue and red filtered through the curtains once more, followed by an ear-splitting '*whoop-whoop*' as two squad cars skidded to a halt. I expected heavy boots on the drive, for the door to slam open and for all of us to be told to '*get on the ground!*' without an answer between us. But that didn't happen. The residents of Briarwood muttered amongst themselves, and then, as one, their voices grew distant.

"They're leaving?" Ava said. I shook my head and made for the front door, followed by the others.

In the flashing colored lights, the mass of people were led like cattle, led by two policemen in front with their weapons drawn. I motioned for the others to follow me and we waded into the crowd, our heads down, moving as one.

"They've got her," someone said, and a tangle of voices answered as the collective pace quickened, all of us speed walking. The crowd paused and I pushed to the front, barging through shoulders and bellies, and froze at the sight before me. Kenny, Pop and Ava appeared by my side.

Angie was on her knees in the center of the street, swaying like a hypnotized cobra. Henderson had his weapon drawn, pointed at her forehead. He looked equally as perplexed. His squad car was parked some meters down, but the interior stood empty. Rebecca Barrows was nowhere to be found. It was as if she'd set up mannequins in an action scene before running away and snapped her fingers, setting time back in motion. Here we were, pawns in her game. I wondered if she'd known she'd get away with her pennies from the very start.

"Easy, easy," one of the officers told Henderson. Henderson's eyes flashed to the man as his mouth quivered, no words coming, but his weapon remained trained.

"You've got her now," the second officer stated, and holstered his own gun before jogging behind Angie and cuffing her. As the metal teeth bit around her wrists, Angie's head fell forward and found me. Spittle fell from her swollen lip, and in her eyes I saw...nothing. Nothing at all. I imagined the look of a freshly lobotomized patient wouldn't be much different. Whatever Rebecca wanted from her, she had already taken.

Then Angie yelled in a singsong, and the gathering neighbors gasped.

"*He* knows," she wailed, her voice like an out-of-tune violin. Goosebumps prickled my flesh. An idiot smile replaced her once-cunning grin. "I've seen His face and it's *alllll* eyes." She followed this with a laugh—the funniest joke in the world. "All eyes!" she repeated. "Sees it *all* at once, *every one of them*, out of time, in time, before time, after time, all the time, all the time, all the *tiiiiiime!*"

"Quiet, Ma'am!" The officer yanked Angie to her feet as her hair fell forward, graciously covering her demented face.

"He's awake now," she said, a flat statement that seemed to sadden her. Then her head lifted, her hair parted, and her blank, glistening eyes once again found mine. "This is the price. He's awake now."

The officer pushed her toward Henderson's idling cruiser as the second cop muttered something into his walkie and approached the crowd.

"Go home, people, please. Give us some room."

More lights lit up the night as the entirety of Briarwood's PD responded and the gathering dispersed in confused, rambling clumps. Those who attempted to stay got physically pushed. The PD weren't fucking around.

A hand gripped my shoulder and I jumped.

"Come on," Kenny whispered. "She's given us an out and we're fuckin' taking it. Move."

I did as instructed, but then a hair-curling laugh erupted from Angie as she was placed in the back of the cruiser and I shivered.

"She's lost her mind," Ava said. "That Barrows lady did something bad to her and Henderson. Think we'll see her again?"

"I doubt it," I said, and, like the first time I saw Angie get forced into a cruiser all those years ago, I turned my back and refused to watch.

We headed for the house as Kenny muttered something beneath his breath.

"What's that?" I asked.

"Guess I just don't wanna see that lady again. Even if she says she owes me. I don't wanna go to Woodmount for as long as I live. I'm *tired*, Joey."

"I hear ya," I said, and he actually chuckled.

"Look, If I don't get home, I'm gonna pass out, man. Too much excitement for one day. Will you call me tomorrow?"

I said I would, and the brick shit-house of a man actually hugged me. My ribs constrained as he pressed me to his deflated, flabby chest but I accepted the gesture all the same, needing the comfort. He pulled me back to arm's length.

"Go on home. We'll talk more tomorrow."

"Right."

He slipped past two elderly women on the sidewalk and headed for his house. I highly doubted he'd sleep a wink. That promise of *something* would keep him awake, like a curse, until he finally raced for Woodmount like his heels were on fire. I should know, I had a jar of promises next to my bed for nights on end. Still, I hoped he had enough sense to control himself. A single dealing with the Crimson Sisters would only be the start of something else.

I've seen His face and it's alllll eyes!

"Joe," Pop said. "Come with me?"

A PENNY FOR YOUR THOUGHTS

I recognized that tone, though a subtle quiver underlined the words. I allowed him his space as he stalked off toward the house. We had much to discuss, me and the old man. And I motioned to Ava.

"You okay?"

She nodded and tucked a stray strand of hair behind her ear. "I'll be fine...just...well, it's a lot to take in, isn't it?"

"You got that right."

She flashed a sad smile. "What's gonna happen with your Pop? You think it's...permanent?"

"I haven't had much time to really think anything. But I guess I'm gonna find out."

"Will you come over tomorrow? So we can talk?"

"Yeah, of course."

"I hope your Pop's okay, Joe."

And then she, too, hugged me. I'd never felt anything as comforting in all my years.

"Me, too," I said, and pulled away. Tears stung my eyes as my overwhelming emotions barged to the surface, all clamoring for the front row.

Tears slipped down Ava's cheeks. "It's just so much to take," she said, and gave a nervous laugh with a shrug. "Fuck, man. This is a *lot*."

"It is. Look, go on home. You gotta get Gomez."

"He's home," she said. "Made his way to the house when Kenny came and got me. I swear, Joe, that dog...he's something *different*, isn't he?"

"He is."

"Something tells me I'm gonna have him for a long time. And part of me wonders why my wish came true without, y'know, the bad side. The payment."

"Maybe that's coming," I said, as much as I didn't want to. "Or maybe He just doesn't care much for our notions of good and bad. Maybe it's all a big joke to Him. Some win, some lose. You might've gotten lucky."

"Maybe I did," she said, and rubbed my arm. "I'll see you in the morning."

After Angie's outcry of *'I've seen His face and it's alllll eyes!'*, neither of us felt the need to elaborate on the 'He' in question. Ava put it perfectly when she said it was a lot.

We left after another small embrace and I turned to find Pop missing. The streets stood empty except for the police and their lights, so I speed walked home beneath stars I no longer quite trusted.

"Pop?" I peered inside the empty living room. A crimson splotch from Angie stained the carpet. The bitch left her mark wherever she went, like a mutt marking territory.

"Pop?"

"In here, Joe."

The airy voice came from the bathroom. I eased open the door, spilling light across the hall, and found him seated on the closed toilet with something clasped in his hands.

"We need to talk," he said, and silent tears spilled from his eyes.

I closed the door behind me. Just me and Pop. Like old times.

"Sure," I said. "Let's talk, Pop."

CHAPTER TWENTY-SIX

"**J**OSEPH...SON." **POP** sniffed, not meeting my eye as he brought his arm up angrily to wipe his nose. It was unlike him, kid-like in action. He cleared his throat and then met my gaze.

I sat on the edge of the bathtub as he continued.

"I've never been a God-fearing man. You know that much. I've always tried to live a good life and do the right thing, but God? No, that wasn't for me. Your mother...she tried. But I've always had too many questions to believe. Right or wrong, you got that from me. Hell, as a kid, you were curious from the get-go. Always the one to question and ask what if, or why not, or..." Pop's eyes reddened. I had a hard time meeting his focus.

"Point is, I was never a church-going man. Whenever I ended up sittin' in the pews, it was because I wanted to make your mom happy. Wasn't because I believed in God."

"Pop, I..." I glanced at the black case in his hands. My heart ached and I didn't know why. No. I *refused* to think about why.

"But I believed in your mother. I believed in her and I believed in you when you were born. Joe, I..." He sniffed again and looked toward the ceiling, away from me before continuing. "Kid, I have loved you from the day you were born and *every single second* after. I know I..." He paused to clear his throat again. "I know I've...*we've* never said it often. It was one of the things...With your mother gone and being on my own, I was just trying to make you strong and sometimes, a *lot* of times, love makes you weak. But just know, son...I love you. Always have.

"Even when you were, you know, when I was helping you detox, I never lost faith in you." He focused back on me. "You're my son. *My son.* I *never* lost faith in you."

My eyes brimmed with tears suddenly and I felt my throat swell. I couldn't reply. Couldn't even think clearly. I knew something was happening and I was part of it, but I couldn't hang on anything except for Pop's words.

"Kid, you know this ain't right, me bein' here now." He took a deep breath and let it free slowly. "I'm an old man and my time was short enough already. But what happened, Joe, that was supposed to be the end of me and we both know it. Ain't right. Ain't *natural.*"

He looked down to the dust-covered case and slowly unzipped it. The sound was so very loud in the bathroom.

"Pop, what if it was a second chance? What if it was—"

"Son, life doesn't give second chances. There aren't any stage rehearsals. This is all we've got so we've damned well better make the best of it." He unfolded the case, and the contents drew a cry from deep down in my lungs. Several thin syringes with orange caps and a small glass bottle with a silver top. A pack of Marlboros and a black lighter completed the collection. Pop shook a cigarette free and lit it. He took a drag as he tilted his head back with his eyes closed, a soft smile on his face as he exhaled. "Been damned near twenty-five years since I smoked. Still tastes..." He opened his eyes. "I suppose the addiction never truly goes away, does it?"

A PENNY FOR YOUR THOUGHTS

I shook my head, trying to focus on my father with blurred eyes. Scalding tears spilled down my cheeks as sweet smoke curled to the ceiling.

"I guess we do what we can. Fight the addiction best as we know how." He took another drag off that stale Marlboro before tossing it into the bathroom sink where it sizzled. He sighed.

Pop uncapped a syringe before puncturing the bottle with its thin needle, turning the entire connection upside down and pulling the plunger almost free. He drew the syringe full to the hilt.

I recognized my mother's insulin straight away. Somewhere, probably from a TV show or a movie, my mind registered the fact insulin had to be refrigerated. This bottle had gone bad long ago.

"Pop?" My voice cracked on a single word.

"It's old, I know. But maybe after all I've been through tonight, there's still enough juice in it to do what needs done." He glanced at the hole in his shirt and the blood stains surrounding it.

He smiled at me as he withdrew the syringe from the bottle. "Twice a day is what your mother needed of this, remember? Only one time in sixteen years did she get so bad she asked me to inject her. Squalled out like a damn banshee when I shot her up because I had no idea what the hell I was doing. After that, she always kept a candy bar in her purse, though I never saw her eat it." He gave a light chuckle as he lay the bag on the bathtub lip, then held the needle toward me. "I'm complete shit at this. But you know what you're doing."

"Daddy?" I hadn't called my father that since before I even knew how to ride a bike and I had no idea why I called him that just then except I had become a child again. I hadn't gone through being an addict or any of this shit. I hadn't been part of robbing a store or being a convict or...

It hit me. Everything hit me then. It all made sense even though I fought and clawed and bit and screamed. You know how people say when they have a scrape with death, their life flashes before their eyes? That moment was like that, but from a different point of view.

My Pop and I in the back yard, tossing a softball in freshly oiled gloves. The smack of the ball hitting the pliable leather. The *smell* of it. Pop and I, standing on a sandy beach, me holding a handful of seashells in a plastic cup.

Pop and I, his car parked outside my middle school, nodding and grinning as I opened the door for my date and walked her away toward my first homecoming dance.

Pop, tossing his car keys to me and telling me to be careful as I drove off on my own for the first time.

Pop, sitting in the courtroom behind me, nodding and being strong best as he could.

Pop, wiping my head of sweat and rubbing my back as I threw up over and over and over again as he cleaned my body of drugs.

Pop. My father. My dad. Always.

I shook my head, my throat beyond tight. I couldn't swallow anymore. There was no lump. It was...

"Son?" He held the syringe out further and I took it automatically, though my hands trembled something fierce.

I knew what he was asking me to do, but how do you do that? How the hell do you do something like that?

I'll tell you how. You turn off. You kill off something inside yourself. You dig and you mine and you find the love you have for that person. You do what they ask because you love them. You do what it is because it's what needs to be done.

I held the syringe and, out of habit, flicked the tubing, even though, considering its purpose, that didn't matter. Pop rolled up a sleeve and flexed his fist a few times as veins thickened in his forearm. Years of effort working his job made them easy to find.

I held his wrist and paused the needle at a vein near his inner elbow. My hands continued shaking. My cheeks boiled with tears. "Pop?"

He nodded and smiled. "Payment's due, son. It's okay." He reached out his other hand and rested it on my shoulder.

I slid the needle into his vein and Pop took it from me and hit the plunger, injecting the old insulin. He withdrew it and pulled the stem of the syringe open to the hilt again, drawing nothing but air. "Line it up for me again, Joe."

"Pop, no."

"It's okay, kid. Just a bit of a failsafe."

I stared at the empty syringe and took it in shaking hands. I tried to steady myself and did as he asked, sliding the needle back into his vein.

Jesus.

I felt Pop's tough-skinned hand rest over mine and he put pressure on my thumb. I hit the plunger before I could rip it free and throw it aside and run from the house.

Make it stop.

My guts turned hollow. My entire being emptied as the plunger hit bottom, pushing the air into his veins. I slipped the needle free.

Pop shook his head and released a slight groan. I watched a bead of blood swell from the injection and he folded up his arm. "Help me up, kid."

I stood on shaky legs and we shuffled out to the living room. Pop, of course, sat in his easy chair. In that short time, I noticed a gleam of sweat on his forehead. He was becoming pale. I knelt down beside him.

"Kid, there's a...in the top drawer of my filing cabinet." He craned his neck toward his small desk in the corner. "All the important papers you'll need are in there. Had them put aside ever since—" He took a sharp breath and his expression tightened. "Since your mother passed." A fresh sheen appeared on Pop's face, his eyes not wild, but unfocused. "Joe?" He reached out, his fingers flexing as he did. "Hold my hand, Son."

I swallowed hard and took his calloused hand in mine. "Pop? Dad, are you...are you scared?" I studied his face, but had to look away. For the first time, I noticed the worn leather on the side of his easy chair. I listened to his breathing get heavier, labored. He brought his free hand up to his chest and pressed his fingers against it, rubbing over his heart. The pause went on so long I looked up at him again.

A gentle smile broke his face and he shook his head slightly. "Scared? No, boy, not at all. Your mother's waiting for me. Sometimes it's just nice to..."

Pop gritted his teeth and a long exhale escaped him, and then a harsh grunt as he arched his back away from the easy chair and stiffened. He let loose a sharp, pained moan and several short breaths.

His grip on my hand tightened and then eased, relaxed, loosened to no pressure at all. His body lowered back against the soft padding.

A PENNY FOR YOUR THOUGHTS

"Pop?" I squeezed, but there was nothing. He stared at the popcorn ceiling of the living room—168 tiles, I knew—and a trace of a smile remained on his face.

"Dad?"

He didn't take another breath.

CHAPTER TWENTY-SEVEN

FOR ME, TIME always slipped. I'd lost days flaked out on a floor or a couch with Angie beside me, hours puking or shaking in bed. Even in prison, studying the cracked cement roof while my cellmate snored like thunder. And as the sun slipped through the blinds with dust motes swaying in the slivers of light, kissing my cheeks dry, I'd lost six hours. I recounted the ceiling tiles twice. It was eleven a.m. by the time I rose from Pop's side and allowed my hand to come free of his. For all the pennies in the world, I couldn't tell you my thoughts that night. All except for one.

At Mom's wake, with her body in the casket, her painted features gave the false illusion of slumber—the handiwork of a trained professional. 'Sleeping,' mourners said. 'Looks just like she's sleeping.' But without that skilled mortician's hand, Pop didn't look asleep. No. Pop looked dead. At last. But peaceful? Yeah. Yeah, he looked peaceful.

I fell out of the house like one of the living dead into the cold air and harsh sunlight. All of Briarwood was out, hassling the flabbergasted policemen as they shoo'd people from the yellow-taped yard of June Randolph. Two medics hoisted a veiled gurney and crab-walked to the back of an ambulance wedged between a couple of news vans. I overheard concerned talk of, 'the crazy woman,' and how, 'June was found in her Daphnes.' The same flowers she'd given my father. I imagined them both kneeling beside a bush in some Vaseline-soaked afterlife with my mother close by as they laughed and trimmed the leaves. Just like the ending of some Kleenex-required film. But then I remembered: Pop looked dead. And June? June toppled straight back with a hole in her head. There was no happy-ever-after for either of them.

"Joe."

Henderson, joined by another officer, jogged to me from June's side of the street as onlookers gawked. He clutched to his belt as he ran, the exercise clearly foreign to his routine.

"Joe, I've been meaning to call down, it's a madhouse out here, I—"

"You don't remember what happened last night, do you?"

"No," he said, and relief washed over him. "How did you know that?"

"I wish I could tell you, man. I really do."

He wiped a palm across his hair, blew a breath as the young officer kept the gawkers at bay. "I remember takin' two ladies from your Pop's in the middle of the night, one of 'em was in charge. I don't know how I know that, it just *felt* right? But, Joe, for the life of me, I can't remember what she looked like, a single thing she said, nothin'. I—I think I'm goin' crazy here, and the Chief's breathin' down my neck for *every last detail*. I've got a report due, I'm only out here—*we're* only out here—'cause we're short on hands and Lowback ain't *never* seen nothin' like this. It's all hands on deck."

A PENNY FOR YOUR THOUGHTS

"I wish I could tell you something useful, man. I really do." My voice cracked, harsh from a lack of sleep and overwhelmed by exhaustion. The air stung my eyes. "But do me a favor, okay?" I said. "I don't mean to add to your chores, but go to Pop's place. The living room. Have those medics with you."

"What are you...?"

"Yeah."

Henderson read my expression and reality hit him. "No." Tension blew from his shoulders. I swear—the whole world loved my Pop. "Just one more damn...Shit, Joe."

"I know."

"I'm—I'm sorry."

The young officer chimed in. "What the hell happened?" He glanced at June's property and then back to me. "She do it? That girl we caught last night, Angie? Do we got a killin' streak on our hands?"

Confusion clouded Henderson's features, he clearly had no recollection of Angie, but I didn't have the time to try and jog his brain.

Did *she do it?* I thought. *Yeah,* I decided. *She did. She killed my Pop. Shot him right in the chest.* And for once, I wasn't lying. Honest as Abe. Angie had shot Pop dead. He'd been gone for some time, in fact. And to the natural world, I'd spent the night with a ghost. Though I didn't say so.

"Please, Henderson," I said. "Just go check it out."

The young officer mouthed a cuss, clearly overburdened by the situation. Beside him, Henderson continued to try and recollect just *who the hell* was Angie.

"Look, I gotta go," I said.

"Where to?"

"To see a friend. I need to be around some people."

He didn't even try and stop me. The young officer just stood in the street as more orders were barked, more cameras flashed, and Henderson continued asking, *"Who the hell is Angie?"* I left the chaos of Briarwood and shambled off to Ava's trailer on Leeds Mill Road. And at the foot of her drive, that loose slab finally grabbed my boot and sent me ass-over-teakettle.

Pop and Gramma Greenfield had a lot in common. Perhaps it was a trait of that generation, a genetic acquirement. But as I loomed over the loose slab with my hands braced, full of piss n' salt and ready to fling the damn thing across the yard—I noticed the etching.

Miss Greenfield had drawn it with a finger, going full circle in the wet cement before pressing the center through—a donut. *Of course* a fucking donut.

I slipped my finger into the rough chunk, the texture nibbling my skin, and hoisted the slab from the drive. I placed it on the lawn before peering down. And then I laughed. I placed my hands on my hips, faced the clouds, and shook my head. The gods weren't the only tricksters, it seemed. Pop and Miss Greenfield were right up there with 'em. Down in the hole lay a single, glistening wheatback penny taped to a water-damaged wish. Just one.

I plucked the wish before heading up the drive, igniting a series of yaps from Gomez as Ava unlocked the door. The little brown pup sprang out and circled my legs, tail whipping so hard, the thing could've taken flight. Ava gave me a sad smile from the threshold, her eyes red and sunken, before she stepped out and pulled me into a hug. We stayed that way for a long time.

"What did you do to my damn yard?" she asked, but her light attempt at humor got no response. That hug had dislodged the thought that *Pop was dead*, and even a chuckle seemed worlds away for me. I sniffled and rubbed her shoulder as I said, "Let's go inside. We need to talk."

And then I told her everything.

We cried. We sat in mourning. We hugged. We drank coffee and stroked Gomez and stared at nothing at all. And time, as it does, slipped by. We did everything but decide on what happens next. Then I showed her the wish, the words beyond legible on the soggy sheet. From my prison visit, I knew two more wishes sat at the bottom of the quarry, resting like Cthulu in that forgotten, sunken city, but I didn't feel the need to tell anyone. Not even Ava. That secret would go to the grave with me and Miss Greenfield. I really was free.

"That's what I did to your yard," I said, flipping the coin around my fingers. The year read 1956, one of Miss Greenfield's first, and a gray-green splotch of mold had eaten half of Abe Lincoln's face.

"Gramma," Ava said, "That sly bitch."

I agreed, but Miss Greenfield's act reminded me of Pop and that made an iron fist grip my stomach. His loss hurt more than withdrawal ever had.

Ava took the coin from me and held it like a squirming bug. "What do we do with it?" she asked. "With so much wrong...so much destruction, what do we make right?"

"I don't know," I said, "But it's all yours, Ava. I'm takin' Pop's road and having nothing to do with it. Besides, for whatever reason, maybe your Grandma starting all of this, *He* seems to like you. Gomez can attest to that."

She studied the coin for the longest time, her brow knitted and her eyes clear. After a while (time, like I said, slipped. Could've been minutes, could've been an hour), she rose and pulled a slip of paper from the dresser by her bed. She wrote slowly, each letter a work of art with the utmost detail. Then she got some tape, finished the job, and said, "Done."

"What did you wish for?"

A soft smile spread across her face. "It's a secret," she said.

I liked that. I liked that a lot.

CHAPTER TWENTY-EIGHT

BEEN A FEW months now since Pop passed away. He never had a real will but I had lawyers sort through everything and after they took their cut, I ended up with a little bit of money and the house. It's quiet there without him and I've been thinking about maybe getting a dog or something. I don't know. I spend most evenings in the living room with the TV on for some noise, though I can't look at Pop's easy chair without missing him. I keep the lamp turned on all the time.

Most nights, I have bad dreams. Sometimes it's of the Barrows woman, other nights, it's Pop walking up the driveway in clothes muddied with grave dirt. On particularly bad nights, I jolt awake and take a walk up on the Lowback Trail. I find a quiet spot up there among the pines and wait for the sunlight to break through the branches—those little stairways to heaven busting with golden beams. I listen to the birds as they wake up and announce morning, for those of us lucky enough to hear.

Sometimes I sip a little from Pop's bottle of scotch as I sit up there, though the bottle is almost finished now. I feel the burn of the liquor and look down into the rushing waters of the river and once in a while I see glints of things, shiny and copper-colored, but I never wade in after them.

Best leave them be, whatever they are.

None of us have seen nor heard from the Barrows woman and I'm damned fine with that. I could go through the rest of my days without looking into the hellfire her eyes held within them. Even Kenny managed to control himself and not go to Woodmount, despite the reward she promised.

I spend a lot of time alone, just walking around town, thinking about everything. I have a little notebook I take with me and write things down when they come to me. Things to think about later, I suppose—whenever the hell that'll be—but not too far off. Like Pop said, we don't get a dress rehearsal in this life.

Couple weeks ago, I ran into Officer Nelson down at Blackie's Diner. He was in Lowback for his cousin's funeral, and we sat and had a coffee and talked for a bit. He told me he was glad I seemed to be doing well. He mentioned the last time he'd seen me at the prison, though he still didn't seem to recollect Angie at all, like she had been wiped clean of his memory.

At one point, as we talked, Nelson took a sip of his coffee, sat it back down, and stared at it quietly. He leaned forward and spoke again, but in a lower voice.

Seems a day or so after I'd been to the prison to see Gramma Greenfield, there had damned near been a full-scale riot at the prison. Everything was going fine, prisoners in the courtyard playin' dominos or cards and whatnot. All of a sudden, *Greenfield Granny*, as Nelson called her, starts screamin' to beat hell, clawin' at her throat and face. He hadn't seen the start of it himself, but a few of the inmates told him there had been shadows swirling like black mercury all around her in a blur. Fuse boxes blew on the main level of the prison and the generator kicked in, triggering the alarms. The old woman's screams grew louder and by the time Nelson rushed into the common room, her body had started turning inside out, flexing like you'd bend a green willow branch to break by workin' it back and forth. I recalled the wish I'd pulled from the loose slab, her wish, and I guess her payment had come due.

"By the time the screaming stopped, that ol' woman's body was busted up enough you could have sent it through the prison laundry and hung it over a plastic hanger."

I let the man's words hang for a bit, and then put a five on the table. I stood up and clapped his shoulder a few times before walking back home. Sometimes, there's nothing else to say.

You can't get through this damned life without carrying some kind of debt. Some's forced on you and others you take on yourself.

But sooner or later, payment comes due.

Rebecca Barrows and the Crimson Sisters had forced Joyce Greenfield to set things in motion. I just hope she's at peace.

Don't hear much from Kenny anymore. Once we got through Samson Gallows' loot, we shared the profits and washed it through Hole in the Dough like we'd planned. But we never made another robbery. He calls me up about once every two weeks or so. He's got a girlfriend. Cinnamon is her working name up at the Twist and Whirl Gentleman's Club, but her real name is Tammy. Nice enough in person the couple of times I was around her, and for whatever damned reason, she seems to adore Kenny. Last time I was over, he grilled some burgers and though I tried not to, I stole a few glances at the girl's more than ample rack. They're about the same size as

Kenny's used to be, and I couldn't help but snicker to myself. I'm pretty sure Kenny knew why but he didn't say a word about it and I damned sure won't.

I started a job at the Lowback Feed Mill a month ago. With Pop's reputation breaking the ice, it was easy to get a job there. I already know it's not a *forever* thing but it keeps Henderson happy at the moment, though he's been pretty easy on me after Pop died. He still has nightmares about a woman whose face he can't quite recall. And his parole calls have become therapeutic for both of us.

Ava and I have been talking about opening up the donut shop for real. She wrote a business plan and even got a logo done up with a picture of Gomez poppin' his head through the donut hole. She's got the fire to do it, but I suppose I'll believe it when I see it.

I visit her often.

She moved out of Briarwood Trailer Park a couple of months ago. Got herself a little two-bedroom house with a small yard. Cute place. Even has a white picket fence around to keep Gomez from running off, though that little mutt is so attached to her, I don't think a parade of fire engines would make him stray too far.

Last time I visited, I took notice of the neat stone path dividing the yard up to Ava's front porch. A rough-edged block of not quite cured cement lay nestled into the dirt by the entrance. I paused and paid attention to the circle scrawled in one side with a little depression in the center. A heart was drawn into the cement just to the right of it.

Donuts are love.

A PENNY FOR YOUR THOUGHTS

It made me smile, and for the first time since Pop's death, my heart didn't ache over everything, but I didn't mention it to Ava when I went inside.

A man's heart holds secrets well enough, I guess, but I tend to think maybe a block of well-laid cement holds them even better.

ROBERT FORD has published the novels *The Compound*, and *No Lipstick in Avalon*, the novellas *Ring of Fire*, *The Last Firefly of Summer*, *Samson and Denial*, *Bordertown* and the short story collection *The God Beneath my Garden*. In addition, he has several screenplays floating around in the ether of Hollywood. He can confirm the grass actually is greener on the other side, but it's only because of the bodies buried there.

MATT HAYWARD is a Bram Stoker Award-nominated author and musician from Wicklow, Ireland. His books include *Brain Dead Blues*, *What Do Monsters Fear?*, *Practitioners* (with Patrick Lacey), and *The Faithful*. He compiled the award-winning anthology *Welcome To The Show*, and is currently writing a novel with Bryan Smith. Matt wrote the comic book *This Is How It Ends* (now a music video) for the band Walking Papers, and received a nomination for Irish Short Story of the Year from Penguin Books in 2017. He is represented by Lane Heymont of the Tobias Literary Agency and can be found on Twitter @ MattHaywardIRE or at his website www.sundancecrow.com

CPSIA information can be obtained
at www.ICGtesting.com
Printed in the USA
BVHW082254130619

551010BV00001B/3/P